T0301115

DEAD
COLD

DEAD COLD

T. F. MUIR

CONSTABLE

CONSTABLE

First published in Great Britain in 2024 by Constable

Copyright © T. F. Muir, 2024

1 3 5 7 9 10 8 6 4 2

A CIP catalogue record for this book is available from the British Library.

ISBN: 978-1-40872-038-7

Typeset in Dante MT by Hewer Text UK Ltd, Edinburgh
Printed and bound in Great Britain by by Clays Ltd, Elcograf S.p.A.

Papers used by Constable are from well-managed
forests and other responsible sources.

Constable
An imprint of
Little, Brown Book Group
Carmelite House
50 Victoria Embankment
London EC4Y 0DZ

An Hachette UK Company
www.hachette.co.uk

www.littlebrown.co.uk

In memory of my brother, Ian, a gentle man,
who never had a bad word to say about anybody.

AUTHOR'S NOTE

First and foremost, this book is a work of fiction. Those readers familiar with St Andrews and the East Neuk may notice that I have taken creative licence with respect to some local geography and history, and with the names of some Police Forces, which have now changed. Sadly, too, the North Street Police Station has been demolished and a block of flats constructed on the site, but its past proximity to the town centre with its many pubs and restaurants would have been too sorely missed by Gilchrist for me to abandon it. Any resemblance to real persons, living or dead, is unintentional and purely coincidental. Any and all mistakes are mine.

www.frankmuir.co.uk

CHAPTER 1

7.15 a.m., Sunday, late March
The Castle Course, St Andrews, Scotland

Detective Chief Inspector Andy Gilchrist turned his face to the wind, a stiff easterly that blew in from the North Sea with bitter fingers cold enough to squeeze tears from his eyes. Thick clouds as dull and grey as a convict's blanket hung low to the horizon, doing what they could to smother a rising sun. Beyond the dark silhouette of the old Scottish town, rain covered the Eden Estuary like sheer curtains, blocking Tentsmuir Beach and the northern shores from view. He shrugged off a shiver, pulled up his collar, and shifted his gaze to the distant clubhouse, already stirring with addicted golfers preparing to do battle with the links and the elements.

From behind, he heard his car door slam, then Jessie stood by his side, blowing into her hands. 'You ever imagine what this place would be like if it didn't rain?'

'Dry?'

'And pleasant.' She clapped her hands together, then stuffed them into her pockets. 'And this is supposed to be spring?' She puffed out her breath. 'The only thing springy about this morning is the clocks have sprung forward. That's something. Come on. Looks like the SOCOs have made a start. Let's see what we've got.'

Gilchrist watched Jessie stride through the damp grass towards tape that flapped in the wind like thin bunting that surrounded the Incitent, the yellow forensic tent erected by Scenes of Crime Officers to protect the crime scene from disturbance. Two female SOCOs he didn't recognise were removing equipment from their Transit van, their gruesome task of going over the area in microscopic detail not yet begun. The police photographer had been and gone, and the slender figure of the police pathologist, Sam Kim, camera in hand – she always insisted on taking crime scene photos of her own – stood by the tent, twenty metres away. As Jessie approached, Sam Kim slung her camera over her shoulder, said something out of Gilchrist's earshot, then stood back while Jessie snapped on her gloves and slipped inside the Incitent.

Silent, Gilchrist pulled on his own latex gloves, flexed his fingers, a sickening feeling already settling in his stomach. Despite having attended countless murder scenes, he'd never become inured to the horror of it all, never been able to shift that rising sense of dread before the initial viewing, the first sight of a murdered body, the mental struggle against the urge to turn away and leave it to others, or study the crime scene with the professional dispassion all investigations demanded. He filled his lungs with clean cold air, and forced his mind to free itself of emotional attachment, knowing only too well that the victim was more than likely someone's daughter, sister, or mother, whose lives would soon be changed forever.

He'd taken the call from Jessie just after six that morning, as he was about to set off on an early morning run along the West Sands, his long-promised attempt to bring some regimented exercise back into his life. He hadn't learned much from her, for the simple reason that she hadn't known the facts herself – only that the body of a woman had been found on the Castle Course, in the rough close to the fifteenth green, by one of the greenkeeping staff tasked with cutting new pin locations before the first golfers of the day arrived.

He scanned the area around him, trying to work out why the woman had been killed out here, in the open, not a car in close proximity, two hundred metres at least, maybe more, from the Fairmont Hotel, and a good fifty metres from the edge of the hotel's entrance road. She wouldn't have come by way of the Castle Clubhouse, he felt certain of that. From what he knew, the Clubhouse was more pro shop than restaurant, serving golfers rather than the public. Even so, they would have to close the course and block off the access road until the SOCOs had completed their forensics examination.

He shifted his attention to the hotel.

Lighted windows dotted three-storey wings that reached out like arms either side of the entrance portico, as if to protect arriving guests from whatever weather Scotland could throw its way. A car park fell away from the hotel, dotted with vehicles parked here and there – plenty of spaces – which told him that the hotel was not filled to capacity. Had the victim and her killer made their way here from the hotel? Gilchrist had already organised a team to question the hotel staff and create a list of everyone on duty last night, including names of all guests. But he couldn't shift the troubling thought that the killer had not been a resident of the

3

hotel, and was there only for an evening at one of the restaurants or bars. Which really opened up the list of suspects to the wind. On top of that, his team would have to question greenkeeping and golf club staff, which caused a niggling worry to stir at the growing likelihood of budgetary constraints.

His peripheral vision caught movement, and he turned in time to see Jessie step from the Incitent and stumble from the scene. She stopped ten metres away, her back to him. Her stillness, and the way her breath heaved and clouded the air, warned him that the crime scene was a bad one. He whispered a curse, then waded through the damp grass, teeth gritted, jaw tight, conscious of trying to keep his own breathing steady.

Sam Kim watched as he approached, but said nothing, just grimaced with a shake of her head, then stepped aside. He steadied himself for a moment, took a deep intake of breath then let it out as he struggled to force all emotion from his being. He had to study the scene with the utmost detachment, learn as much as he could from that initial viewing, but even so, there was only so much a person could stomach. He chanced another look at Jessie, but she still had her back to him. He could do with catching one of her black humour quips that could lighten the intensity of even the bleakest of moments. She seemed to sense his eyes on her, for she held her head to the side for a long moment, as if waiting for him to say something, then turned away.

He was on his own.

He took one last deep breath, then entered the tent.

CHAPTER 2

The first thing that struck Gilchrist was the smell, the air thick with the cloying aroma of shit, fresh and raw and strong enough to coat the tongue. The second was blood. Lots of it. Everywhere. As if someone had emptied a bucketload. An adult human body contains over a gallon of blood – depending on the individual's size and weight – and from what he could see, every last ounce of that life-supporting fluid had been drained from this victim. It pooled in congealed puddles by her body, painted rain-flattened grass all around, coloured her skin from head to toe.

Whoever killed her must have been splattered with the stuff.

He forced himself to have a closer look, struggling to make sense of something that didn't seem right, as if his nervous system was too overloaded to work it out, and was trying to shut down his brain. The victim was a young woman in her late teens, early twenties, as best he could tell by the slimness of her waist, the muscled tone of her skin, the swell of her buttocks. She lay naked on her stomach, legs apart, her rectum and pubic area a mess of clotted blood and faeces. He couldn't see any open wounds; her calves, thighs and buttocks appeared undamaged, the skin taut and devoid of cellulite. She'd kept herself in good shape. Her arms, too, had fine muscle tone, and lay outstretched above her head, as if she were about to take a headlong dive into the dune grass. In contrast to the rest of the body, her hands were clean, her fingernails square-tipped, painted white, one nail on either hand contrasted blue-and-white-crossed to represent the saltire. But it was her hair that confused him. Long and blonde and thick with blood, it spread across the nape of her neck and shoulders in a congealed mass that looked like . . . that looked . . .

He felt the hot nip of bile sting the back of his throat as his stomach spasmed, but he gritted his teeth, fought it down, and managed to preserve some level of professional dignity. He wiped his sleeve across his mouth, conscious of someone entering the tent.

'Who in their right mind would do this?' Jessie said.

He had no answer, managed only to shake his head, fight off another spasm.

Without a word, Jessie bent down, pushed her gloved hand through what should have been hair at the back of the neck, and eased a handful of intestines loose. He wanted to tell her not to touch the body, leave the poor soul alone, but his voice was trapped in his throat. He took a step back as she let the string of guts slip through her fingers, slippery and thick as bloated worms.

'You seen anything like this before? Guts and everything?'

He had. Not long after he'd joined the Force. But it had been suicide by train. What he did remember was witnessing the victim's intestines being bagged by the side of the track. He shook his head. 'Can't say that I have. Not like this. No.'

Jessie pushed to her feet. 'I'd say we've got some nutter running wild.'

He nodded. 'She's naked.'

She looked at him, and frowned. 'I can see that.'

'I mean, where are her clothes?' It was all he had the strength to say.

Jessie shook her head, glanced around her, then stared at the body again. 'Maybe he took them with him.'

'Why?'

'Wanking material? Sniffs at her knickers? Who knows?' She shrugged. 'But have a look at this. I think he's taken more than her clothes.' She stepped over the victim's left leg, and reached for her hand. 'No rings. But I'm thinking she was married. Or maybe engaged.' She fiddled with the ring finger. 'See that? The tan mark? That's from a ring, but it's been removed. She's got a nice tan, too, so I'm thinking she's maybe just back from holiday.' She glanced up at him. 'What do you think?'

He didn't know what to think, only that one of his team – the family liaison officer – would have to let the victim's next of kin know, and how on earth could the FLO look the family in the eye and offer such news, knowing the manner in which she'd been killed?

Jessie stumbled to her feet again, opened the tent and shouted to Sam Kim. 'You got all you need?'

Kim tapped her camera, and nodded.

'You might want to come in and take some more,' Jessie said. 'I'm going to turn her over.'

'Leave that to the SOCOs,' Gilchrist said.

'Just a quick peek. I want to see her face. Might be able to ID her. I'm thinking the sooner we catch this nutter, the better.'

Ordinarily, Gilchrist would insist on leaving the body for the SOCOs, but the police photographer had been, and Sam Kim had taken an additional set, and the SOCOs were still fiddling with their equipment, so he said nothing while Jessie bent down, adjusted one of the victim's legs, slipped a hand under the waist, another under the shoulder, and gently, very gently – he would grant her that – eased the body over and onto its side where it balanced for an unsteady moment before slumping into an awkward position, not quite flat on its back.

At first glance he struggled to identify the wounds. Congealed blood and grass and some other stuff that looked like lumps of mud, but more likely faeces, or maybe the contents of her stomach, stuck to the skin making it impossible to determine what was an open wound or smeared blood. But as he stared at the body, his mind working through the visual mess, he came to see that most of the marks were open wounds, slits all about the same size – four inches or so – telling him that a wide-bladed knife could be the murder weapon, and already asking the question – who would bring a knife like that out here, or more to the point, where had the knife come from? Even as his mind ticked the mental box to instruct his team to focus on the hotel's kitchen staff, he found himself counting the stab wounds on the victim's neck and chest. And as his gaze drifted the length of her, he forced his eyes away from the open gash across the stomach where the body had been eviscerated, and counted six more open wounds around the pubic area.

'Fuck sake,' Jessie whispered, and glanced up at him. 'You seen this? Her eyes?'

Gilchrist pressed his lips tight.

'The bastard's cut her eyes.' She whispered a hissed curse. 'This guy's gone and lost the plot.' She turned her attention to a wound on the neck, and said, 'Her throat's not been sliced open,

8

but stabbed. See? So I'm thinking that wound's been done post-mortem.' She ran her hand over the chest. 'Ah fuck,' she said. 'You see this?'

He found himself leaning closer.

'Both nipples have been sliced off,' she said, and whispered another curse as she raked her fingers through the grass where the body had lain face down.

'He'll have taken them as trophies,' Gilchrist said. 'Along with her rings, too.'

Jessie hissed yet another curse, then said, 'It's a small mercy, if you think about it. He could've cut her boobs off, too.' She sniffed. 'Isn't that what they used to do in the Wild West to Indian women? Cut off their boobs and use them as tobacco pouches?'

Gilchrist shook his head, and watched Jessie work her fingers around a group of open cuts in the middle of her chest. 'Not sure which one of these would've been the fatal wound,' she said. 'What do you think?'

Despite himself, Gilchrist leaned closer to study six wounds in the centre of the chest, bunched so close together that several overlapped. What could drive someone to carry out such a frenzied attack? How angry would you have to be? If the woman had been stabbed in the chest first, she would surely have died from only a couple of blows. Even as his thoughts processed that, he struggled to make sense of the sequence. It seemed that she'd been naked before being attacked, although he could have that wrong. But if so, had she willingly walked out here to have consensual sex, say, then stripped herself naked before being killed? Surely not in this weather. Even though spring was in the air, March nights in Scotland often hit sub-zero temperatures. Or had she been dragged by her hair, screaming and kicking? Too

9

many questions, not enough answers. But the answers would come, he felt certain of that. He just had to focus on the facts, the evidence, which first of all meant trying to make sense of the wounds.

'You could be right,' he said. 'If this was where she was first attacked, then the only blessing was that she was dead before he cut her open.'

Just then, Sam Kim stepped into the tent, camera at the ready, and he was only too willing to step outside for a breather while she captured the horrific scene for posterity.

CHAPTER 3

Jessie followed Gilchrist through weather-flattened dune grass until they came to the fifteenth green. The flagstick shivered in the wind, which now blustered in from behind them, as if to hound the gulls and terns seawards.

'Penny for your thoughts?' she said.

He breathed in hard and deep, then let it out in a defeated burst. 'Why?' he said. 'That's what I'm thinking. Why kill someone like that? Why keep stabbing her again and again when you must surely know she's dead?'

'Rage?'

'That goes beyond rage,' he growled. 'That's out and out insanity.'

'He's off his meds, that's for sure. But you know what I'm thinking? I'm thinking she knew him, and he knew her. Not just in the passing. But lovers.'

He turned to face her. 'I'm listening.'

'There's no way she'd come out here on her own. Last night, it was pissing it down. And blowing a gale, too. I'm thinking it's that age-old chestnut – jealousy.'

11

'They were in a relationship, and she broke it off?'

'More like, they were in a relationship, and she got shagged on the side.'

'And he found out about it, lured her out here, and killed her?'

'Yeah.'

'There's a lot of ifs, buts and maybes in that lot.'

'I know, I know, but to my way of thinking it kind of explains the missing ring.'

'Why?'

'The ring means something to him. It has to. Why else would he take it?'

'Trophy?'

'No, that's what serial killers do, and I don't think we're dealing with a serial killer here. I think we're looking for some jealous nutter who can't control his temper.'

Gilchrist stared off to the horizon. The sun was doing what it could to break through the clouds, but the way the wind was blowing, they might not see it until later in the day. What Jessie was saying made sense. But it was only one answer from a thousand possibilities. 'I didn't notice any other jewellery. Did you?'

'Didn't see any.'

'How about earrings?'

'*Shit*. I never noticed, what with the . . . you know . . . the stuff. Want me to check her ears? See if they're pierced? She might have a couple of studs. Who hasn't these days?'

Gilchrist had seen enough blood and guts for the day, so said, 'Let's wait until the body's back in the mortuary.'

Jessie said nothing, just turned her gaze to the tent.

'What are your thoughts about her clothes?' he said.

'Aye, well, that's another matter.' She faced the sea again, ran a hand under her nose. 'But if you ask yourself – what's he going to do with his *own* clothes? I mean . . . unless he was starkers, they've got to have been covered in blood. His hands, too. He would've soiled anything he touched.'

'Unless he was wearing gloves.'

'With that mess back there?' She shook her head. 'He would've needed to have been covered from head to toe in full forensic gear to avoid getting anything on him. I'm thinking it's more like the guy's only now realising what he's done, and asking himself – what am I gonnie do with these clothes? How am I gonnie clean the mess in my car?'

'You think he's driven here?'

'Well he wouldn't have got the bus, would he? And he wouldn't have called for a taxi. So, yes, he's driven here, and driven back, and this morning he's waking up wondering how the hell he's going to clean it all up.'

Gilchrist glanced back at the forensic tent. Sam Kim had finished taking more photos, and was striding back to her car. Off to the side, one of the SOCOs had widened the crime scene area, and now stood about thirty metres away, deep in the rough, holding the police tape in one hand, and trying to catch the attention of Colin, the lead SOCO, with the other.

'Looks like they've found something,' Gilchrist said.

'Maybe her clothes?' Jessie said, and chased after him.

By the time he reached the SOCO, his shoes were wet through. 'What've we got?'

'Looks like a man's sock, sir.'

Gilchrist leaned down for a closer look at a black sock, half-calf length, saturated, a red Pringle logo at the ankle, lying on top of a clump of dune reeds, as if it had been placed there to dry in the sun – if it ever emerged from the clouds. He cast his gaze around, half-expecting to find its companion, but saw nothing. What he did see he might never have noticed if he hadn't been looking from that spot – a pressing of the winter grass to one side, then the other, not windblown damage, but from someone wading through the rough.

He pushed himself to his feet as his eyes followed what he could only describe as the faintest of trails. Was that what he was looking at? A trail made by the killer walking away from the victim's body? As his gaze shifted farther through the long grass, he thought he saw how the killer had left the scene; stumbling through the rough, across the dunes, then onto one of the fairways where the walk to a car in the Castle Course car park could be done with relative ease, and well out of sight of prying eyes of guests of the Fairmont, or anywhere else for that matter.

But why leave a sock? Was it the killer's? And why here?

Another look at the forensic tent with the Fairmont Hotel in the background, and he thought he saw the outline of some answer, maybe not an exact answer, but one that ticked all the boxes, in a manner of speaking. 'He stripped off,' he said.

'Andy?'

He stared at Jessie. 'He stripped. He's taken his clothes off. *Here*. Stuffed them into a bag and walked back to his car in the nude. It was raining last night, so he'd be soaked, and more importantly, his skin and hair and face would be cleaned of any blood.' He smirked at Jessie. 'And it was wild and windy, too.'

She stared down at the sock as realisation rose within her.

'That's right,' he said. 'He dropped one of his socks in the pitch black, and didn't notice.' He turned to the SOCO. 'Bag it, and secure this area.'

CHAPTER 4

By midday, the SOCOs had confirmed that the spot where the sock had been found was almost certainly where the killer had stripped off his clothes and stuffed them into some carrier bag of sorts, most likely a plastic bag, maybe two – one for his own, the other for the victim's. A closer examination of the sock identified spots of blood. Blades of grass under the sock revealed minute traces of blood, too, protected from the elements by the sock itself. The SOCOs would find other traces of blood in the immediate area, Gilchrist felt certain of that, showered off the killer by last night's downpour. But in the cushion of trampled grass, there was no chance of finding footprints, and he had to settle for the fact that the sock and minute traces of blood were the only evidence they were ever likely to find. A great result when you thought about it, and a lucky one, too, but he knew from experience they had a long way to go before they ID'd the killer – if they ever could.

Both the sock and the samples of blood had been sent off for DNA analysis, marked urgent, with a request by Gilchrist to have the results back by the end of the day – fat chance of that happening. But Sam Kim had proven herself to be a demanding forensic pathologist, and if anybody could expedite DNA results, she could.

CCTV footage from the Castle Course clubhouse came up empty, no signs of any late-night driving anywhere near the car park, leaving Gilchrist to wonder if the killer had parked somewhere remote from the clubhouse and walked farther through the wind and rain in the nude to some destination, as yet unknown. He didn't like that thought, as it opened up the possibilities by an exponential factor, but two uniforms were tasked with tracing CCTV footage from adjacent properties.

Even so, he felt his investigation was best focused on the Fairmont Hotel. He'd already instructed a team of four uniforms to obtain the names and addresses of all guests checked into the hotel last night, and to create a list of individuals who attended any of the hotel's restaurants or bars. Bar or menu receipts would help identify those who weren't overnight guests. Had there been any events on last night – wedding reception, birthday party, work outing? Had anyone seen a couple by themselves in a bar, in a restaurant, in the spa? Had anyone noticed anyone arguing, seen a disturbance of any kind? And check the kitchen staff, he'd instructed. Find out if any knives are missing – deep bladed, like a butcher's knife. Had any of the kitchen or hotel staff not turned up for work, called in sick, acted strange, done something different?

All those questions and others, he'd asked his team to focus on.

Seated in his BMW in the car park overlooking the Castle Course, holding a coffee courtesy of the hotel, Jessie said, 'Do you think the killer knows he's dropped a sock?'

Gilchrist gave her question a moment's thought, then shook his head. 'Once he'd stuffed his clothes into the bag, I don't think

16

he'd check its contents before getting rid of them. He wouldn't want to risk contaminating himself.'

'But what if he knew he'd dropped it, and couldn't find it in the dark? What then? He wouldn't have risked using a torch in case someone saw him.'

'Out here? I doubt he'd worry about that.'

'You don't think he brought a torch with him?'

'He could've used the light from his mobile phone. Everyone's got a mobile these days, haven't they?'

'Which makes you wonder what he did with *her* mobile.' She looked at him, the light of an idea glinting in her eyes. 'If he's bagged all her clothes, *everything*, including her purse, her rings, *and* her mobile, then we might be able to track his movements from her phone.'

'He would've removed the SIM card.'

'You think so? Butterfingers drops a sock in the dark? What chance would he have of trying to remove a SIM card? Especially if it's an iPhone. You need to have one of those wee pin-thingies to open them. But once we ID her, and we will, we can get her mobile number and track his movements.'

Jessie was right. He saw that. But she wasn't taking the logic far enough. The killer would've had a mobile of his own, which he might have left in his car after he phoned the victim to lure her to her death. If his theory was correct – and that's all it was at this point, a theory, and a wild one at that – then they would've met in the dark, where no one could see them, the killer *sans* mobile, the victim fully clothed and kitted out. Then a walk across the grass – what had he said to persuade her to do that? – plastic bags and murder weapon hidden inside his jacket? An argument ensues, and in a rage he removes the broad-bladed knife and stabs her over and over and over, to death.

17

Except . . . he had it wrong. This was no spontaneous killing. This was premeditation of the first order. The killer had come fully prepared. He'd lured his victim deep into the golf course rough. He knew what he was going to do, and he knew how he was going to get rid of the evidence. Stripped naked, wading through the dune grass, he would've known he could be tracked by her mobile. So he got rid of it. He had to. How else was he going to make his escape without leaving any tracks? Well, other than those he'd left through the dune grass—

'Earth to Andy? Hello . . .?'

He turned to face her. 'You're right,' he said. 'But wrong, too.'

'Sounds like a Chinese proverb coming up.'

'She would've had a mobile. Which he took. Let's go with that. And her purse. And her ring. And whatever other jewellery she was wearing. But he doesn't care about her purse. He'll take whatever cash she had, and keep the jewellery. The ring means something to him. You said that. Maybe he's got it in a safe place at home, or somewhere out of sight that only he knows about. But he has to get rid of her phone. Not keep it. Not for any length of time. And he won't get rid of it with the clothes—'

'Why not?'

'The clothes he can dump later, in some construction skip in town somewhere, or a city, Glasgow, Edinburgh, maybe in England, or even far out at sea, although keeping them underwater for any length of time might be a problem, so maybe not at sea—'

'Slow down, Andy, what're trying to tell me?'

'That he ditched her mobile. He didn't take it with him.'

'So where is it?'

He opened his car door. 'That's what we're about to find out.'

18

CHAPTER 5

If Gilchrist thought he could solve the case by finding the victim's mobile phone, he was sorely mistaken. By the time darkness settled in, he was no further forward. Both he and Jessie had scoured the rough from the spot where the killer had stripped, all the way over the dune grass to the Castle Course car park. He'd tried to visualise what the killer would have done in the dark, where he would have discarded her mobile. But the possibilities seemed endless, not to mention the likelihood that he had it wrong, that the killer might have taken her mobile to his car, where he had one of those pin-thingies Jessie mentioned, and removed the SIM card, thus killing any chance of tracing it stone dead. And the longer he thought about it, the more sense that scenario made.

Even so, he'd called in the sniffer dogs, two of them, who were still criss-crossing the area with canine enthusiasm. With night settling in, it was only a matter of time until they had to call it a day. The dogs would start again first thing in the morning. But the longer the mobile went undiscovered, the more likely his theory was wrong.

The victim's mobile could be anywhere.

'God, I'm knackered,' Jessie said. 'Never walked so much in my life. And look at these dogs. They're having the time of their lives.'

Gilchrist said nothing, deep in the misery of his own thoughts. He noticed DC Mhairi McBride exiting the hotel, and for a moment the faintest glimmer of hope surfaced that she might have found some new lead. She'd been put in charge of obtaining details of all hotel guests, both outgoing and long-staying; names, addresses – home and email; phone numbers – mobile and land-line, if any; reason for visit, any comments of note, etc; and for overseeing initial interviewing. Never afraid to take control or voice an opinion, Mhairi had complained to Gilchrist by late morning that she needed at least two more uniforms to handle the steady flow of guests checking out. He'd done as she'd asked, without question.

She caught his eye and headed his way.

'Any luck?' he asked.

'Don't know if you'd call it luck, sir, but the best I've got is two separate reports of a young couple having some kind of disagreement over dinner in the restaurant last night. Not shouting out loud, or anything like that, but more as if they weren't enjoying each other's company.'

'Were they staying at the hotel?'

'No, sir, only a dinner reservation.'

'You get their names?'

'Only the man, sir. The table was reserved under his name.'

'And you don't know who his female companion was?'

'No, sir.'

'Right,' Gilchrist said, sensing the first chance at a break in the investigation. 'Were you able to find an address?'

'Yes, sir. Got it from his credit card company. He lives close by in Anstruther, sir.'

On the drive to Anstruther, doubts began to swell in Gilchrist's mind. If the couple had a dinner reservation, and the man was the killer they were looking for, and Gilchrist's theory about the sequence of the murder was correct, then why would he park his car in the Castle Course car park? Surely he would have parked it in front of the hotel? And if he and his companion had left the hotel together, and not gone straight to his car, but walked off into the rough where they'd found the body, where would he have hidden the murder weapon? And the plastic bags? And how would he manage to return to his car stark naked?

By the time he pulled up in front of the address in Gardner Avenue, and stood on the front step, Jessie at his side, he had all but convinced himself that they'd set out on a wasted journey. Still, you never could tell what a face-to-face could uncover.

The door opened to a barefooted man – late twenties, early thirties – wearing jogging shorts and a sweat-covered T-shirt. A towel hung around his neck, and his hard breathing told Gilchrist that he'd just finished a run, or some strenuous exercise. Gilchrist introduced himself and Jessie, then said, 'We need to speak to Mr Poynton, Derek Poynton.'

'That's me, yeah.'

'We'd like to ask you a few questions about last night.'

'What about last night?'

Jessie said, 'Are you going to invite us in, or do we have to stand all night on the doorstep?'

'Why? What's up?'

'Maybe best we talk inside,' she said. 'In case the neighbours notice.'

Poynton frowned, but stepped aside to let Jessie sweep past him.

Without a word, Gilchrist followed her along a narrow hallway and into a tidy lounge, in the corner of which stood an exercise bike. When Poynton entered, Jessie kept up the quips. 'Keep yourself fit, do you?'

'Not as fit as I should. Why? What's this about?'

'You were out last night at the Fairmont?'

'So?'

'So you had dinner for two. You and your girlfriend?'

'She's not my girlfriend.'

'Who is she, then?'

'A work associate.'

'Do you normally treat work associates to meals in five-star hotels.'

'I didn't treat her.'

'Your credit card says you did.'

Poynton let out a tired sigh. 'We always split the bill. She gives me cash, and I put it on a card.'

'Why?'

Poynton opened his mouth as if to say something, then turned to Gilchrist. 'What's this about, please?'

Gilchrist jerked a smile. 'We're trying to establish the whereabouts of the woman you shared a dinner reservation with last night.'

'Why?'

Gilchrist ignored the question. 'Can you tell me her name?'

'Carey Conners.'

'And she works with you.'

'We're work associates, yeah.' Another heavy sigh. 'Look, I don't understand why you're here. I'm just off the phone with her.'

Well, there he had it. As good a dead end as any. 'Do you have her number?'

He and Jessie waited patiently while Poynton retrieved his mobile, accessed it, then read out the number.

Jessie jotted it down without a word.

'Before we leave,' Gilchrist said. 'We heard you didn't enjoy each other's company last night.'

'Says who?'

'Was that true? You argued?'

'We didn't argue at all. Carey was a bit down on herself. She'd been looking forward to catching up with a friend of hers. She'd invited her to join us, but she didn't show.'

Jessie said, 'Your reservation said table for two.'

'I didn't know Carey had invited her until we got there.'

'This friend got a name?'

'Jennifer Nolan.'

'Phone number?'

'You'd have to ask Carey for that.'

'Oh we will. Don't you worry about that.'

Poynton grimaced at Jessie, and shook his head. 'Jeez, you guys . . .'

Gilchrist stepped in, and thanked Poynton for his help. 'Before we leave, is there anything you noticed last night that seemed . . . strange?'

'In what way?'

'Maybe something or someone that seemed out of place?'

'Can't think of anything.'

Gilchrist nodded, and held out a card. 'If anything comes to mind, give me a call. Anytime. Thanks again. We'll see ourselves out.'

CHAPTER 6

Gilchrist placed the call to Carey Conners through his car's speaker system. She confirmed what Poynton had told them, until he asked, 'And this friend you'd invited to join you. Jennifer Nolan—'

'She's no friend of mine,' she snapped. 'Not any more.'

Jessie raised her eyebrows, and mouthed an Oh.

Gilchrist kept his tone level. 'So you hadn't invited her to join you?'

'No. She invited herself. Said she wanted to sort it out. I told her it couldn't be sorted and she could go to hell. But she insisted on apologising face to face. So I said, if you think that's going to change my mind, you've got a long think coming.' A gruff sigh told Gilchrist she'd finished her rant.

'Apologising for what?' he said.

'It's personal.'

'Would you prefer to come to the station where you could tell us about it in person?'

A pause, then, 'We were on holiday, see? Five nights in Tenerife. It's hot in March. And we got a good deal. Cheap as chips. I've got a friend in the travel business. She's always fixing us up for deals. Once every—'

'Jennifer,' Gilchrist interrupted, 'wanted to apologise to you for *what?*'

She gave a heavy sigh, then said, 'Our last night, we went to this nightclub. We were drinking cocktails, giving it big licks. We were all pished, but Jennifer was off her face. She gets like that sometimes. I fancied this guy. And I could tell he fancied me. But I had to pass because Jennifer'd had enough and thought we should go back to the hotel. So I goes to the loo for a pee. And I'm only gone a minute. And next thing, Jennifer's outside getting shagged by this guy. I couldn't believe it. I gave him up for her. And then she shags him behind my back, first chance she gets? I tell you, I was livid.'

Gilchrist waited a few beats, but it seemed as if Carey had exhausted her rant. 'So,' he said, 'then what?'

'I went back to the hotel.'

'And left Jennifer?'

'She didn't need my help.'

'You said Jennifer was off her face. Was there any possibility that she'd been . . .' He struggled to find the right phrase. 'Coerced into having sex against her will?'

'Not a chance in hell. She knew fine well what she was doing. It was written all over her face, the *bitch*.'

'I see,' Gilchrist said, then pressed on. 'You said you were *all* very drunk. There were more than you and Jennifer?'

'Four of us.'

'Names?'

'Karen and Lianna.'

First names would do for the time being. Keep it simple. They could always come back for more details, because the fact that

25

they'd been to the Canary Islands in March, which might explain the murdered woman's tan, had him wanting to dig deeper. Even so, he felt he had to pry with care. 'And what did Karen and Lianna think about what Jennifer had done?'

'I don't think they even noticed.'

'But Jennifer got back to the hotel safely,' he said, more statement than question.

'They all staggered in about an hour later.'

'And did you and Jennifer have a talk about it the following morning?'

'Aye, that'd be right. We haven't spoken since.'

'Must've been a nice flight home,' Jessie quipped.

Carey offered nothing more, so Gilchrist pressed on. 'If you and Jennifer haven't spoken since the event at the nightclub, how did she know that you and Derek were meeting at the Fairmont?'

'Derek must've told her.'

'Derek knows Jennifer?'

'I guess.'

'So did Derek suggest to Jennifer that you and she try to make up?' he asked, just to test the waters, see if Derek had been speaking the truth.

'He said he hadn't. He's friendly with Lianna, so maybe he mentioned it to her and she mentioned it to Jennifer. What does it matter? She invited herself, and that's it.'

Was Carey deliberately missing the point, or was she pretending to be obtuse? 'What I don't understand, Carey, is – if you haven't spoken to Jennifer since the holiday, and Derek didn't mention anything to her, how did she know about your dinner at the Fairmont, and manage to communicate with you that she wanted to sort it out, as you said, face to face?'

26

'Text message.'

Duh. Of course. In the digital age of mobile phones and limit-less apps, and music and videos downloads available at the touch of a key, the art of texting had wiped letter writing from the face of the earth. Even basic phone calls had taken a back seat to the pervasive text-messaging phenomenon. He should've guessed, but in his own defence he would argue that he was old school. He forced his thoughts back on track.

Asking for details of what Jennifer had texted wasn't going to help him, he thought he knew that much. But he needed to talk to Jennifer in person, to clear his mounting suspicions that she could be the murdered victim. A dubious conclusion, he would be the first to agree. But you had to start somewhere.

Had Jennifer turned up at the Fairmont unannounced to offer Carey an apology? Had her boyfriend found out about her having sexual intercourse outside the nightclub? And if so, how? Had Jennifer confessed, or as he was now beginning to understand, had Carey, her over-jealous, over-reactive holiday mate, spilled the beans to him in a spiteful act of revenge? Or maybe she was married. The tan mark on her ring finger suggested she could be, or was engaged at least. Seemed he was finding more questions than answers once again.

'So . . .' he said, 'after Jennifer texted you, did you text her back?'

'No.'

'Did you hear from her again?'

'No.'

'Was Jennifer married?'

'Nobody would be stupid enough.'

27

'I take it that's a no.'

'No. I mean, yes, it's a no.'

'Boyfriend?'

'Several?'

'Any long-standing ones?'

'Don't know and don't care.'

He glanced at Jessie who sliced her hand under her chin in an *End the call* signal, and mouthed *Waste of time*. Well, he had to agree. She couldn't care less about Jennifer, and it would take more than a face-to-face apology to rekindle their broken friend-ship. 'If you could give me Jennifer's contact details,' he said, 'we'll take it up with her directly.'

'I've only got a mobile number for her.'

'That'll do.'

She read it out to him, while Jessie wrote it down.

'One final thing,' he said. 'Do you have any photographs of Jennifer?'

'I used to.'

'What does that mean?'

'I deleted them.'

'Why?'

'It's not like we were best friends or anything. She's more friends with Lianna.' A pause, then, 'What's this all about anyway?'

'Thanks for your help,' Gilchrist said, and ended the call.

'What a bitch,' Jessie said. 'Bet you a pound to a penny that she dobbed her in to her boyfriend.'

'I thought you said she was married.'

'She had a ring. That's all. They wear them on any fingers these days.'

'One thing I did notice,' he said. 'She . . . the victim . . . didn't have any tattoos. Did you see any?'

'Too much blood. Maybe we should call that bitch back, and ask her.'

'Don't bother. Contact Jennifer on that number instead.'

CHAPTER 7

Jessie had no luck phoning Jennifer Nolan. The call rang out and went to voicemail, and Jessie left a short message – 'This is Detective Sergeant Janes of St Andrews CID. Call me as soon as you receive this. It's urgent.' – which in one way could be taken as good news, Gilchrist thought. If she was the murdered woman, he would've banked money on her mobile being dead, its SIM card removed or destroyed. Still, he could have it all wrong.

'Get Jackie to find an address for her.'

'Will do, but now we're here, do you fancy sharing a fish supper? I'm still watching what I eat. I'll buy.'

Anstruther Fish Bar was locally renowned, some might say internationally renowned, for the quality of that most simple of British dishes, fish and chips. And come to think of it, he hadn't eaten since breakfast, a failing of his that Irene often badgered him about. 'Sure,' he said, 'but it's my treat.' He powered up his car and set off.

By the time they arrived at the seafront, Jackie had texted Jessie with Jennifer's address. 'There's a surprise,' Jessie said. 'She's a neighbour of yours. Lives in Crail. Kirkmay Road. You know it?'

'Vaguely,' he said. 'Enter it into the satnav while I get the fish supper. What're you having? The usual? Haddock?'

'In breadcrumbs. No vinegar. And loads of salt. Here.' She shoved her hand into her pocket, but Gilchrist had already stepped outside and was crossing the road. She thought of texting her son, Robert – deaf from birth, with no possibility of ever hearing – and asking if he would like her to bring him a fish supper, but she'd left a pizza in the fridge for him before she left home that morning. Besides, she had no idea how long it would take to interview Jennifer, if they were able to locate her, that is.

And with that thought, she called Carey again.

'One more question,' she said, without introduction. 'Did Jennifer have any tattoos?'

'Why don't you ask her yourself?'

'Because I'm asking you.'

'What's this about?' she said, and Jessie thought she caught the faintest shimmer of remorse in her voice. Remorse at having been so hurtful to her friend – not speaking to her, refusing to accept her apology? Or remorse at having done something far worse, like telling her boyfriend she'd been unfaithful to him?

'You told him, didn't you?'

'Told who?'

'Jennifer's other half.'

'No, no, I didn't, I swear.'

Maybe some of that sixth sense of Gilchrist's had rubbed off on her, but she sensed Carey was holding back, hiding something. 'So what's her other half's name then?'

'I don't know. That's what I'm telling you. I only . . .' She choked back a sob.

31

Jessie waited for several seconds before saying, 'You only what?'

'Please don't tell me something's happened to her.'

'You only *what*, Carey?'

'I only sent a tweet. Just the one. But I took it down the next morning.'

'And what did the tweet say?'

'I can't remember exactly. I was drunk. But it wasn't nice.'

'What's your Twitter handle?'

'Why? Has something happened to Jennifer?'

'Your Twitter handle, Carey.'

She told her.

Jessie jotted it down. 'When did you send the tweet?'

'That night on holiday, after I got back to the hotel from the nightclub.'

'What date?'

'We flew back over a week ago, on the seventeenth, so it would've been sent on the sixteenth, and deleted on the seventeenth.'

'So . . .' Jessie said, returning to her original question. 'Tattoos, or no tattoos?'

'Tattoos.'

'Where?'

'Down below. Just the one. A love heart, I think.'

'What do you mean, down below?'

'Her private area.'

'Her vagina, you mean?'

'Yes.'

'In it, around it, close to it, or what?'

'I don't know. I never saw it. She just told me.'

32

'Anything else you didn't tell us about her?'

'No. I can't stop thinking about her. I didn't mean to—'

Jessie ended the call, then phoned Jackie. 'Can you recover deleted tweets?'

'Uh-huh.'

'See if you can recover a tweet from this Twitter handle that was sent on the evening of the sixteenth of March and deleted the following morning.'

'Uh-huh?'

'And let me know as soon as you find something out. Thanks, Jackie. You're a star.' She ended the call. If anybody could recover a deleted tweet, it would be Jackie Canning, *researcher extraordinaire*, as Andy often called her. A civilian employed by the police, who knew her way around computers and the internet as if she'd been born to it, she split her time between her home and the North Street Office in St Andrews, which granted her access to the PNC – the Police National Computer – and other restricted databases. Other than her cerebral palsy, which hindered her mobility for which she had crutches, the main difficulty for Jackie was her stutter, which was now so bad she'd effectively given up speaking. Uh-huh for yes, nuh-huh for no, was about her limit, although Andy seemed to be able to expedite answers, sometimes with just the shrug of his shoulders.

The door opened, and Gilchrist slid into the driver's seat holding a paper bag, which he passed to Jessie. The mouth-watering aroma of cooked chips filled the cabin.

She peeked inside. 'You've got enough here to feed an army.'

'I've got lemon sole for Irene,' he said. 'She loves fresh fish. And there's a supper for your Robert, with extra chips. And some paper tissues for your fingers.'

'Jeez, Andy.' She made a fuss of offering to pay, but he was having none of it. 'Well, seeing as how you're driving, I think I'll sneak a few chips now. You want one?'

'You've talked me into it.'

He fired up the ignition and set off for Crail, while Jessie slipped a chip into his opened mouth. 'Hot hot hot,' he said, and had to suck in hard before he could chew it.

Jessie brought him up to speed with the latest from Carey, and said, 'I've got Jackie trying to recover that tweet she sent.'

'Call Sam Kim,' he said, nodding to the car phone. 'See if she can confirm the tattoo.'

When Sam Kim answered, Jessie said, 'We think we might be able to ID the woman on the golf course. She should have a tattoo somewhere in her vaginal area.'

'No tattoos,' Sam Kim said.

'Are you sure?'

'Positive. It's unusual, especially in the younger generation now, to have no tattoos of any kind. It was one of the first things I looked for. I expected to find one, but I can assure you, she has no tattoos anywhere.'

'Shit,' Jessie said. 'For a moment there, I thought we had her.'

Gilchrist said, 'Have you found anything that might help us ID her?'

'A small mole on her left side, close to her armpit. But other than that, her skin is blemish free. I'm working on a digital image of her face. Her eyes have been stabbed, so I'm trying to blank them out. Won't have it ready for this evening's news, but you should be able to show it to the public tomorrow morning, if you haven't ID'd her before then.' She let out a heavy sigh, then said, 'I've never seen anyone so brutally murdered. Thirty-eight stab

34

wounds in total. I'd say the fatal wound was one of those to her chest, so most of the others would've been made after her heart had stopped.'

'Thank God for that.'

'But that's not the worst of it.'

He tightened his grip on the steering wheel, and braced himself. 'I'm listening.'

'The human body has roughly seven to eight metres of intestine. The small intestine is about six or so metres long, and the large about a metre and a half.'

Gilchrist whispered a curse. He knew what was coming.

'This body's large intestine is intact,' Kim continued, 'but is missing approximately two metres of its small intestine.'

'Oh dear God.'

'Is there any chance it's been missed in the search around the body?' Kim asked.

'None.'

'Well, there's no other explanation for it. Whoever killed her, took two metres of intestines away with him.'

Gilchrist pulled to the side of the road, and drew to a sharp halt, the memory of the slaughtered woman all too clear in his mind. He wiped his hand over his mouth and stared hard at the phone. 'Why on earth would he do that?'

'The only way to answer that, is to find whoever killed her, and ask.'

CHAPTER 8

It felt odd driving through the back streets of Crail again, as if he were returning home from a long spell away. Although he hadn't moved out *per se*, he now spent almost all of his time at Irene's in St Andrews, staying there most nights, while his own home, Fisherman's Cottage, lay fully furnished but unoccupied. He'd resisted renting it out. The additional income would be nice, of course, but the thought of someone living in his home had the feeling of putting a permanent stamp on something that may turn out to be short-lived.

Familiar sights slid by in the evening gloom as he took a lazy detour through the old streets, taking his time, relishing the sense of being back in the old fishing village. He found he was in no rush to head to Irene's, and although Jessie had nibbled half of her chips, his and Irene's fish supper would have to wait until they'd at least tried to talk to Jennifer Nolan.

He found her address on Kirkmay Road, and kept his car windows open – to clear the smell of fish and chips from the cabin. He and Jessie stepped into the cold March night. From a first glance, he could tell no one was home. The curtains were open, the windows dark with no interior lighting. Everything about the house, as they walked along the path, seemed cold and deserted. In contrast, homes either side appeared welcoming, warm and lived in.

'Looks as if she's out,' Jessie said.

'Ring the bell anyway. You never know.'

After three attempts, she shook her head. 'Let's try the neighbours. Maybe they can tell us something.'

But forty minutes later, he was none the wiser as to Jennifer's whereabouts. What he did learn was that she lived by herself, wasn't married, and didn't appear to have a steady boyfriend, although she had been seen being picked up in a car a number of times by a man with a shorn head and a heavy growth, which could describe about 80 per cent of all Scotsmen these days. None of the neighbours could tell them which make or model of car the man drove, although two confirmed that Jennifer owned a white Ford Focus, registration number not known, or not remembered, although one thought the numbers zero and six were part of it. So where was her car now? She'd last been seen on Saturday morning, driving into St Andrews where she liked to do her shopping. And that was it.

No one knew what she did for a living, where she worked, or what she did with her days during the week. Despite the worrying fact that she was becoming more unlikely to be the murdered woman, even though she had no tattoos anywhere – and her SIM card was still active, even though she was not answering her mobile – Gilchrist found himself becoming more intrigued. Was it just coincidence that she'd gone missing the same day an eviscerated body was found on the golf course? Coincidence seemed the likely reason. But if you didn't believe in coincidence, where did that put you? More to the point, how did that change the course of your investigation? No matter how he tried to rationalise it, he felt certain that if the victim was not Jennifer Nolan, then the two women had to be linked in some way, but how, he couldn't say.

What he had to do was concentrate on what they had. A mutilated body from which they might be able to confirm the width and length of the knife's blade, which in turn might lead them to its place of purchase. A man's Pringle sock, from which they might be able to lift the DNA, presumably the killer's. He felt confident of that. And the most tenuous of all, if you thought about, a long list of overnight guests and hotel staff and other revellers out for a Saturday night. Surely someone somewhere had seen or heard something. He trusted Mhairi to have overseen the interview process and collection of DNA samples thoroughly, so felt hopeful of her uncovering some new lead.

With his original focus on Jennifer Nolan being the most probable murder victim, and her boyfriend the prime suspect, he'd hoped they might not have to analyse everyone's DNA. In today's cost-conscious Police Force multiple DNA tests could make the bean counters sweat in their sleep. But now with his own rising doubts surrounding Jennifer, it seemed that he'd have to go through with the DNA analyses after all.

On the drive back to St Andrews, Jackie surprised them. She texted Carey's deleted tweet to Jessie who scanned through it. 'She really is one nasty bitch, that Carey. Listen to this. "Holiday ruined. Boyfriend shagged by best friend." And there's a photo of someone who could be Jennifer. Looks like she's in bed asleep. I mean, who takes photos of their mates when they're asleep?'

'I thought she didn't know her that well. Wasn't that what she

38

said?' He thought for a moment. 'Does the photo look like our victim?'

'Impossible to tell.'

'Forward it to Sam Kim. She might be able to make a good comparison.'

'Will do.'

'Is that all the tweet said?'

'No. There's more. She calls her out. Jennifer Nolan is a slut and a shagging cow, followed by a string of emojis, mostly negative. Jeez, what a bitch.'

'Once the tweet's out there,' Gilchrist said, 'can anyone read it?'

'If you have a Twitter account.'

'Which could include Jennifer's boyfriend?'

'I'd say so, yeah. And he'd blow a fuse after reading that.'

'If he ever read it, you mean.' He thought for a moment. 'Can you tell who's read that tweet, or how many people have read it?'

'Six thousand, four hundred and twenty-nine people have seen it, according to Jackie. Which is a lot, I think. But it'd be a task and a half to list everyone who'd seen it, especially if we don't know who her boyfriend is, or his Twitter handle. You can't tell the person from their Twitter handle, as they mostly use all sorts of names and stuff. We'd be wasting our time trying that.'

He slowed down as he drove through Kingsbarns, and found himself resisting the urge to pull into the Inn for a quick pint. He'd told Irene he would be home by six, but already it was closer to seven. And besides, it was Sunday evening, and Jessie needed to get back home to Robert with his fish supper.

Beyond the village, he powered up to seventy, braking hard into bends, powering just as hard out of them. He wouldn't describe himself as a fast driver, rather a driver who didn't like to hang around on an open road. As he swept past the entrance to the Fairmont Hotel, his mobile rang – ID Mhairi – and he put her on speaker.

'What've you got for us, Mhairi?'

'Nothing definitive, sir. But one of the kitchen staff, a sous-chef, has been off sick for four days, and no one's been able to contact him.'

'Is he local?'

'Rents a place in town. But that's not all, sir. Apparently he'd been acting strange for the last week or so – moody, argumentative, aggressive – and then he didn't turn up for work on Thursday. He left a message that morning, saying he was sick, and that's the last anyone's heard from him. I'm not sure about him, sir, but I thought I should run it past you.'

'Thanks, Mhairi. It's worth talking to him. Do you have a name?'

'John Green.'

'Address?'

She gave it to him, and if his memory served him, it was somewhere off the road to Cairnsmill Caravan Park.

He brought Mhairi up to speed with their thoughts on Jennifer Nolan, and how she might not be the victim after all, and Mhairi did likewise on her interviewing and swabbing for DNA. But other than John Green, she had nothing significant to add.

'Right,' he said. 'Send off what you've got for DNA analysis. Get them to expedite the results. I'll talk to Smiler about the budget. And I want all interview reports on my desk first thing in the morning. Get your team to work overnight, if they have to.'

'Will do, sir.'

Chief Superintendent Diane Smiley was Gilchrist's immediate boss, and ran the North Street Office with a tight laundered fist. She could have shares in a national cleaning service from the way she dressed, as if every article of clothing had been bought five minutes earlier. But where it came to the Office's budget, you would think it was her personal bank account she was overseeing. From time to time, Gilchrist had to bend the rules in order to properly resource his investigation of the day.

As he drove along Lamond Road, no more than a few minutes from Jessie's home in Canongate, he said. 'You know . . . I've been thinking that we're missing something. It could be that we're wrong about the killer being a male.'

Jessie sucked in her breath. 'I'm not so sure, Andy. Some of those knife wounds are deep. It takes strength to kill someone like that.'

'In the heat of the moment? Adrenaline flowing? Anger rising?'

'What about the sock? It's a man's. I'm sure.'

That almost stopped him. 'Cold night. Woollen socks for warmth.' But as he listened to himself, he knew he didn't sound convincing. 'So where's Jennifer?' he tried. 'Why is *she* missing all of a sudden? On the same day a woman's body turns up hacked to bits? It doesn't work for me.'

'You think she might be the killer?'

'Don't you?'

She pondered his words as he swung into Canongate and drew to a halt outside her home. 'Maybe she was an accomplice. That would work for me. But I have to say, I'd like to talk to her.'

'We need to find her first.'

Jessie looked towards her home for a long moment, as if deciding whether to go in or head to the Office. The living room lights were on, which told him that her son was in.

'Robert must be hungry,' he said. 'Go on. We'll talk about it in the morning.'

She turned back to him. 'I'll call Jackie. Get her onto that Ford Focus. If she can find the registration number, we can do a search on the ANPR. Try and track it down in real time. That would be a good start.'

Automatic Number Plate Recognition technology used cameras to read number plates in real time and instantly check them against national or local database records of vehicles of interest, with all data being stored and retrievable for one year. Honest law-abiding citizens were mostly unaware that their car journeys could be retrieved on screen at the press of a few buttons. But to modern-day criminals, ANPR could be the digital tool that inarguably placed them at the scene of a crime, which in turn created the criminal sideline of vehicle cloning, and number plate registration manipulation, all in an attempt to fool the cameras.

'Do that,' he said. 'But you'll need to zap his fish supper in the microwave.'

'Hot or cold. Robert doesn't care. Appetite like a horse most of the time.'

'Go home, Jessie. Feed your son. I'll see you in the morning.'

The door opened to a blast of cold air. She gave him a toodle-do wave, then scurried up the drive. He waited until she opened the door and stepped inside, before he pushed into Drive and eased off. He had one last thing to look into before going home.

CHAPTER 9

John Green's address led Gilchrist to a row of bungalows at the back of Morrisons. He switched off the ignition, and eyed the building. Like Jennifer Nolan's, Green's home appeared deserted. No lights on, no car parked outside, although the curtains were drawn, which gave him hope that Green could be home, sitting in the dark. Of course, there was always the worrying possibility that he might not have answered calls from his employer because he'd moved out, or perhaps was no longer alive.

But first things first.

He rang the doorbell, then stood back and eyed the windows, searching for the tiniest flicker of twitching curtains, the faintest movement of flitting shadows. Another ring, another count to twenty, and he had to conclude that Green wasn't home. As a final check, Gilchrist leaned down, opened the letterbox and peered in. Nothing. No hint of coffee or burnt toast either, or worse, the tongue-coating smell of putrefaction. Nothing out of the ordinary. Just the solid silence of an empty home.

He let the letterbox slap shut as he stood upright, and was about to return to his car, when he stopped. Had his ears deceived him? He stood still, head cocked to the side, every fibre of his senses on alert. He thought he'd heard movement from inside, the quiet thud of a door being closed, or the gentle press of a foot on a stairway.

He turned back to the door, leaned down and opened the letterbox again.

'I know you're home, Mr Green. Open up. I want to talk to you.'

He snapped the letterbox shut, then pressed a finger to the doorbell and held it there to the count of ten, then twenty, and was about to give up at thirty, thinking that his mind had played tricks, when the lock clicked and the door swung open, and a young man stripped to the waist, shorn head, heavy beard growth, faced him, eyes alight with barely concealed anger.

'What's your fucking problem?' he growled.

'John Green?'

'You deaf or what?'

Gilchrist held out his warrant card, and introduced himself. 'I'd like to ask you a few questions.'

'What about?'

'Inside?'

'Here'll do.'

Gilchrist returned Green's glare with a hard look of his own. But the young man wasn't for backing down. It looked like asking questions on the front step would have to do. 'You're a sous-chef at the Fairmont Hotel.'

'Used to be.'

'I was told you called in sick.'

'Who told you that?'

'Are you?'

'Am I what?'

'Sick.'

'What the fuck's it got to do with you?'

'Are you saying you're not going back to the Fairmont? That you've left your job?'

'Are you no listening to a word I'm saying? What the *fuck's* it got to do with *you?*' He stepped back as if preparing to slam the door shut, but Gilchrist beat him to it, stamped his foot on the threshold.

'Where's your car?' Gilchrist said, hoping his non sequitur might throw Green.

'What?'

'Where's your car parked?'

'Are you for fucking real, or what?'

'Oh I'm very much for real, don't you worry about that sonny Jim.' He'd put some hardness into his tone, and watched the young man's eyes narrow when he said, 'A woman's body was discovered on the golf course in the early hours of this morning close to the Fairmont. Did you know her?'

'You think I killed her?'

'I didn't say that.' He watched indecision shimmer behind the dark eyes. 'I'd like to ask you a few questions. That's all.' He waited a couple of beats, and said, 'Inside?'

This time, Green stood back.

Gilchrist brushed past him into the dark interior, and waited until the door closed behind him. 'Do you always sit in the dark?'

'I was asleep until you tried to batter the fucking door in. Here.' A switch clicked, and the place lit up.

They stood in a short hallway surrounded by three closed doors – two either side and one at the far end. Green faced him, legs apart, arms folded, lips tight. At six foot one, in the land of the short arses, Gilchrist could be considered tall. But Green stood a good few inches taller. Six-pack abs, swollen biceps, and shoulders out to here, warned Gilchrist that the man worked out. A square jaw and chiselled features added to the male model image. But the eyes were too close together, the forehead too high, downgrading handsome to just plain. And not a tattoo in sight, which pulled up an image of the dead woman.

'What d'you want to ask?'

'Are you always this angry?'

'Like I said, I was asleep, and I don't like getting wakened up by some nutter with his thumb glued to the fucking doorbell.' He took a deep breath, then let it out. 'Car's parked at the end of the road, because the street's too narrow and I don't want it scraped by bin lorries and lazy council bastards who don't give a fuck. I called in sick on Thursday because I was feeling lousy, and I'm not going back because I can't stand the sight of the head chef who thinks being the boss gives him the right to shout and swear at me all night fucking long. I don't know anything about a woman's body being found in the Fairmont, because I haven't set foot outside since I called in sick. And if they ever phone again, I'm going to tell them to take a flying fuck to themselves.' He glared at Gilchrist. 'Any other questions?'

'Do you know Jennifer Nolan?'

Gilchrist had thrown the question out there, just to gauge a reaction, and watched in silent disbelief as Green puffed out his lips, squished his eyes half-shut, and shook his head in slow motion, as if struggling to search the deepest parts of his memory banks.

'No,' he said at length, still shaking his head. 'I don't think I know her.'

Gilchrist thought it might be worth squeezing another lie out of him. 'What do you have for breakfast?'

'What?' Green scowled at him, back to Mr Angry. 'What the fuck's that got to do with anything?'

'Cereal? Cornflakes? Rice Krispies?'

'Bran flakes, if you must know.'

'With fruit?'

'Sometimes.'

'Bananas?'

'Yeah, for fuck sake. So what?'

Gilchrist shrugged. 'You called in sick on Thursday. So you haven't set foot outside since Wednesday, so you said. And tomorrow's Monday. So I'm thinking your milk must be going off. Your bananas, too.' One beat, two beats. 'Well . . . are they? Your milk and bananas? Going off?'

Green could have given a hundred different answers – I use long-life milk. I buy litre bottles at a time. I've had no bananas for days. I keep tinned fruit in case I run out. I skipped breakfast the last few days – each of them satisfactory. Instead, he eyed Gilchrist as if he'd appeared before him by magic, and swallowed a lump in his throat.

'What's your car's registration number plate?'

Green rattled it off, as if relieved at the change in tack.

'Make and model?'

'Audi S6.'

'Black?'

'Dark grey.'

'Alloy wheels?'

'Of course.'

'Nice.' Gilchrist jerked his lips in a makeshift smile. 'Right. That's it. Thanks for that, John. Sorry to trouble you.' He reached for the door handle. 'If I think of anything else, I'll be in touch. Okay?'

'Yeah, sure.' Green faced him with a puzzled frown, as if knowing he'd been tricked but without being able to work out how.

Gilchrist waited until Green shut his front door, before he drove off and did a three-point turn at the end of the street. A dark grey Audi with alloy wheels and number plate as recited, sat parked boot-end in, beside three other cars, gleaming showroom new under the overhead street lights. Green hadn't lied about his car. That much was true. But Gilchrist was willing to bet he hadn't uttered a single word of truth about anything else.

He passed Green's house again, now returned to its original state of darkness, and made a mental note to have Jackie look deeper into the man's past.

CHAPTER 10

Irene was sound asleep on the sofa when Gilchrist entered, in front of the fire, rug around her legs, paperback askew on her thigh. He didn't wake her up, but carried their fish suppers into the kitchen and laid them on the counter top. He filled up the kettle, switched it on, then walked through to the lounge.

Her subconscious awareness must have heard him, for she stirred as he approached, and opened her eyes. She smiled when she saw him. He smiled back, leaned down and pressed his lips to hers.

'You okay?' he said.

'Must've nodded off.'

'Fed up waiting for me?'

'I didn't say that.' She reached for his hand.

Although the room was warm – they kept the heating turned up all day, and the fire on most days – her fingers felt cold. She shuffled on the sofa, fluffed up the rug around her legs, folded her paperback shut. 'Tell me about your day,' she said. 'What was so important that you had to rush off to work on a Sunday morning?'

What he loved most about Irene was the concern she showed for him. She cared for him in a way that no one had ever cared for him before; neither of his parents, and certainly not his late wife, Gail, who'd seemed to consider him as little more than someone to earn an income, pay the bills, and keep the garden tidy, although he would be the first to agree he was no Titchmarsh. Instead, Irene wanted to know how he was feeling, what he was thinking, what he wanted to do, where he wanted to go, and more often than not, what he had done with his day. She wasn't prying, or trying to catch him out doing something behind her back. None of that. She was simply interested in him as a person, as a friend, as a lover.

But with that, came the other side of the coin, and what he hated most about himself – the need to sometimes smother the truth about his job, tell white lies, keep the most difficult parts of his day hidden from her. He had no wish ever to relate to her the gruesome side of his profession, the gory details of a murder victim, or how someone's life being brutally cut short seemed to be affecting him more deeply the older he became. But he had to convey a certain element of truth because, like everyone else, Irene could catch the news on the TV.

Sometimes there was just no hiding it.

He placed his hand to her forehead. 'You feel flushed,' he said, then ran his hand over her hair, short and soft, and smiled. 'It's growing back in.'

'And it's a different colour. It's white. Pure white. I didn't expect that.'

'You can always colour it, if you don't like it. But I think it rather suits you.'

She smiled at his compliment. 'And I think it's going to be curly. Which is odd. I've always had straight hair.' She tapped the seat beside her. 'Give me a cuddle.'

He sat beside her, placed his arm around her shoulder, and let her fall into him. He kissed the top of her head. 'It's tickly, too,' he said, and smiled when she chuckled.

'So . . . I take it you had a difficult day.'

He exhaled with a heavy sigh. 'You could say.'

She thought for a moment, then said, 'Will I hear about it on the news?'

'Most likely. Maybe best to catch it on the morning news, not tonight's.'

'Oh dear. Was it . . .?'

He squeezed her shoulder, pulled her tighter to him. 'Let's not talk about it. So . . .' He brightened his tone, forced himself lively. 'I've brought us a fish supper for tea. Lemon sole and chips. From Anstruther. Your favourite. It'll need a quick zap in the micro-wave, though.' He paused for a moment. 'What's up?'

'You shouldn't have, Andy. I'm sorry, but I made myself a sand-wich. Ham and tomato. I couldn't wait. I made a couple of extra. They're in the fridge. I thought you might like them.'

'Perfect,' he said. 'Ham and tomato sandwiches it is. The fish suppers'll last until tomorrow. We could even have them for breakfast, if you'd like. And why not?'

She laughed with him at that.

He squeezed her shoulder, pressed his lips to her head. 'It's good to see you've got your appetite back.'

'Not really. A couple of bites, and I feel full.'

'But it's better than how it used to be. I remember when you couldn't even face a cuppa. And the thought of a biscuit could turn your stomach.'

'Thank God that's behind me.' She puffed up her cheeks, then exhaled. 'That's a time I want to consign to history, and forget about.' She gave an involuntary shiver, tugged the rug tighter. 'But it's the lack of energy I can't stand. I feel so tired most of the time. It's as if my body's never going to get its strength back.'

'It's your body telling you how to recover. I keep telling you that. You have to take it really easy, sleep as much as you can.' He lowered his voice in imitation of being forceful. 'And you certainly don't need to go around making sandwiches. I can do all that for you.'

'But only if you're here.'

He hadn't failed to catch the nip in her voice, and resisted the urge to defend himself. Detective chief inspectors didn't have the luxury of picking and choosing what investigation they wanted to work on. They just had to get on with it. Even so, he found himself regretting not having spoken to her during the day. He should have given her a quick call, asked how she was doing, told her he was running late, that he didn't know when he would be home, he was tied up at the start of an investigation in which the body of a young woman had been found. He couldn't leave the team, he had work to do, and he would bring home a fish supper later, or another takeaway if she wanted.

Instead, he'd let that day's events override his thoughts.

The start of a murder investigation was always critical, where every lost hour could set the team back days. It was an empirical fact that if a breakthrough wasn't made in those first twenty-four hours, then each hour after that increased the likelihood of the investigation stalling, or even failing altogether. Even so, there really was no excuse for not making just a quick call.

'You're right,' he said. 'I should've phoned.'

'Yes, you should have. You know I don't want to interrupt you during the day. I never know where you are, or what you're up to. It's just . . . it's just that . . . sometimes I get lonely.'

Somehow that word stung. He hated to think of her being lonely, and knew he should be there for her. But the job always seemed to push his personal life to the side. 'I know. I'm sorry. But I don't want you ever to feel that you can't call me. Anytime. *Anytime* at all. It doesn't matter what I'm doing, or where I'm at, I'll always have time to talk to you. All right?'

She nodded.

'No,' he said. '*All right?*'

'Yes. All right.'

He retrieved his arm from around her shoulder. 'The kettle's boiled. Can I talk you into having a cup of tea?'

'That sounds nice.'

He pushed to his feet. 'I think I'm going to have a few chips on my ham sandwich.'

'On the side, you mean?'

'No. In it. It's what I call a Gilchrist chip supper.'

She smiled at his silly joke.

'Oh,' she said, 'I forgot to tell you that Joanne called. She spoke with Maureen today, who said Jack's coming home.'

Irene and Gilchrist's daughters, Joanne and Maureen, had been friends long before they'd introduced their parents to each other, an act for which Gilchrist would be forever grateful. He threw a couple of teabags into the teapot, then picked up the kettle. 'Jack's coming home? I never knew he was away. Did you?'

'No I didn't. But you know what kids are like these days.'

'Jack's not a kid. He's an adult, and a father, and he needs to start acting like one.' His sudden flush of irritation took him by surprise. He filled up the teapot, then removed a jug of milk from the fridge. 'I don't mean that, of course, it's just that Jack has this

53

family and other life that he seems unwilling to share with me, with *us*,' he added quickly.

'Do you think it might have something to do with him living in Sweden?'

'No, because he lives in Edinburgh. Doesn't he?'

Irene removed her rug, and pulled herself to her feet. 'I thought so, too,' she said. 'But Joanne told Maureen that he's flying back from Sweden tonight. In fact, he should be landing about now.' She shuffled her way into the kitchen, and flopped into a seat at the breakfast bar. 'That's better,' she said with a tired sigh. 'Why am I so exhausted?'

'It'll take time to get your strength back. It might not seem like it, but I think you're doing incredibly well.' He placed two cups on the counter, and filled them with tea.

'I think you've every right to be concerned, Andy. I know what you mean about Jack, but whether you like it or not, there's nothing you can do about it. He and Kristen have their lives to get on with, and a beautiful daughter to raise.' She took a sip, then returned the cup to the counter top with care. 'There comes a time in every parent's life, when you just have to let your children go. Let them lead their own lives.'

'To screw it up as they see fit.' He hadn't meant to say it with such vehemence, but *damn* it, why couldn't Jack give him a call to let him know what was going on? He would've gladly met him at the airport. If only he'd known. Then he realised that Jack was only doing to him what he was doing to Irene – not keeping him abreast of things.

Irene placed her hand over his. 'Andy. Look at me.'

He did.

'Jack's a good man. You know he is. He's made a life out of being an artist, doing his own thing, and a successful life at that, which few of us can say. Love Jack for who he is, Andy, not for who you would like him to be.'

Somehow, hearing those words struck home. Was that what he was doing? Trying to mould his son into how he perceived a son should be? And was that why his relationship with Maureen always seemed to be on edge, too? An interfering father who couldn't let go? All of a sudden he felt ashamed of how he'd spoken. He squeezed Irene's hand. 'You're right,' he said. 'You're oh so right.'

She giggled at that, came in close for a hug and a peck on his cheek. 'You should never underestimate the power of a woman.'

'I might have many faults. But *that*, I can assure you, is not one of them.'

'You know your place, then?'

'I most certainly do.'

It pleased him to see her smile, the never-ending exhaustion from earlier months now appearing to be on the wane. Her pain, too, was being managed well. He'd been told before, years earlier, when his late wife Gail had first been diagnosed with cancer, that once you had that despicable disease, you were never fully cured, no matter what treatment you had. The best you could ever expect was for it to be in remission, and just live with it. And that's what he needed to do with his own life now. He thought he saw that. Just get on with it. Live it to the full. Don't let other familial matters take control. Despite her promising recovery, Irene still had difficult days ahead of her, post-chemotherapy.

And whether he liked to admit it or not, by association, so had he.

CHAPTER 11

Monday
North Street Office

Gilchrist spent the following morning reading police interviews of the hotel staff and overnight guests, including those who'd only spent an evening at the restaurants or bars. He didn't have all the reports in yet. The process was resource-intensive, on top of which a number of guests had returned home, while others still had to be tracked down. He'd assigned Jessie the task of collating a full contact list, with a deadline to get back to him by midday, or no later than mid-afternoon if she ran into difficulties.

He'd also instructed Jackie to give him an initial report on Green – was he marked on the PNC, or the SCRO, the Scottish Criminal Records Office? Did he owe the taxman, was he behind on his rent, did he have points on his driving licence? – that sort of thing, rather than instructing her to spend time digging deeper into the man's employment history and financial records.

That could come later, if need be.

Sam Kim also provided him with a facial of the dead woman, with her eyes digitally recreated. One look at it, and he'd rejected it flat out. 'It doesn't look right,' he told her.

'There's a limit to what I can do,' she said.

'Why don't you place a blank rectangle over her eyes? That way you're not trying to reconfigure her looks in any way.'

She'd agreed, and within fifteen minutes sent him another image, which he approved for immediate release to all major Scottish news channels, along with a statement confirming that the body of a young woman had been found on the Castle Course, close to the Fairmont Hotel, alongside a phone number for anyone who might have any information to contact the police with complete anonymity. No mention at all of how she'd been murdered. He'd set it up so that all calls would be answered by a team at Glenrothes HQ, and he didn't expect to hear anything until shortly after the midday news.

Just before midday, he received Sam Kim's post-mortem report, accompanied by a folder of photographs that showed the victim's mutilated body in sickening close-up detail. He forced himself to study them, taking note of those around the genital area in particular, searching for that mystery tattoo. She'd taken photographs of the body in situ, as well as at the mortuary, before and after cleaning the body of blood and faeces and other detritus. Gilchrist let out an involuntary gasp of disgust at the stab wounds in and around the woman's vagina. He counted eight in total, open wounds that sliced and criss-crossed that area in cuts two inches long, with one of them deep enough to show bone. The only blessing, he was sure of it, was that the woman must have been dead when those wounds were inflicted.

But why? Why stab her there? What was to be gained? Surely not for some perverted sexual pleasure. He'd come across vicious

57

acts before which defied decency and imagination, but nothing like these. Had they been carried out for revenge, or to vent anger? But whatever the cause, who would harbour such rage? There had to be a reason for the brutality, but at that moment, he couldn't see it, as he struggled to fight back a rising surge of bile.

He pushed to his feet, and stumbled towards the window. He managed to grasp the handle and open it, and sucked in cool, fresh air as if his life depended on it. It took several minutes to steady his breath, and he ran a hand over his mouth, dabbed spittle from his chin. He glared at the open folder of photographs on his desk, from a safe distance, as if willing it to close itself and fly from his office, taking its vile contents with it—

'You okay, Andy?'

He almost jumped at the sound of Jessie's voice, then nodded to his desk. 'If you call looking at that lot normal, then yes, I'm okay.'

Jessie picked up the folder, and flipped through the images. 'Jeez,' she hissed, 'we have the mother of all sick psychos out there. What the hell? I never realised it was as bad as that yesterday. Why would he cut out her intestines? And stab her eyes? And mutilate her genitalia?'

'Those are the burning questions.'

'He wouldn't have done that for sexual pleasure. I just can't see that. I mean . . .' She cursed under her breath. Then she looked at him, and shook her head. 'I don't see this as a serial killer starting out on a murder spree. I see this as a one-off. I'd bet my reputation on it, for whatever that's worth. This is revenge. Pure and simple. And by the looks of it, I'd say boyfriend, ex-boyfriend, lover, partner? Someone close to her? She's not married, right?'

He nodded. 'We don't think so. But I had a chat with John Green last night.'

'You did?' She closed the folder, returned it to his desk. 'What did he have to say for himself?'

'Mostly lies.'

'You think he did it?'

'I didn't say that. But he's hiding something. That I do know.'

'Want me to have a go at him today?'

'Not yet. I've asked Jackie to look into him. Let's see what she comes up with first. Maybe you could chase her up.'

'I'm on it.'

He nodded, closed the window, and returned to his desk, somewhat surprised to see Jessie still standing in his doorway. 'You look as if you want to tell me something.'

She frowned. 'That list of contacts you asked me to prepare.'

'You completed it?'

'Almost there.' A pause, then, 'I'm not sure if it's worth mentioning, but something's niggling. I think it's that sixth sense of yours rubbing off on me.'

'Let's hear it.'

'I spent the morning getting copies of all our reports, then cross-referencing the names of everyone who was at the hotel on Saturday night, overnight stays, evening guests, staff coming on shift and leaving shift, making sure we hadn't missed anyone. The hotel even had three separate deliveries. Got the driver's names, and they've already been interviewed. But there's nothing there, as you'd expect, I suppose.'

'And the others?'

'Well . . .' She scratched her head. 'Probably doesn't mean anything, but there's one guy we haven't been able to track down. Leandro Hutton. We've got his mobile, which he isn't answering. He runs his own business, and his PA, that's personal assistant to

59

you and me, says he hasn't come in today. And she hasn't heard from him since Friday morning, and doesn't know where he is.'

Gilchrist frowned. 'What sort of business?'

'Hutton Insurance Services. It's a small business. Three insurance agents who advise clients on insurance options, then purchase insurance contracts. Mostly brokerage services, but commercial, which means it specialises in high-risk customers, like the marine, oil and gas industries.'

'So he makes a lot of money for not doing a lot of work.'

'Got it in one.'

He thought for a long moment. 'Why doesn't his PA know where he is? Isn't that what personal assistants are supposed to do?'

'I've had a chat with her. She sounds a bit too familiar, for my liking.'

'Meaning?'

'She's shagging him.'

'Ah. Right. Of course. I should've known.'

'No, seriously, Andy. I can tell. Women know these things.'

'I'm not going to argue with you. But shagging aside, let's make a point of talking to him. We need to find him and eliminate him from our enquiries. If we've anyone spare, get them onto it right away. This could be the break . . . we're . . .' He paused, then said, 'What? What's up?'

'I don't think we should throw all our resources at him.'

'Why not?'

'I don't think he's who we're after. He was one of a party of four on Saturday night. I've checked with the other three, and their stories match. They played a round of golf in the afternoon, then had drinks in the bar. They stayed overnight at the hotel, two rooms, then dinner in the restaurant, back to the bar, then off to bed around midnight.'

'And you've confirmed that one of them didn't wander off in the middle of the night and commit murder?'

'I've got Mhairi going through CCTV footage of the hotel entrance. Haven't heard back from her yet, but I've a suspicion they're going to turn up clean.'

'That sixth sense again?'

'I'll hunt him down if you want. But . . .' She shrugged her shoulders.

Gilchrist walked to the window and stared into the car park below. What Jessie was saying made sense. It sounded like Hutton had nothing to do with the murder. But if you ask – why doesn't anyone know where he is, or why can no one get hold of him? – then you had to come up with the only logical answer, at least to his own way of thinking – because he's hiding something.

But what? That was the question he needed to have answered.

Which put him in a bit of a quandary. Resources were tight, and becoming tighter, so he couldn't just pull someone out of the pack and send them off on a mission to find Hutton when all they were likely to achieve was to turn up nothing and deplete his budget.

He turned to Jessie. 'Where's his business located?'

'Dundee.'

'Right. Get over there and pin that PA to the wall, and don't come back until she tells you where he is?'

'I'm on my way.'

'Jessie?'

She paused at the doorway.

'I meant pin her to the wall in a metaphorical sense.'

'Of course you did,' she said, then turned and trundled down the stairs.

CHAPTER 12

Jessie parked her Fiat 500 in the Multistorey car park in Gellatly Street. The offices of Hutton Insurance Services were more than four blocks away in Nethergate, and the sun had forced its way through the clouds as if to fool Scotland into thinking summer was just around the corner. It had been a long time since she'd last walked the pedestrian thoroughfare, and it felt good with the sun on her face.

She took her time, browsing shop windows, and suspecting Andy would likely have words with her if he found out she was dithering. She'd heard that as men aged, the more mellow they became, but it seemed Andy was an anomaly. Not that he was aggressive in any way to her, or brash or forthright, but rather he seemed more driven than before, as if he knew retirement was on the horizon, and he had only so much time left before he had to let it all go. She'd once thought of retiring, too, or more correctly, walking away from the Force. But that was when she worked with Strathclyde Police in Glasgow. Like the idiot she knew she could sometimes be, she'd let herself be seduced by one of the senior detectives. Maybe seduced wasn't the right way to describe it, more like a quicky with her knickers to her knees up against an office desk. God, she shuddered at the thought, and how close it all had come to being the end of her career, before she'd had a chance to get started. But the move to Fife Constabulary to work alongside DCI Gilchrist in St Andrews CID had been a lifesaver. She owed Andy a great deal, more than just for saving her career, but for encouraging her to be the best detective she could be, and for giving her a free rein now and again to let her do her own thing – a privilege, which she realised with a shiver of shame, she was currently abusing.

Time to get back to business.

She stepped off the pedestrianised walkway onto Nethergate, and phoned Hutton's offices to confirm his PA hadn't gone out for lunch, or if she had, where she was. She hadn't, and five minutes later, Jessie skipped up a flight of steps – well, trundled up them would be more accurate – to find herself well and truly out of breath at the top landing.

She gave herself some time to recover, then pushed the door open and entered a tidy reception area – cream walls and ceiling, light wood flooring, skylight window; clean and bright. But not a person in sight, only four closed doors, and a small table with two chairs for visitors to sit and wait. No magazines or reading material, which gave the impression that visitors might be welcome, but weren't encouraged to stay long. The air hung thick with the choking scent of pine, and she located the culprit, an air freshener stuck to the wall next to a doorbell button with a sign that invited visitors to press it for assistance.

Jessie did, and heard a hard buzzing from somewhere deep within.

A door opened behind her, and she turned to face an attractive woman with brunette hair tied back, and black-rimmed specs that made her look like the perfect secretary. Mutton for lamb, was her first thought. A black skirt, six inches too short, showed more fat knee than was good for her. She'd been a head-turner once, but that was years ago, maybe decades.

She showed her teeth for a nanosecond – super-white and dentist-straight – and said, 'Can I help you?'

Jessie flashed her warrant card and introduced herself. 'I'm here to speak to Mr Hutton's PA.'

'That's me.'

'Name?'

Her forehead creased with fake concern. 'Andrea,' she said. 'How can I help?'

Jessie decided to go straight for the heart. 'Where's Leandro?'

'Mr Hutton?'

'Do you know any other Leandros?' she said, and received a demure smile for an answer. She waited a couple of beats. 'Well?'

'I'm afraid Mr Hutton hasn't come into the office this—'

'That's not what I asked.' She gave her what she hoped was one of her don't-you-mess-with-me-you-stupid-bitch stares, and said, 'I asked . . . *where* is Leandro?'

'I'm afraid I can't tell you.'

'Afraid you can't tell me? Or afraid you don't know?'

'Oh,' she said, as if puzzled by the question. 'I'm . . . I'm . . . I simply don't know.'

'So where do you think he *might* be?'

'I don't know that either.' She pursed her lips, gave a tiny shake of her head. 'Who did you say you were again?'

'Detective Sergeant Jessica Janes. St Andrews CID.' She handed over a business card. 'That's my details for when you write in to complain.'

'Why would I do that?'

'Because you're not telling me the truth.'

'I am. I don't know where Mr Hutton is.'

'So you keep telling me. But I'm asking where you think he *might* be.'

'I . . . I . . .' She shook her head.

'Look, Miss . . .'

'McKay. And it's Ms.' The word buzzed with the tiniest hint of anger.

'Look Ms McKay,' she buzzed in return. 'Let me be clear on this, so there can be no misunderstanding. I'm investigating a murder, and I need to speak to Mr Hutton as a matter of priority. If you're holding anything back from me, you could be implicated by association, and end up in court to answer some very serious charges. *Very* serious.' She was stretching it, she knew, but it was intriguing to watch the meaning of her words shift behind the eyes.

'Oh. A murder.' Hand to lips, then a shake of the head. 'I'm sorry, but I really don't know where he is. And that's the truth.'

'Phone him.'

'I already have. He's not answering.'

'Text him.' She stepped closer. 'And I'll tell you what to text.'

'My mobile's at my desk.'

'Let's go,' Jessie said, and stepped towards the door.

'Wait,' she snapped, her voice high, which told Jessie that she didn't want others in the office to know the police were here. 'I'll get it.'

'Any longer than ten seconds, and I'm coming in.'

Without a word, Andrea opened the door, and returned in record time.

'Right,' Jessie said. 'Text the following: The police are here. They want to talk to you. What do I tell them?'

They didn't have to wait long, less than a minute, before Andrea's mobile beeped.

'Let's see it.' Jessie read the text – Taking a few days off. Tell them I'll be back next week – then said, 'Ask him where he is.'

Which received the prompt reply – Where do you think?

Andrea looked at Jessie, as if wounded. 'What now?'

'That's easy,' Jessie said. 'You tell me where you think he's at.'

Andrea looked to the door, then her mobile, then back to the door again, as if trying to work out what to do next, or more likely, which lie to tell. Then, decision made, said, 'He has a holiday home where we . . . eh . . . eh . . . where he . . . where he sometimes goes to relax.'

'Address?' Jessie jotted it down on her notebook, then gave Andrea her coldest stare. 'If Leandro Hutton has gone when I get there, then I'll know you've warned him off. If you do that, I can assure you that you'll be in the deepest shit you've ever been in, and I'll see to it personally that the entire book is thrown at you. You can kiss goodbye forevermore to dirty weekends in the boss's holiday home.' She lowered her head and stiffened her tone. 'In the meantime, switch your phone off. You're not to take any calls from him or anyone else. Is that clear?'

It was.

CHAPTER 13

Shortly after one o'clock, Gilchrist felt confident he knew who the murdered woman was. Several calls had come in after the midday news confirming her to be Nicola Johnson, Nici for short, twenty-two years old, a first-year student at St Andrews University studying English and History. Originally from Edinburgh, she had moved to Fife in her late teens after the death of her mother, claiming she couldn't live in the same house as her father. She kept in contact with her younger brother, Rory, who had eventually convinced her to study at St Andrews. Rory was a second-year student at the university, and had been one of the first to contact the police after seeing Sam Kim's censored headshot on the news. He'd agreed to travel to the Bell Street Mortuary in Dundee to formally identify her body.

Which worked well with Gilchrist, for he needed the murder victim to be conclusively identified so he could put to rest his concerns over the missing Jennifer Nolan being the victim. He arranged with Sam Kim to meet him and Rory at the mortuary at 2 p.m.

Rory turned out to be tall and gangly, with short blond hair, and a handshake that was damp and limp. He seemed well dressed for a student, but many students at St Andrews came from wealthy families eager to have their children graduate from the same university as William and Kate.

'I've brought these,' Rory said, holding out a pack of photographs held together by a rubber band.

Gilchrist slipped the elastic off and worked through them. A young woman smiled out at him, the picture of health, wearing a cycling outfit and crash helmet. The next several were more of the same, taken on what looked like a cycling holiday in Scotland – brooding hills in a grey background, cloud-laden skies, gloved fingers gripping rain-dabbled handlebars, skintight Under Armour outfits, eyes and teeth and sunburned skin all gleaming with the youthful energy of life. Others showed happy groups of three, four, and the last one, a couple standing by their bikes, side by side, the skin-hugging grip of their cycling leggings leaving not a lot to the imagination. Dying young was something that could not be further from their minds.

From the images, Gilchrist was unable to tell with certainty that this was the murdered victim. Lying face down on rain-battered grass with intestines thickening her hair, he'd been unable to see the woman's face. Even when Jessie rolled the body over, he'd struggled to take a look. And then to be photographed on Sam Kim's PM table, the image censored across the eyes, all but negated any sense of recognition for him.

He tapped the full-length photo of the couple by their bicycles. 'When were these taken?' he asked Rory.

'Last summer. A group of us cycled to the west coast.'

'Who's she standing with here?'

'That's me.'

'Ah.' Gilchrist looked at the image again, and thought he saw the similarity – slim build, tight physique, same narrow face. 'You both look fit,' he said.

He nodded. 'She used to cycle five days a week.'

'Used to?' he asked, and hoped he hadn't stuck his foot in his mouth – of course it's past tense, she's dead.

But he breathed a sigh of relief when Rory said, 'She kind of lost interest after that cycling holiday.'

'Why?'

'Don't know. She wouldn't say. Just didn't want to put in as much effort.' He jerked a shoulder, like a nervous twitch. 'I think she was seeing someone. I think that's why she lost interest in cycling. But I don't know for sure. She could be a bit of a loner. She pretty much kept everything to herself.'

'Do you know who she might have been seeing?'

'No. Sorry.'

'Would anyone know?'

Another twitch of the shoulder. 'Maybe Ann. She'd be her closest friend, I suppose. They're in the same course . . . *were* . . . in the same course at uni.'

Gilchrist let a few beats pass, then said, 'Ann who?'

'Ann Templeton.'

'Is she in any of these photos?'

'No. She wasn't a cyclist.'

Gilchrist nodded, then glanced up as Sam Kim entered the room. He introduced Rory, then stood back as she slid the curtain back to expose a viewing window. A supine body lay under a white sheet, covered from head to toe.

'If you're ready?' she asked Rory.

He swallowed, with some difficulty, then nodded.

She opened the door and let him enter first.

Gilchrist didn't follow, but watched through the window. He couldn't hear what was being said, but knew that Sam Kim would handle it with professional sympathy. She would not let Rory see any of the body wounds, or let slip details of the attack, and would certainly make no mention of the evisceration. He watched her ease the sheet back, which let him catch a glimpse of the girl's face. Sam Kim had done what she could to mask the knife wounds to the eyes, but there was only so much that make-up could do. Rory stiffened for an awkward moment, then his body slumped as he nodded his head. Gilchrist never liked to see a man cry, but at least he could now put a name to the victim.

When Rory emerged from the room a few minutes later, he wiped a hand under his nose, sniffed, and shook his head. 'Why would someone murder her?' he said. 'I don't get it. Nici wouldn't hurt a fly.' His eyes pleaded for Gilchrist to give him an explanation, tell him something, *anything* to help make sense of it. But all Gilchrist could do was tighten his lips and shake his head, and find himself wondering what had drawn Nici to the Fairmont Hotel, when all along he'd been trying to find Jennifer Nolan. Had he missed something? Had Nici's surname been in any of the reports he'd read? He couldn't recall, and made a mental note to have Mhairi look into it, and follow up with Jessie once she got back from Dundee.

His thoughts were interrupted by Sam Kim saying, 'Do you have any other questions for Mr Johnson?'

Gilchrist forced his thoughts back on track, and nodded. 'This Ann Templeton,' he said. 'Do you have a contact number for her?'

Rory frowned, then said, 'Hang on. She'd be one of Nici's friends on Facebook.' He removed his mobile from his back pocket, then tapped the screen with both thumbs as fast as any typist. 'Here she is,' he said, and turned the screen to Gilchrist, to an image of a young woman pouting her lips at the camera, a glass of something bubbly in one hand, her other hand giving a V for Victory sign. The background could have been any pub in Scotland.

'How do I get hold of her?' he said.

'I can DM her for you. What would you like me to ask her?'

He wasn't sure what DM-ing someone meant, but didn't want to show his ignorance. 'Tell her to call this number as a matter of urgency.' He read out his mobile number, then softened his tone. 'She might not know about your sister. Tell her I'm with the police and that I need to speak to her about Nici.'

Rory thumbed his mobile again, then said, 'That should do it.'

While Sam Kim took Rory to the side to explain the procedure involving his sister's body – it wouldn't be available for burial or cremation until the police were satisfied they had all the information from it that they needed – Gilchrist phoned Mhairi.

'Just had her ID confirmed,' he said. 'She's Nicola Johnson, or Nici for short. Did her name come up in any of your interviews?'

'Doesn't ring a bell, sir. Would you like me to check?'

'Yes, and get back to me as soon as you can. She was a student at St Andrews Uni. Get the team working on her social media – Facebook, Twitter, and any other stuff that's out there. Who were her friends? What was she doing? Where did she go? And who with? I want the works. And get a copy of her mobile phone records. See who she last spoke to, or texted. And who called her? Have our IT guys look into it, see what they come up with. Got that?'

'Yes, sir. I'm on it.'

With that, he slipped his mobile into his pocket, said his farewells to Sam Kim and Rory, and returned to his car. Knowing the victim's name opened up new lines of enquiry. Even so, his mind was spinning with confusion. Too many names, each seemingly unrelated to the other. Was it all coincidence? He didn't know. What he did know, was that he didn't believe in coincidence.

That being the case, where did that leave him?

CHAPTER 14

Jessie parked her car half-on half-off the pavement, and switched off the engine. She stepped outside into a chilling wind, and eyed the house. A holiday home, Hutton's PA slash weekend-pussy-on-the-side had called it. But if this was a holiday home, what on earth did his main residence look like?

The bungalow – purely by definition; it was constructed on one level – had a slated roof that rose on the shallowest of pitches to ridge tiles that seemed to divide the building in two large spans, front and rear. Two pairs of six skylights, grouped side by side, provided enough sunlight to keep the living areas bright all day long, even in Scotland. A fancy car, low and sleek and silver-grey, which reminded her of a James Bond film, was parked on the cobbled driveway. In contrast, the front lawn lay thick with flattened grass and windblown leaves scattered over the garden in sodden brown piles. Flowerbeds that edged the lawn looked as if they hadn't seen the sharp edge of a hoe since the summer months.

At the front door, Jessie rang the bell, then leaned down and clattered the letterbox just for the hell of it. A figure appeared through the vestibule glass like an out-of-focus shadow, then manifested into a man wearing black needlecord chinos and a blue polo neck sweater, thick enough to weather a deep freeze. Maybe the central heating was done in.

'Can I help you?'

She held up her warrant card, introduced herself, and said, 'Leandro Hutton?'

A puzzled, 'Yes?'

'You got a minute?'

He shrugged with a frown, then stood aside. 'Of course. Come in, come in.'

As she brushed past him, she caught the musky fragrance of some aftershave she was sure must cost a fortune.

'Straight through to the living room,' he shouted after her.

At the end of the hall, she entered what she took to be the living room. Three- and four-piece sofas and assorted chairs, posh enough to be the pride of any architect-designed home, filled the space. One wall had full-length ceiling-to-floor windows that overlooked a slabbed patio area, which had to be larger than Jessie's home in Canongate. A four-panel folding door was opened wide – hence the need of an arctic sweater – beyond which a set of upended garden chairs lay side by side on the patio. Some electrical contraption, with hoses and cables unwound around it, stood off to the side.

From behind her, she heard Hutton enter the room. She turned to face him, which was when she noticed his hands. 'What's with the latex gloves?' she said.

'Just about to power-wash the garden furniture.'

'Don't you need garden gloves for that?'

'Too thick. Can't feel the switches. So . . .' He rubbed his hands, and gave a shiver. 'What's this all about, then?'

'I think you know why I'm here.'

He frowned, shook his head. 'I'm sorry, you've lost me.'

'None of your friends been in contact with you?'

'Not when I'm here. I turn my mobile off.'

Lie number one, she thought. 'No TV?'

'Barely watch it.'

'Radio?'

'Don't have one. If I want to listen to music, I stream it on my mobile. Which I turn off when I'm here. As I said.'

She hadn't been interested in whether or not he listened to music on the radio, rather she'd been prying to see if he caught the news. But something about the manner in which he spoke to her warned her that he might have known that, too. She decided to cut closer to the bone, and said, 'You played golf on the Castle Course on Saturday, then spent the night at the Fairmont Hotel.' She jerked her lips in a quick smile. 'With your three drinking buddies.'

'Yes,' he said, stretching it out to two suspicious syllables.

'We've taken statements from all three, and I'm here to take a statement from you.'

'About what, exactly?'

'We'll get to that.' She spent the next five minutes asking him details of his overnight stay, and not expecting his version of events to be any different from the others, which turned out to be the case. She closed her notebook, and said, 'Thanks for your time, Mr Hutton,' and pushed to her feet. 'We've been taking voluntary DNA swabs from everyone at the hotel,' she added. 'Simply to eliminate them from our enquiries.'

'DNA?' he said. 'Why? You haven't told me what this is about yet.'

'A body was found on the Castle Course close to the hotel. We've launched a murder enquiry.'

'Oh my God! That's the first I've heard of it. That's awful, just awful.'

Lie number two was not quite the Oscar-winning performance she'd expected, but it was not bad. Maybe the grand finale was still to come. 'So if you wouldn't mind letting me take a sample for DNA analysis. Just to eliminate you. Purely procedural. That's all.'

'I thought you said it was voluntary.'

'I did. And it is.'

'Well in that case, I don't see why I should be compelled to provide a sample.'

'As I said, to eliminate you from—'

'Yes, I know, but what guarantees do I have that you would destroy the sample once I've been eliminated from your enquiry? You say it will. But I've only your word for that. I don't think it's morally ethical that you keep an innocent person's DNA on file for posterity.'

'I agree. And we won't. And you have a right to decline, of course.' She lowered her head and eyed him over an imaginary pair of specs. 'But if you do, I have to ask – why?'

'It's the principle of the thing. That's all. I don't think it's right. It's wrong, having people's DNA kept on file like that.' He gave her a smile of squeezed eyes and wet lips, as if to let her know that was the end of it.

'As I said, once you're eliminated from our enquiry, your DNA profile and the DNA profile of every other innocent person will be destroyed.'

'Again, I only have your word for it.'

'It's standard procedure.'

'So you say.'

'So you're not willing to give a voluntary sample?'

'No.'

Jessie held his gaze for longer than she hoped would be comfortable. But he stared at her without a shimmer of uncertainty, a man confident of his rights, certain that no one would challenge him. God, she thought, what a wanker.

'Okay,' she said. 'Do you have anything you'd like to add?'

He puckered his lips, shook his head. 'Nope.'

She nodded. 'Not even to ask who the victim was?'

'Oh. I'm sorry. The DNA stuff just . . . you know.' He jerked a sad smile. 'Have you found out who she was?'

'I didn't say the victim was a woman.' She held his eyes for three long beats, then said, 'I'll see myself to the door.' She left him standing there, silent, with the thought firmly planted in her head that she would get his DNA one way or another.

CHAPTER 15

Tuesday
North Street Office

Ann Templeton phoned Gilchrist while he was having breakfast with Irene. He took the call in the living room.

'I would've called last night,' she said, 'but I was so upset when I heard about Nici's murder. I mean, I couldn't believe it. Neither could Rory. We're all so shocked.' She sniffed, then started sobbing, and he had to wait thirty seconds or so before he sensed she'd recovered her composure.

'I understand you and Nici were close,' he tried.

'We've known each other since we were in our teens. She fell out with her parents, especially her father, and left home not long after her mother died. She was strong willed that way. We shared a flat in Dundee for a while, until she moved in with her boyfriend. Don't know what she saw in him. Bit of a creep, if you ask me.'

Gilchrist's ears pricked up at that. 'When did she move in with her boyfriend?'

'Over three years ago. Closer to four, I think.'

'Got a name?'

'Timothy Johnson. I remember it, because they had the same surname, which Nici thought was really cool. She said it was fate that they'd met. But I told her she was being silly. We kind of fell out for a while after that, but we made up again.'

'And was she still living with Timothy?'

'God, no. That ended after nine months. She told me how wrong she'd been to have let him into her life the way she had. I'd never seen her so upset. For the longest time she wouldn't tell me what had happened, but eventually she did. She said he lied to her all the time, and nothing she ever did was good enough for him. There was always something wrong, calling her stupid and useless and all that sort of stuff that just grinds you down. It ended when she'd arranged a get-together with her brother, Rory, and Timothy refused to let her go. That's when she saw the light, and decided to leave him, which didn't go down well.'

'What do you mean?'

'He went ballistic, is what he did. Told her he would follow her, that he would be watching her every minute of every day. Told her that she belonged to him, and that he would beat up any man she went out with.'

'And did he?'

'She never met anyone else. She concentrated on her cycling instead. I think it was her way of getting him out of her life.'

Gilchrist gritted his teeth. Domestic abuse, one of the most insidious of crimes, and one that often went unreported. The logic of such domineering relationships still puzzled him. Despite years of physical or mental abuse, many women failed to report their partners or their husbands to the relevant authorities. He'd often thought fear of retribution was the reason, but he'd seen

79

too many women return to their abuser, despite having had the opportunity to leave and get on with a new way of living. It seemed almost like the old adage – better the devil you know. He let out a frustrated sigh at the hopelessness of it all, and said, 'Did Timothy ever resort to violence against Nici?'

'She said he didn't, but I'm not so sure. When she moved in with him, I kept in touch with her, tried to meet up at least once a week. But every now and then she'd text to say she couldn't make it. Next time we met, she would be wearing heavy make-up. But one time she couldn't hide the swelling. I questioned her about it, but she denied anything ever happened. In the end I just stopped asking.'

Gilchrist let the rationale of Ann's words filter through his mind. Nici had broken up with him about three years earlier. Was three years too long to hold a grudge? If not, then Timothy Johnson should be his prime suspect. He made a mental note to have Jackie look into the man's background, but his intuition was warning him not to expect much: why wait three years for revenge, if that was his intention? Still, it was a box that needed ticked.

Back to the present.

'Did Nici date anyone recently?' he asked.

'I don't think so. After finishing with Timothy, Nici changed. She became introverted and preferred to keep herself to herself. I encouraged her to go out more, which was when she upped her cycling, and threw herself into keeping fit.'

Gilchrist pressed on, prodding here, poking there, but soon realising he was getting nowhere. 'One final question. Did Nici ever mention Jennifer Nolan?' He threw it out there, fishing at his best.

'I don't think so, no.'

'John Green?'

'No.'

Well, as good a dead end as any, he supposed. He thanked Ann for phoning, told her he was sorry for her loss, and if she thought of anything else, to give him a call. He would need to speak to Mhairi as soon as he arrived at the Office.

He found her at her desk, eyes glued to her computer monitor. She looked up at him and said, 'Have you spoken to Jessie? She was trying to contact you.'

'Been busy. Do you know how she got on with Hutton's PA?'

'Got an address for Hutton out of her, and paid the wanker a visit.'

'Wanker?'

'That's what she said.'

'I'm listening.'

'Said she didn't get on with the guy, and that he refused to give a DNA sample.'

'Did she say why?'

'Didn't trust the police to dispose of his sample once he'd been found innocent.'

Fair enough, he thought, and made a mental note to tackle Jessie on it. 'So, how's your end coming along?'

Mhairi ingathered a pile of reports, tapped them into a tidy bundle. 'Five more DNA results, and that's nearly everyone taken care of. Except Hutton, of course.'

'Anything leap out at you?'

'Sorry, sir. No hits, I'm afraid.'

This was what he'd feared. Budgets being swallowed by wasted DNA tests. He'd have a tough time justifying the expenditure to Smiler. But he'd have to cross that bridge when it turned up. 'Okay,' he said, 'once you've got the remaining few, hand everything over to me, along with your final report.'

'I'm on it, sir.'

He nodded, gave a quick smile, then returned to his office, the thought of having to confront Smiler about the expense of useless DNA sampling pulling his feelings low.

But dammit, what else was he supposed to do?

Back at his desk, he fired up his computer and noticed he'd received an email from Jackie. He opened its attachment, scanned through the first few pages of a twelve-page report on John Green – copies of birth certificate, driving licence, numerous ANPR images of his Audi S6 – then decided it was simpler just to print it out. Maybe he was still old school, but he much preferred to read printed material, pages he could touch and scribble on, rather than reading scrolled words on a computer screen.

While the printer clicked alive, he phoned Jessie.

'Mhairi said you were trying to contact me?'

'Yeah, but I've nothing to report really. Hutton's alibi ties in with the other three, but he refused to give a DNA sample.'

'I heard.'

'Not sure if it was a wasted trip, though. He's hiding something. I don't know what it is, but I'd like to find out.'

'You think whatever he's hiding has anything to do with this current investigation?'

It took five seconds of silence before she said, 'No,' with a hard finality that told him all he needed to hear.

'Forget him, Jessie. Smiler's going to have my balls on a plate once she gets the bill for the million DNA tests we've already run. And not one bloody hit so far. We can't carry on fishing on a hunch. Call it a day. You're needed here.'

The line died.

'Bugger it,' he said, and threw his mobile onto his desk.

CHAPTER 16

By midday, Gilchrist was no further forward in his investigation. All DNA analyses fast-tracked by Mhairi had come back with no positive results, which told him that the killer was not employed by the hotel, or been an overnight or visiting guest. His highest hope had been the blood-stained sock he believed had been dropped by the killer in a rush to leave the scene. Despite it having been out all night in heavy rain, lab technicians had tested the sock for DNA, and got a result. But that, too, pulled up nothing on the PNC.

CCTV footage in and around the hotel showed nothing suspicious, even around the time of the murder, estimated to be in the small hours of Sunday morning. Annoyingly, or so Gilchrist thought, the hotel's CCTV footage turned out to be of low quality, and on a storm-riven night, visibility had been less than fifty yards. Footage from the Castle Clubhouse was of no use, too, the fifteenth green being too distant for CCTV cameras to pick anything up. If the killer had sought a more secluded place in which to murder someone, he would have been hard pressed to find one.

And Jackie's report on John Green didn't help. Her search had uncovered numerous John Greens, some with middle names, others with just initials. Passport photographs, social media downloads, and those whose birthdates put them about the same age as their suspect, narrowed the list considerably. But even so, of their suspect, nothing of historical significance turned up.

Despite Gilchrist's gut telling him that Green had been lying, the man seemed to have led a trouble-free existence. Just as he'd asked, Jackie confirmed that Green was not marked on the PNC or the SCRO, and that he owed the taxman nothing. Nor was he behind on his rent, or have any points on his driving licence. Several ANPR images showed Green's Audi in various spots around town, but no images were available during the days leading up to the murder, which told Gilchrist that the car hadn't moved from its parking spot at the end of the street in all that time.

Despite his team's best efforts, they could find no record of Green's employment history before being a sous-chef in the Fairmont. Gilchrist recognised that he'd asked Jackie to look into Green as a matter of urgency, so she might still be digging. Even so, from what she'd found, he had to conclude that Green was telling the truth, that he'd been home unwell, with his car parked at the end of the street for the duration.

He pushed away from his desk and walked to the window.

In the car park below, puddles rippled in a stiffening wind. A number of window boxes on the back sills of the buildings opposite displayed the last of the pansy colours – whites, purples, yellows. Tulips eager to bud sprouted next to dying crocuses in others. Overhead, folding clouds rolled across a threatening sky.

In an hour or so, maybe less, the town would be battered by heavy rain – at least that was the forecast.

He turned his back to the glass and eyed the reports and photographs scattered over his desk. What was he missing? An energetic and fit young woman with her life ahead of her had been slaughtered in the most brutal way, in the middle of a rain-soaked and bitter March night, out in the desolate wilderness of a links golf course, stripped of clothing, belongings, jewellery, phone.

Phone. He'd been so focused on the DNA analyses and interview reports that he'd been remiss in not chasing up on the outcome of Nici's social media contacts. But he'd heard nothing back from Mhairi or the IT guys. Did that mean Nici's mobile number had given up nothing?

He reached for his office line and called Mhairi.

'Nici Johnson's mobile,' he said. 'Have you found it?'

'No luck, sir. We have it pinging off a mast close to the Kinkell Braes just after one o'clock on Sunday morning. And that's the last. It looks like the SIM card's been removed. But I've got a record of her mobile calls, sir. Last incoming call was at ten forty-three on Saturday night from a number registered to Ann Templeton. That call lasted two minutes and thirty-one seconds.'

'And before that?'

'Nothing of interest, sir. The IT section made a list of the numbers of all incoming and outgoing calls, with a note of the account holders' names beside each. We're in the process of contacting each account holder.'

'Does the name John Green appear anywhere?'

'Hang on while I check,' she said, then came back quickly with, 'No, sir.'

Somehow, hearing that deflated him, even though he knew it shouldn't. After all, John Green had been in bed all weekend – so he said.

'As you would expect, sir, she texted much more than she phoned. I've requested a printout of all text records, but haven't received anything back yet.'

'What about her contact list?' he tried. 'Anything in that?'

'Again, sir, I haven't got that back from the IT section. As soon as I receive it, I'll let you know. Would you like me to send you a copy when I do receive it, sir?'

'Please. And Mhairi?'

'Yes, sir?'

'Well done. And keep up the good work.'

'Thank you, sir.'

He returned his phone to its cradle, and reclined in his chair. Mhairi was proving to be a useful member of his team, continuing to use her own initiative, and moving things forward without having to ask. It was time she considered applying for promotion, he thought, and he made a mental note to bring it up at the first opportunity with Smiler. But just the thought of meeting Smiler had him pushing to his feet, and heading to the stairwell.

Time for a coffee, or a bite of lunch at Irene's.

He turned into College Street, the narrow cobbled road that connected North Street to Market Street, on one corner of which stood the Central Bar, and on the other, Costa Coffee. Despite the cold weather and a heavy breeze, tables and chairs had been set up outside the Central, as if to persuade passersby that winter was a thing of the past, and warmer days were just around the corner. At that moment the skies opened, somewhat timely he thought, and decision made, he turned left and entered the Central from the Market Street entrance.

It never failed to amaze him how many people had time to spend lunchtime in a bar, not to mention having the money to pay for lunch and drinks. Early afternoon, Tuesday, and he estimated thirty or so seated around the place, eating, drinking, chatting, many of them – mostly the younger ones – on their phones texting, maybe even gaming, for all he knew.

He took a seat at the bar and ordered soup of the day and a pint of 80 Shilling. He pulled out his mobile, found the number in contacts, and dialled it.

After eight rings, his call was transferred to voicemail. He was about to hang up, then changed his mind. 'Irene, it's me. I hope you're okay and that I haven't disturbed you. I was going to swing by for a cup of tea and a quick bite, but it's pouring down, so I'll see you later. Bye. Love you.'

He ended the call as the barman placed his pint in front of him. He took a sip, then eyed his mobile, not sure if he should make the call or not. Another sip, which turned into a mouthful and took it almost to halfway, helped him make up his mind. Despite having called the number infrequently, he knew it by heart.

Jack answered on the first ring. 'Hey, man, how're things?'

Gilchrist went through the customary platitudes with his son before arriving at the purpose of his call. 'Mo told me you flew back from Sweden yesterday.'

'Yeah. Got in late afternoon.'

'Where are you staying?'

'A friend's in Edinburgh.'

'Anyone I know?' Which received a hard chuckle, followed by silence. 'So how's your studio doing?'

87

'Not bad. Good days, bad days, the usual, you know.'

He almost complained that he didn't know what *the usual* was, because Jack and he rarely phoned each other any more. And any time they did speak or meet, it always seemed to have been as a result of Gilchrist's efforts. But he shifted the subject. 'And Kristen and Linna? How are they keeping?'

'Good. Good. Yeah, they're keeping good.'

'Will they be flying over, too?'

'No. No. They're still in Sweden. But doing well. Both keeping good. Yeah.'

'So . . . how long are you staying in Edinburgh?'

'Difficult to say, Andy. A week or two. A month, maybe. Maybe longer. You know. Probably best just to suck it and see.'

'Okay.'

'Yeah.'

Which more or less drained Gilchrist of anything else he wanted to ask. But he clung onto one last hope. 'So . . . will you be coming up to St Andrews anytime soon?'

'Difficult to say, Andy. Difficult to say. Probably not. You know. Stuff here.'

'Okay.' A pause, then, 'Maybe Mo and I can drive down to Edinburgh someday. Meet up for a pint or three.' He threw in a chuckle just to keep it light. But it seemed he was on his own.

'Sure. Yeah. That'd be good. Yeah, man. That'd be good.'

'Well I'll eh . . . I'll give you a call, Jack, try to set something up with Mo . . . Soon?'

'Yeah. Do that. Yeah. Listen, man. Good to talk. Got to go. Catch you. Okay?'

'Okay.'

But the line was already dead.

Gilchrist slipped his mobile into his pocket, and stared at his pint. Jack hadn't said much, but he'd said enough to let him know that his son was hiding something, maybe even in some kind of trouble. But just what he was hiding, or how much trouble he was in, was the question that needed answering.

CHAPTER 17

When Gilchrist opened the door to Nici Johnson's flat and stepped inside, he was struck by the fragrance, an almost overpowering aroma that reminded him of gift shops at Christmas. The air was thick enough to taste, redolent of potpourri and cinnamon. He found the culprits; pewter-lidded glass containers that sat on top of window sills, side tables, bookshelves, coffee tables, even one on the floor tucked behind the sofa.

'Jesus,' Jessie said. 'Did she buy all this stuff in bulk?'

'What else do you notice?' Gilchrist said.

'That I'm choking and about to boak?'

'Aside from that.'

Jessie looked around the room, then walked to an ornately framed mirror on the wall, raised her arm and ran a latex-gloved hand along the top of the frame. She shook her head as she studied her fingertips. 'Not a speck,' she said. 'So I'm thinking she's a neat freak.'

'Agreed.' Gilchrist let his gaze shift around the room. Paperbacks stood to attention, all arranged from left to right in authorial alphabetical order, on shelves that looked freshly

90

painted. Another shelf housed hardbacks – histories, biographies, literary prize winners – again in order, in the corner of which sat one of the ubiquitous potpourri containers.

The walls, too, looked bright and fresh, no wallpaper, just off-white paint rollered on nice and thick. Framed black and white photographs ran in three parallel rows along one wall – six on the top, five in the middle, and six on the bottom – each ten by eight frame level and lined up perfectly with the others, as if they'd been put up using a spirit level and plumb bob.

'See this?' Jessie said, pointing to a boxed shelf in which sat two SLR camera bodies – Nikon, Canon – each with the shutter aperture covered by a plastic dust cap. 'These might interest you. Aren't you into photography?'

'More Irene's cup of tea,' he said, and lifted the Nikon off the shelf. He turned it over, pressed the shutter button to the sound of a solid click. An F3, one of the top single lens reflex cameras in the eighties, and one of the more expensive. He returned it with care to the shelf. 'This is before Nici's time,' he said. 'Why's this got your attention?'

'Nothing, really,' she said. 'Neat freak. The place looking like it's had the living shit polished and hoovered out of it.' She shrugged. 'Photos on the wall? Camera arty-farty stuff on the shelves? Makes me wonder, so it does.'

'About what?'

'About what photos she's got on her phone.'

'Well, that's easy. It's missing, likely never to be found. And its SIM card's probably destroyed. So we're never going to be able to find out what's on her phone, are we?'

'You ever heard of the Cloud?'

'What's that? A group?'

'It's digital storage. It's where everyone files their stuff now, because there's not enough space on computer hard drives any more.'

'Ah,' was all he could think to say.

'Jeez, Andy, you really need to get up to speed with IT gizmos and stuff.'

'I leave that to the experts,' he said, and held her gaze. 'So . . .? This cloud?'

'I'm betting she's got a ton of photographs, not printed out, but stored in perfect alphabetical order in some perfectly archived file somewhere in the Cloud.'

'And how do we find this archived file?'

'As you said, we leave that to the experts.'

He let his gaze roam around the room while his mind worked through the logic of what Jessie had told him. Would Nici's archived photographs help them solve her murder? He couldn't see how they could. Yet, on the other hand, having a look through them might be more than just a box to be ticked. He'd learned from experience that you never could tell where something would lead you.

He turned to Jessie. 'Get our IT team onto that.'

'They're already on it,' she said.

'Well give them a kick up the backside in that case. Tell them it's urgent.'

Jessie gave him a flickered smile, then turned away, phone in hand.

Gilchrist left her to it, and entered Nici's bedroom. For all its neatness, the flat was small and compact, large enough for only one tenant. From what he'd learned of Nici and seen from her tidy apartment, he had a sense that living by herself suited her. A single bed hugged one corner of the room. The walls were devoid of the usual teenage-girl posters of boy bands and pop idols, which he supposed was because Nici had been a young woman in her early twenties, who'd outgrown her teenage desires. He spent a few minutes opening and closing drawers, noting sweaters, socks, undergarments, all neatly folded, and all fresh and clean, some still with their price tags on. He closed one drawer as Jessie entered the room.

'I bloody knew it,' she said.

He turned to face her. 'Knew what?'

'The bed's made.' She shook her head. 'I mean, just look at it. You could bounce a coin off that duvet and it would hit the ceiling. What did she pay a month for this place? Jeez, you can hardly swing a cat in here. And where does she keep the rest of her clothes? I don't see a wardrobe in here.' She nodded to the bedside table. 'Find anything in that?'

'No clothes, if that's what you mean.'

Without a word, Jessie kneeled on the floor, lifted the edge of the duvet to expose two drawers that slid out from under the bed. 'Ah, here we are.' She pulled one open. 'Looks like she's got her summer clothes stored in this one,' she said, easing blouses, shorts, swimwear aside. She closed the drawer and opened the other. 'Tell you what though, she wasn't afraid to spend money on clothes. This one's still got the price tag on it.' She whispered a whistle. 'Eighty quid for a skirt? Jeez, the only way I'd buy an eighty-quid skirt would be in a charity shop where you might be able to haggle it down to ten, maybe a fiver.'

She smoothed the skirt flat, and opened the other drawer. 'Looks like winter stuff in this one.' She peeled back a couple of folded sweaters. 'Feel the texture. Cashmere. Oh, my goodness. I could be happily buried wearing this.'

She was about to shut the drawer, when Gilchrist said, 'Hold on.' He leaned forward, slid his hand down the side of the clothes, and removed a leatherbound booklet, about the size of a mass-market paperback. 'A diary,' he said, and noted the date. 'And it's this year's.' He opened it, and felt a flush of disappointment at the crisp stiffness of the pages, as if it had never been opened. A flick through January's blank pages proved him right. He flipped through more pages while Jessie pressed closer for a peek.

'Anything?' she said.

He shook his head. 'It's blank,' he said, and handed it to her.

'Well why hide it in a drawer under the bed if there's nothing in it?'

'Maybe she forgot she had it.'

He was about to walk from the room, when Jessie said, 'I'm thinking it's a Christmas present from someone she didn't like.' Something in her tone stopped him. He frowned at the smirk on her face.

'What don't I know?' he said.

She held out the diary, opened at the front cover. In the top left-hand corner, in thin looping handwriting, the simple words:

For making memories
Love always
TJ

'The only TJ I can think of,' she said, 'is Timothy Johnson.'

Gilchrist grimaced. 'Therein lies the problem.'

'What d'you mean?'

'If the TJ in the diary is the Timothy Johnson that Nici used to go out with, emphasis on *used to*, then she's no longer his girlfriend, and hasn't been for three years. And if that's the case, why would he suddenly pop out of the blue and give her this year's diary?'

'Trying to get back into her knickers?'

'According to Ann Templeton, Nici would have nothing more to do with him.'

'But this diary shows that *he* wants something to do with *her*.'

'Only if TJ stands for Timothy Johnson.'

'Aye, well, there is that,' she said, and looked at the diary as if defeated.

'Bag it anyway. Forensics may be able to lift TJ's fingerprints off it.'

'That's a bit of a longshot.'

'But at least it's a shot.' He cringed at the improbability of it all, then said, 'We need to double our efforts in locating Timothy Johnson. If we're right about the initials, then that diary puts him in recent contact with Nici. And if he's half as abusive as Ann Templeton says he is, then it makes him a strong suspect for Nici's murder. Get onto Mhairi, and have her and Jackie focus on finding him.'

'I'm on it.'

'And get the IT guys to go through Nici's social media with a toothcomb. She once lived with Timothy Johnson. So I can't believe there isn't a photograph of him somewhere. And get them to look into her Cloud, too, or whatever it's called. I'm beginning to think that might be the only way we're going to find this mysterious Mr Johnson.'

Jessie nodded, walked from the room, mobile to her ear.

As Gilchrist followed her, he stopped in the doorway and let his gaze scan the room once again. He was missing something.

They both were. He was sure of that. But what they were missing, he could only guess at.

Timothy Johnson seemed to be the key now.

Find TJ, and everything would slot into place.

If it were only that simple.

He turned, and followed Jessie from the building.

CHAPTER 18

Gilchrist's debriefing earlier in the evening had turned up nothing new. The IT section assigned three computer analysts to scour Nici's social media and access her archived files in the cloud, looking for any connection to Timothy Johnson, but so far had turned up nothing, which had Gilchrist frustrated almost to the point of anger. Jessie had already left for the day, having promised to give Robert a lift to the airport – *He's flying to Manchester for a few days with his girlfriend* – which left Gilchrist to take out his frustration on Mhairi.

'Nici had moved in with him several years ago, right?'

'Right, sir, yes.'

'So he must've meant something to her at one point in their relationship, right?'

'Right, sir. But it seems that their relationship lasted only six months or thereabouts.'

'Even so, when you're young, six months in a relationship is a long time, isn't it?'

'I would say so, sir, yes.'

'So why can't we find any photographs of them together? What am I missing?'

'I think what you might be missing, if I may, sir . . .'

He held her gaze, tried to soften his tone. 'I'm listening.'

'. . . Is that Nici broke up with Timothy, sir. Not the other way around. She left of her own accord after realising she was in an abusive relationship. Now, sir, with respect, if you put yourself in her shoes – an abused woman facing her male abuser who we would have to assume is physically larger and stronger than she is – then what Nici did, sir, ending their relationship then walking away, took tremendous courage. Not many woman would have the mental strength to do that, sir.'

'Okay. I get that.' He almost shrugged his shoulders. 'So . . .?'

'Well, if that was me, sir, and I'd just done what Nici had done, then the first thing I'd do would be to delete any and all historical contact with him, including everything I had on Facebook, Twitter, and any other social media. I'd also rip up every photograph of the pair of us together, or of him individually, then I'd shred them to pieces, make a nice little pyre, and burn them. Sir.'

Gilchrist raised his eyebrows, and mouthed a silent 'Wow', then felt his lips spread into an involuntary smile. 'Remind me never to fall out with you, Mhairi.'

'Yes, sir,' she said, then blushed at her comment.

If Mhairi's thoughts were correct, then it didn't look good for the investigation. Not just one more hurdle to overcome, but one that might stop them cold. All of a sudden he felt tired, mentally. And stiff. He lifted his arms to shoulder height, and stretched, then glanced at his watch – just after eight – more than a little surprised when he realised what time it was.

'Why don't we call it a day, Mhairi, and hit it fresh first thing in the morning?' He didn't wait for her answer, but turned and walked from the room, removing his mobile from his pocket, already feeling remiss at not having phoned Irene sooner.

Rather than drive straight back to St Andrews from Edinburgh Airport, Jessie took a detour. Well, not a detour *per se*, more like taking a long way home for a shortcut. At the end of the narrow lane, she drew to a halt outside Leandro Hutton's bungalow, switched off the lights, and killed the ignition.

Blackness fell around her like a thick blanket.

She waited several minutes to let her eyes adjust to the darkness, then rolled down the window. Not a sound. The night air seemed stilled by her very presence. Nothing stirred. She opened the door, stepped into the country chill, and stood still for a worrying moment as she scanned the shadows around her, feeling the oddest sense that she was not alone. She gave an involuntary shiver, whispered to herself there was nothing to fear, no one was home, it's all in your imagination. Then she eased the car door shut with a dull thud for a click that seemed to echo around the woods like a hammer hit.

The driveway lay deserted, which almost convinced her that Hutton had returned to the matrimonial home. Of course he would have. There was no need to hide any more. She'd shown him her hand yesterday. If he continued to refuse to give a DNA sample, there was eff all they could do. Well, not quite eff all, because Jessie had taken a dislike to Hutton, and was convinced he was hiding something. Why else would he refuse to give a sample? There had to be a reason. So to Jessie it didn't matter if Hutton was alibied to the hilt – playing golf and staying overnight at the Fairmont with his drinking buddies – she was going to get his DNA sample whether he knew about it or not.

She entered the property and stepped off the driveway onto the lawn with the oddest sense that Hutton was still here, and had parked his car in the garage and was now sitting in the dark, watching her creep around his garden. Her gaze instinctively shifted to the eaves of the house, its looming shape silhouetted against the forest backdrop. She'd noticed CCTV cameras yesterday, several of them, one in each corner of the building, high up, tucked under the eaves, and one at the front door. If any were connected to lights with motion sensors she could find herself in deep shit. Just that thought almost had her retracing her steps. But she stood still for the count of thirty, swore under her breath, and whispered, 'Fuck sake, Jessie, just get this done and dusted.'

She crept forward, deeper into the property, eased her way along the side of the house, pushed open a gate that hadn't been locked, then stepped into the black expanse of the back garden. Only then did she slip on latex gloves and switch on her pencil torch. The beam slid along the rear of the house, shivered up the wall, darted down to a slabbed path, then swung across the patio like a narrow searchlight until it found its way to the garden furniture, then beyond to a row of recycling bins at the far corner. She gave the patio area a wide berth, just in case motion sensors had been installed at the sliding doors, and reached the recycling bins without mishap. She lifted the lid of the first bin, and shone her torch into its depths.

Empty. Shit.

The next bin was empty, too, which had her mumbling under her breath. Was the guy another neat freak who took his rubbish home with him? Which made sense, if she thought about it. If he didn't stay here for months at a time, then that was the sensible thing to do, rather than leave the bins' contents to decompose and stink, only to be removed the next time he was here. But her concerns were blown away when she opened the last bin to find a black plastic bag sitting at the bottom.

She reached down and pulled it out.

The bag had been tied in a loose knot, which she unravelled with ease. Rather than tip its contents onto the ground, she opened it and shone her torch inside. At first, all she could pick out were discarded cardboard containers from a Chinese takeaway, a pepperoni pizza box, three tins of baked beans, four empty wine bottles, and two champagne – so much for being a conscientious recycling homeowner – scrunched up paper towels, an upended flower pot with its dead plant still rooted in it. She was on the verge of calling it a day, or more correctly, night, but rummaged deeper, until there, there they were – two latex gloves pulled inside out from being taken off.

'Got you, you bastard.' She removed an evidence bag from her pocket, stretched into the bin and, with the tips of her own latex-gloved fingers, lifted the discarded gloves from the bin, and placed them with the utmost care into the evidence bag. She didn't really believe that Hutton was involved in Nici Johnson's murder, and she hadn't mentioned to anyone what she was intending to do. The current murder investigation needed every person giving it their full attention, and if Andy ever found out what she'd done, she knew she'd get a right bollocking from him. But Hutton's refusal to give a DNA sample had simply stuck in her craw, a loose end that needed tied down, a box that needed ticked – as Andy would often tell her.

Well, she would tie that loose end down and tick that box, and if the sample turned up nothing, then she'd keep her mouth shut and never say a word to anyone. But as she retraced her steps along the driveway, placed the evidence bag into the boot of her car, she couldn't shift that stirring feeling in her gut – that sixth sense of Andy's rubbing off on her – that she was going to turn up something unexpected.

Why else would Hutton have declined to give a sample?

There had to be a reason. Surely. But with just those thoughts, the slightest shiver of doubt crept into her mind. Bloody hell, she thought, what on earth was she thinking? Without a warrant, any DNA results would be inadmissible, and what she'd just done could have her facing a disciplinary charge. Or worse, she could find her integrity over this and other cases being questioned in a tough grilling in court.

Did she have it all wrong?

Well, by this time tomorrow, she would know for sure.

She switched on the ignition, and eased her car down the country lane.

CHAPTER 19

Irene was upstairs in bed when Gilchrist arrived home.

Her bedside light was on, dimmed low. He tiptoed in stocking soles to the side of her bed intent on removing a paperback that lay open-paged on the sheets by her shoulder, when she stirred awake.

'I didn't mean to wake you,' he said. 'Sorry.'

She gave him a kind smile and a whispered, 'That's okay.'

He lifted her book, and laid it face down on the bedside table, then sat on the edge of the bed and took hold of her hand. 'How d'you feel?'

'Tired.' She offered another smile. 'But okay. Nothing to worry about.' She shuffled herself up the bed, and he helped by fluffing up a pillow behind her head, and easing her into a half-sitting position. 'Ah, that's better.' She squeezed his hand. 'Have you eaten?'

'I'll have something in a minute.'

'I made a salad, with some cold meat. It was all I could face. I left you a plate on the breakfast bar. I didn't know when you would be home. And there's last night's fish supper if you want to heat it up.'

'Got tied up at the Office. Sorry. It's . . . eh . . . it's hectic at the moment. So I couldn't really break free to give you another call. Sorry.' Which seemed to be all he could think of saying.

'Well, at least the salad won't go off.'

'I'd better eat it then, before it gets warm.' He chuckled at his silly joke, and squeezed her hand. 'Can I get you anything?'

She looked around the room, as if searching for something. 'What time is it?'

'Five past nine.'

'Oh. I'd better get up. There's a programme on the TV I want to watch.'

'I can record it, if you'd like.' He eased off the bed and pushed to his feet.

'I much prefer to watch it live.' She pulled back the duvet cover and slid her feet to the floor. 'Can you put the kettle on, and I'll make us a cuppa? Oh, and before I forget, Mo called. Did she get hold of you?'

'No. Why?'

'She didn't say. She called earlier in the evening, asking for you.'

'She didn't think to phone my mobile?'

'Well, she knows how busy you are, of course.'

He gave her a quick smile, but his lips felt tight. He wasn't sure if her comment was innocent, or her way of letting him know that she was becoming sick and tired of his working late. But wisely he said nothing, and helped her on with her dressing gown, then took her hand and led her downstairs.

Once Irene was seated in front of the TV, the fire on high, and a cup of tea with a digestive biscuit on a plate by her side, Gilchrist excused himself – Going to have a shower – after all, the salad could wait.

Upstairs, he phoned Maureen.

'You called earlier?'

'Yeah, Dad. It was just . . . have you spoken to Jack yet?'

'I phoned him this morning. Why?'

A pause, then, 'I got a call from Kristen this afternoon.'

'Is she back in Scotland, too?'

'No. That's the problem. She's still in Sweden.'

A couple of beats before he said, 'Sorry, Mo. You've lost me. What's the problem?'

'I didn't want to phone you at work, because . . . well . . . well I just didn't.'

'You've got me on the phone now. So what's up?'

Maureen sent a heavy sigh down the line, then said, 'Kristen says she can't get hold of Jack. He's not answering his phone. She's left umpteen messages. And texted him, too. But he's just ignoring her.'

'Okay,' he said, stretching the word. 'We all know what Jack can be like, especially if he's drinking. Is that the problem? He's back in Scotland, and hitting the bars, doing a pub crawl around Edinburgh for old times' sake?'

She tutted, which told him he'd got it wrong. 'He needs to speak to Kristen, Dad,' she said with some force in her voice. 'It's as simple as that. I've tried calling, too, but he's not answering. Can you please get hold of him tonight, and tell him to phone her? It's urgent.'

A cold wave flushed Gilchrist's body from head to toe, as the logical outcome of what Maureen was saying washed over him like an arctic wind. Surely never. Oh, dear God, no. Not that. Not their daughter. 'Don't tell me something's happened to Linna.'

The line fell silent for several seconds, and he felt the air leave his lungs.

Then Maureen was back with, 'Not directly, Dad.'

He sucked in air for all he was worth, his mind struggling to work through the fog that seemed to have enveloped his sense of logic. Not directly? What did that mean?

'So . . .' he said. 'So . . .' But the words wouldn't come.

'Linna's okay,' Maureen said. 'She's okay, Dad.'

'Thank God,' he gasped. 'For a moment there . . .'

'Please, Dad, just phone Jack and tell him to call Kristen as a matter of urgency.'

He pressed his mobile hard to his ear, turned and paced the room. Maureen wasn't telling him the truth, the whole truth, and nothing but the truth. And so help me God, he was going to find out what was going on. *Not directly.* Those were the key words.

'Okay, Mo.' He thought he knew the answer, but asked just the same, this time with some venom in his tone. 'What the hell has Jack done?'

'This is why I didn't want to call you at the Office, Dad.'

'Tell me, Mo.'

'Just tell Jack to phone Kristen. Please, Dad, please.'

'It's Linna, isn't it?'

Silence.

'Has Kristen gone to the police?' he said.

The line filled with the heavy sigh of defeat. 'Not yet. But if she doesn't hear from Jack by midday tomorrow, she says she will. She says he's left her no choice.'

Perhaps he didn't know Kristen as well as some fathers knew their son's other half, but he thought he knew her well enough to feel certain that when shove came to push, she would bulldoze herself into action, full pelt, no holds barred.

'Has she said she would press charges?'

'Oh, for fuck sake, Dad.'

'Has she?' Firmer that time. The truth, or else.

'Yes. She said she would have him charged with kidnapping.' Another pause. 'I'm really worried, Dad. Do you know what the sentence for kidnapping a child in Sweden is?'

He didn't, not off the top of his head. But like other civilised countries, children's welfare was paramount, and sentences for endangering a child's life were usually high. 'Get hold of Kristen,' he said. 'Tell her I need until this time tomorrow night. Midday's too soon. She has to understand that. Nine o'clock. Tomorrow *night*. Got that?'

'I'll do what I can, Dad, but I don't know if she'll agree to that.'

'Tell her, Mo. Tell her I'll do everything in my power to talk some sense into that excuse for a son of mine. And tell her not to worry about Linna. If I have to take her from Jack myself, I'll do that.'

'Okay, Dad. I'll call her. In the meantime, try to settle down. Okay?'

'Don't worry about me, princess. I'm as calm as can be.'

'Thanks, Dad. Let me know the instant.'

The line died.

Gilchrist gripped his mobile tight, struggling with the urge to smash it against the wall and shout at the top of his voice. He took a couple of deep breaths to settle himself, then set about focusing on the problem at hand. What the hell was Jack thinking? Or more worrying, what kind of person had Jack become? This was not the way his kind-hearted, artistic son behaved. He'd

raised Jack from birth, and in all that time, even through the difficult years, he'd seldom heard him raise his voice. Even as he
thought about it, he couldn't remember the last time they'd had
cross words. They'd disagreed of course – who hadn't? – but
never to the point of raised voices, or worse, physical violence.

But no matter how he tried to rationale it, what Jack had done
was serious. To take his daughter from her mother, then to fly her
to another country, and clearly without the mother's consent?
That was kidnapping. A good solicitor might be able to argue
against that. Jack was Linna's father, after all. But even so, Jack
really had dug a hole for himself.

Gilchrist raked his fingers through his hair. This was so out of
character, it screamed of mental instability. Or, when he thought
more clearly about it, drug misuse. If that was so, then God help
Jack if the Swedish authorities got their hands on him.

He stared at his mobile. He had to phone Jack. Right then and
there.

He dialled his number, and cursed when he got a dead tone.
Bugger it. This was worse than he'd thought. Jack had powered
off his mobile, or worse, removed his SIM card, and was in effect
now running from the law. He pressed his knuckles to his mouth.
Fuck it, fuck it, *fuck* it.

He puffed up his cheeks, blew out some air. He didn't want
anyone else involved, but he really had no other options. He
dialled another number he knew by heart, and when it was
answered on the third ring, said, 'Dainty?'

'Speaking.'

'I need your help.'

CHAPTER 20

7.15 a.m., Wednesday
North Street Office

Jessie entered Gilchrist's office, then stopped in the doorway.

He looked up from his computer.

'Are you okay?' she said.

'Yeah. Why?'

'You look like . . . I was gonnie say shit . . . but you look worse than that.'

'Didn't sleep too well last night.'

'Another late-night curry?'

He jerked a half-hearted smile.

'Good morning to you, too. Got you the usual. A large latte. Fatty, not skinny. And I asked for an extra shot. Looks like you could use it. Here. Didn't get you a muffin, as I'm trying to lose some weight.'

He wrapped his hands around the cardboard cup, breathed in the coffee aroma. And the warmth, too, felt welcome. The temperature had dropped overnight, and a haar frost had settled like a light dusting of snow. At that time in the morning, the Office heating had just kicked in. He still had his scarf around his neck. 'Just what I needed,' he said. 'Thanks.'

'I'm too good to you. You know that, don't you?'

He smiled, and wobbled his head. 'Maybe.'

'You wish.' She took a sip of her own coffee, and said, 'Just heard from Mhairi that Jennifer Nolan's car's been located. That white Ford Focus. Remember?'

'And Jennifer?'

'Still missing.'

He held her gaze for several seconds, then said, 'I don't see the connection yet. But I'm sure there has to be one. There just has to be. It's all too coincidental. Don't you think?'

'It's strange, that's for sure.'

He stared out the window, then back to Jessie. 'So Jennifer's car's been abandoned?'

'They told me you were good. Come on. Drink that on the way.'

Gilchrist drew to a halt behind a white Ford Focus parked off the B9131 about two kilometres north of Anstruther. Two cottages less than twenty yards apart – one ahead of the Focus, the other behind – could make anyone driving past think the car's owner lived in one of them. It had taken one of the residents to call it in last night, before officers on duty could confirm it was the car they'd been looking for. They'd then run tape around it and set it up as a crime scene, until instructed differently.

'No damage,' Jessie said. 'Looks like it's been parked here with care.' She tried the driver's door. Locked. Other doors, too, were locked. She walked to the boot, gave the handle a tug, but

110

without a key she was wasting her time. She peered inside. 'Nothing lying around. No key in the ignition. Nice and tidy. I think we've got another clean freak.'

Gilchrist scanned the open fields around them. If Jennifer had parked her car and locked it up, where would she have gone? Other than the cottages, they could be in the middle of nowhere. It didn't look like the place you would park to walk the dog. So why park here? Had she met someone, a lover perhaps, and jumped into his car for a bit of sex on the side? But she lived by herself, so there was no need for any juvenile backseat flings. And even if she had, why not return to her car and drive home?

No, he thought, this car has been abandoned here because Jennifer was in trouble. And he didn't like the looks of it. She was missing, and no one had heard a word from her. But her car showed no signs of struggle, nothing amiss on the inside, just carefully parked, doors locked, then . . . what?

He turned to face Jessie. 'Who called it in?'

'A Ms Smith. At number three.' She nodded to one of the cottages. 'That one there.'

'Who lives in the other one?'

'Don't know that, yet.'

'Find out, will you?'

'Already on it.'

By the time Gilchrist had reached the front door and given it a hard rap, Jessie had caught up with him. 'Ferguson,' she said. 'A pair of pensioners.'

Gilchrist nodded acknowledgement, then turned at the sound of locks turning.

The door opened wide to a woman in her fifties, powdered face, mascaraed eyes, and blonde hair that looked too perfect to be her natural colour. He thought the white jodhpurs were a tad over the top, but they matched her woollen sweater. Her outfit was topped off by a tartan jacket with matching waistcoat, and a purple cravat that plumped out under her chin.

He showed his warrant card, introduced himself and Jessie, then said, 'We're looking into the disappearance of a young woman. Her car, the white Ford, is parked along the road. I understand you reported it to the local police last night.'

'I did, yes.'

He caught the accent, east coast Scottish, with a hint of upper-class elocution. 'When did you first notice it parked there?'

'Sunday night, when I walked with Casper.'

'Casper?'

'My dog. A Leonberger.'

Jessie said, 'Where's Casper now?'

'Out the back, having a good sniff around.' She flickered Jessie a smile, then returned her attention to Gilchrist.

'Did you notice anything unusual about the car?' he said.

'Other than it had been left overnight unattended? No.'

'Did you happen to see the driver?'

'No.'

'Hear anything around the time it was parked?'

'I couldn't tell you exactly when it was parked.'

'What time did you walk Casper?'

'Eleven-ish.'

'And it was parked at that time.'

'No. It wasn't.'

Gilchrist frowned. 'Excuse me, I thought—'

'It wasn't parked there when I *took* Casper for a walk. It was parked there when I brought him *back* from his walk.'

He glanced at Jessie, pleased to see she had her notebook out. 'Can you be more specific about the times?' he said.

'Not really. I didn't have my watch on.'

Jessie interrupted with, 'What was on the telly when you decided to walk Casper?'

'The ten o'clock news had just finished. So . . .'

'So ten minutes to put your gear on and grab Casper's lead,' Jessie said. 'That about right?'

'Yes. I . . . I would say so. Give or take. Yes.'

Jessie scribbled into her notebook. 'And how long was Casper's walk?'

'I don't really know. I never time it.'

'Best guess. An hour? Two hours? Ten minutes? What?'

'Oh, I would say . . . less than an hour, maybe.'

'Forty-five minutes?'

'About that, yes.'

'So, sometime between ten forty and eleven twenty-five, let's say, someone parked that Ford Focus up the road. That about right?'

She glared at Jessie as if seeing her for the first time. 'About that, yes.'

'You take your phone with you when you walk Casper?'

'Sometimes.'

'And last night?'

'Yes.'

'Call anyone?'

'What? Look . . . I'm not sure I like your attitude young lady.'

'Janes. Detective Sergeant Janes. So . . . did you call anyone?'

'I don't see what my personal calls have to do with anything.'

Gilchrist eased forward, a signal for Jessie to step back. 'We're trying to locate a missing person, Ms Smith, whom we strongly suspect has been murdered. Anything you can give us, anything at all, that could pin down the exact time that car was parked there, might provide us with vital information that could help us solve the case.'

'Oh, I see.'

'If we looked through your phone's call log together, it might help jog your memory, remind you of something that could perhaps give us a lead.' He smiled. 'Would that be all right?'

'Well, yes, of course.' She removed her mobile from her tartan jacket. 'I phoned Tom as soon as I left the house.' She tapped the screen, and said, 'Here it is. I called him just after eleven, eleven oh seven to be precise, and the call lasted twenty-two minutes.'

'So you left later than ten-forty,' Gilchrist said, more statement than question.

She stared at him for several beats, then frowned, as if some thought had just come to her. 'I remember now. I had to go to the bathroom first, then I couldn't find my keys, so I must've left the house closer to eleven last night.'

'Maybe even five past?'

'I suppose. Yes.'

'And when you hung up with Tom, how long until you returned home?'

'Only another five minutes. No more.'

'Which means,' Jessie said, scoring her pen across her note-book, 'that your walk with Casper started at eleven-oh-five, and ended at around eleven thirty-five. Give or take.' She looked up and smiled. 'That about right?'

'If you say so.'

'I do. Which gives us a half hour window in which someone drove that Focus, parked it, then walked off.' She held the woman's gaze, and said, 'Anything else you can recall? Did you see anyone walking away? Hear any other cars arriving or leaving? Anything at all?'

'I'm sorry, I don't recall any such thing.'

Gilchrist smiled. 'Thanks for your help, Ms Smith.' He handed her his business card. 'If you remember anything else, please give me a call.'

Back in his car, Gilchrist switched on the ignition, pulled into Drive, and said, 'You really didn't like her, did you?'

'I can't stand uppity bitches. Did you see the jodhpurs? I mean, who in their right mind wears jodhpurs with a tartan jacket?' She coughed out an angry gasp. 'You know who she reminded me of?'

'Who?'

'Queen Becky, the pompous bitch.'

Gilchrist thought it best to say nothing. He'd heard from a reliable source within the Force that Doctor Rebecca Cooper's leave of absence might be coming to an end, and with it, Sam Kim's temporary position as police pathologist.

He gritted his teeth, and drove on, determined to keep his silence.

CHAPTER 21

By midday, Jackie had printed out three ANPR screenshots of Jennifer Nolan's Focus leaving St Andrews on the B9131 to Anstruther. The quality wasn't great, but clear enough to confirm she was driving by herself. Significantly, the timing of the last screenshot, before she drove into the countryside where there were no CCTV cameras, more or less worked in with Ms Smith's night-time dog walk – 11:07:46. Mhairi estimated Jennifer could have parked her car sometime between 11:20 and 11:25 last night, depending on how fast she was driving.

So it all kind of worked in.

'There's nobody in the back seat, is there?' he asked.

'Don't think so, sir. But can't say for sure.'

Which really didn't help. But Jennifer appeared not to be driving fast, so he figured she was not under duress, and driving of her own accord to some prearranged meeting point, likely to have been outside Ms Smith's cottage. Then where had she gone?

Or more importantly, who was she meeting?

Had she walked into the countryside, met someone, then been driven off in another car? And if so, why? What was the point of all the subterfuge, the late night-time meeting out in the Scottish wilderness? He didn't have an answer. Well, not one that he liked.

It was Mhairi who broke his mental stalemate. 'She must've met someone, sir. It would take about an hour to walk into Anstruther, and maybe two hours to walk back to St Andrews. And why would she have driven all the way out here, just to walk back? So, with that in mind, I thought of looking at it from a different angle, sir.'

'I'm listening.'

'We've not been able to find her from her mobile phone records, sir, because they're inconsistent. She's either been powering it down, or removing the SIM card. But the logs do show that she used her mobile that night once only, after ten-thirty. So I'm thinking that call would've been when she spoke to the person she could've been meeting.'

'You have that person's number?'

'It's a burner, sir, so we don't know who she was calling. But we can confirm that the burner pinged two masts around the time of her call, and in the same general location.'

'Which strengthens the likelihood that she was driving to meet him. Or her.'

'Yes, sir.'

'Well done, Mhairi.' He grimaced. 'That's all good and well,' he said, 'but without knowing who she was going to meet, we're still in the dark.'

'There's more, sir.'

He held her gaze. 'I'm listening.'

'Well, sir, once we had the timeline, I asked Jackie to check ANPR records for any vehicles travelling north or south on the

B9131, but allowing ten minutes leeway either side of when we calculated the Focus might have been parked.'

'And . . .?'

Mhairi glanced at him then, and he caught a flicker of doubt in her eyes. 'We can't say for sure, sir, but we have two cars that travelled the same route as Jennifer and fit into the timeline. Whether one of them stopped to pick up Jennifer, we can't know for sure. All we can say is that they must have passed the spot where she'd parked.'

'Show me,' he said.

Mhairi turned to her computer, worked the mouse and pulled up several screenshots of two different cars; one a black Audi – in the darkness of the image, maybe dark grey – the other a white van. He eyed the van, his intuition stirring. No signage on the side panel, no dents on the bodywork, no stickers on the windows, nothing out of the ordinary, just one of tens of thousands of ubiquitous white vans that crowd the nation's streets day in day out. Was there any better vehicle in which to pick someone up without being noticed?

'Can you zoom in?' he said, and peered closer as the van filled the monitor. 'The registration number. That could be a six or a G. What do you think?'

'Jackie's already searched DVLA records, sir. It's a G, and the van's registered in the name of an electrical company. SSE Electrics. A one-man start-up company owned by Steven English.' She clicked the mouse, and the van zoomed out. 'Steven English has no form, and his business has only one year's tax return. So he's legit. But you might find this more interesting, sir.'

Another click, and the Audi took over the screen. 'That's an image taken from the last CCTV camera before heading south.'

She clicked the mouse, and another image of the Audi appeared on the screen side by side with the first image. 'And that's it at the other end of the same road.' She pulled back to offer Gilchrist a clear view. 'What do you think, sir?'

He leaned closer, staring at the first image, then the second. The Audi was low and sleek, and a slight reflection on the windscreen from an earlier downpour hindered visibility. He let his gaze shift from one image to the other, until he thought he saw it.

'Is that a passenger in the second image?' he said.

'We think so, sir. It's not clear, but the first image is better, and clearly shows the driver by himself. So, it's possible . . . although not definite, sir, that the passenger could be Jennifer.'

He stared hard at the screen. 'What's she doing? Is she lying down on the front seat?'

'Don't know, sir. That's why we're not sure if it's Jennifer, or even a person at all. But there's definitely something in the front seat. Now here's where it gets really interesting.'

He watched Mhairi as she worked the mouse, intrigued by the clarity of her logic, and her willingness to work off her own intuition. Her gaze danced across the monitor, as one of the images swelled to fill the screen, then zoomed in on the registration number plate.

'Jackie's checked that number, sir, and it's registered to a Range Rover in Bristol. We can't say for sure if any of the numbers have been tampered with tape, or if it's a complete fake number plate. All we know is that it doesn't match the Audi.'

Gilchrist focused on the windscreen. From that angle, the driver's face was not much more than an out-of-focus blur, but a dark shadow around the lower part of his face could be a beard, or . . . could be nothing more than just a shadow.

But it was the dark image to the driver's left that had him peering closer. Was that a person, or was it a large bag, a holdall, or something similar? Or was it . . . and a flush of ice swept down his spine . . . something more worrying? Was he looking at Jennifer Nolan's body in the passenger seat? He really couldn't say, and found himself struggling to redirect his thoughts. He pulled back from the screen, shook his head.

'What do you think, sir? You think it's Jennifer?'

He returned Mhairi's cool gaze. He didn't know what to think. It seemed that they'd started off investigating one murder, and somehow found themselves embroiled in a missing person's case which was surely but steadily turning into another murder investigation. But one thing he did know – if two seemingly disparate events happened at that same time, then they had to be connected. He couldn't see the connection, and didn't know how to match them up. But the connection was there. He was sure of it. He just had to find it.

He turned to the screen again. Was that Jennifer in the front seat? Or something else? Who was the driver? And was that a shadow or a beard?

Only one way to find out.

'Get our IT guys to enhance that image,' he said. 'And get Jackie to work out some permutations of that registration number, see if it's been tampered with, or not. She's good at that.' He gritted his teeth, and stared hard at the monitor. 'We need to find that car.'

CHAPTER 22

By one o'clock, Gilchrist hadn't heard back from Dainty, so he phoned him.

'Fuck sake, Andy, your ears must be burning. Just about to give you a call.'

Gilchrist had a pen at the ready. 'Let's hear it.'

'Jack's studio's closed, and he's not at home. But my man in Lothian managed to locate him in Morningside. He appears to be living in a flat off Lothian Road.' He read out the address, then said, 'But it's not all plain sailing.'

'Meaning?'

'My man mentioned nothing about seeing a baby. Are you sure she's with Jack?'

Gilchrist blew out his breath. This was not the question he wanted to be asked. Jack would have known that Kristen would come after him. Had he handed over his daughter to someone for safekeeping? But logic dictated that Jack would keep Linna with him at all times. What father could take his daughter from her mother, then have someone else care for her? What would be the point of that? All those thoughts flashed through his mind in a split second, leaving him with the feeling that he didn't want to explain his rationale to Dainty. So, he ignored his question, and said, 'Who owns the flat off Lothian Road?'

'Stone Oak, a company based in Glasgow. Apparently the owner's a right cheapskate who wants maximum rent for minimum outlay. The place could do with a lick of paint, or a right good gutting, but it's currently being rented to two students; Magda Petersen and Ailsa McIntyre. Names mean anything to you?'

'No,' he said, although if Magda Petersen was Swedish, that might explain why Jack was staying there. Could Magda be a friend of Kristen? It seemed possible. 'And your man's seen Jack, has he?'

'Knows him from his studio. Bit of an art collector himself. There's no mistake, Andy. Jack's there.'

Gilchrist thanked Dainty, ended the call, and pushed to his feet. The memory of his call with Maureen last night stirred alive in his mind. He'd insisted that Kristen didn't report Jack to the Swedish authorities no earlier than nine o'clock tonight, and a glance at his watch warned him that he was running out of time – fast. The quickest way to resolve it – if indeed he could resolve it at all – would be to speak to Jack by phone. But Jack had removed his phone's SIM card, and even if he could get through, it was odds on that he would ignore the call, or disconnect at the first opportunity.

Damn it, Jack, what the hell are you thinking? But there was one way he could find out. He swore under his breath again, then grabbed his jacket from the back of his chair.

Gilchrist was less than fifteen miles out of St Andrews when the image came to him, a thought that flashed through his mind with the speed of a lightning strike. Something in that image had triggered some buried neural connection in his subconscious, because he couldn't recall noticing it, and now here it was, some shapeless memory that floated to the forefront of his thoughts like a shadow out of darkness.

He made the connection on his car's phone.

Mhairi answered on the second ring. 'Yes, sir?'

'That Audi, Mhairi, could you call up that screenshot again, and check something out for me?'

'Give me a minute, sir.' A few clicks in the background, then, 'I have it, sir.'

'Zoom in on one of the wheels, and tell me what you see.'

A pause, then, 'I'm not sure what I'm looking for, sir. I've got the front wheel, but the image isn't good enough to read the make and size of tyre.'

'It's an alloy wheel though, isn't it?'

'Yes, sir.'

'With a distinctive pattern?'

'I'm not sure if it's a distinctive pattern or not, sir. But I'll look into it.'

He couldn't recall the alloy pattern, only that something about it was odd, maybe one of those fancy spoked alloy wheels that boy-racers loved. 'Not all alloy wheels have the same pattern,' he said, 'but something about that pattern is unusual, I think. There might not be too many black Audi's with that exact alloy wheel. Could be a good starting point to narrow the search.'

'I'm on it, sir, and I'll let you know what I come up with.'

He ended the call, then phoned Jessie. 'You busy?' he said.

'As a blue-arsed fly. What else?'

'You know how to work the camera on that phone of yours, don't you?'

123

'I'm not going to take a selfie for you, if that's why you're asking.'

'Nothing as simple.'

'Okay.' Serious now. 'What are you looking for?'

'John Green.'

'What about him?'

'I think he's due a second interview.'

'Want me to bring him in?' she said, hope rising in her voice.

'Not so quick. But visit his home, ask a few questions, make him feel a bit uneasy, then ask him about his car.'

'What about it?'

'It's an Audi.'

'Okay. So . . .?'

'It's parked at the end of the street. Take a few photos of the wheels. They're alloy.'

'What's that?'

'A type of wheel. All cars have them fitted nowadays. But they're all different, and some are manufacturer specific.'

'Do you want me to make a show of taking the photos?'

'Yes, but don't make it too obvious. Make it look as if you're trying to do it without him noticing. I need you to take a photo of the number plate. And close up of anything that suggests the plate's been removed recently.'

'Like what?'

'Like scrape marks, or something. A loose screw. I don't know. Use your initiative.'

'All right. Settle down. I'm just making sure I don't screw up. Excuse the pun.'

'And once you're done, show the photos to Mhairi.'

'And that's it?'

'Mhairi'll bring you up to speed.'

Jessie grunted, then said, 'This another one of your longshots, is it?'

'Let's just say it's an educated guess.'

'How educated?'

He didn't want to tell her it was kindergarten level, or that he was shooting at hidden targets in the dark, or that his sixth sense was telling him that Green wasn't who he said he was. Instead, he said, 'Therein lies the problem,' then ended the call, and settled down for the remainder of the drive to Edinburgh, and the unavoidable confrontation with his son.

CHAPTER 23

Gilchrist found the address Dainty had given him, managed to squeeze into a tight space between two cars, and better still, open the door without denting the paintwork. Parking spaces seemed to be narrower than they used to be, or cars wider. Maybe both.

From the outside, the address looked like any one of a thousand tenement buildings that had been modified throughout the nation's cities for second or third homes that housed students or the less affluent of society's citizens. The list of names by the entrance buzzer looked as if it had been there since the turn of the century. Cheap print, poor penmanship, and a city's worth of dirty fingerprints all but obliterated the residents' names, but he thought the worn letters 'Ma' for a flat on the second floor could be the first two letters of Magda Petersen.

He pressed the buzzer for a flat on the top floor, then another one next to it, and had to wait several seconds before the door clicked, and he pushed it open. A quick trot up the stairs, and a printed nameplate outside a second-floor flat confirmed Magda Petersen lived there. An untidy handwritten scrawl beneath it belonged to Ailsa McIntyre. He was about to press the doorbell, when he thought better of it.

The problem with Jack was that he was smart, and could be as devious as the devil if he put his mind to it. Gilchrist remembered him as a wee boy, four or five years old at the time, who could come up with a lie as quick as a flash to deny wrongdoing. He once threw a stone at a neighbour's window, then swore with childhood innocence that it was Maureen who'd broken the window. When Gilchrist pointed out that Maureen was in town with Mum, Jack blamed the neighbour's son in the space of a heartbeat. When that was proven wrong, he then blamed it on a man who'd thrown a stone from a car. What had struck Gilchrist at the time was how convincing Jack had been, and what an extraordinary and lively imagination he had at that age.

His worry now was that Jack had warned Magda and Ailsa not to answer the door, or take any calls, or do anything that might give away his presence. But as a guest in their flat, would they do as told, or would they ignore him, maybe even tell him to piss off? He thought that maybe his best bet would be to return outside and wait and watch and hope that someone might step out for shopping. After all, if Jack was staying there with Linna, he would need to buy all sorts of things that babies needed on a daily basis – provided he hadn't brought a week's worth of supplies with him. Christ, talk about longshots. But all arguments aside, he chose patience as his best option, and retraced his steps, exited the building, and found a spot on the opposite side of Lothian Road where he could stand by himself in the cold, making sure he kept out of sight of prying eyes from above.

He worked out which windows belonged to Magda and Ailsa's flat – two of them with matching curtains, as it turned out. He wasn't sure if anyone was home, so he waited on the other side of the street, searching for signs of movement within, but hoping someone might step outside instead. He wouldn't know Magda or Ailsa, but he could confront anyone who left the building, and find out what was what.

It took just over twenty minutes before he caught the faintest sign of movement at the window closer to the end of the building, the flicker of a curtain, the passing of a shadow, for just a moment, then nothing. So, someone was home. That much he knew. But who?

Ten minutes later, with no one having entered or left the building, he'd had enough. He crossed the road, jogged up the stone stairs again, and without giving pause for second thought, pressed the doorbell. He stood facing the peephole in the hope that if Jack saw him, he would realise he'd been found out, that it was pointless continuing to hide; the game – or whatever he wanted to call it – was up. A flickering shadow at the peephole told Gilchrist he'd been clocked, and he stepped back in anticipation of the door opening. But thirty seconds later, alone on the landing, he realised he was being ignored.

Another stab at the doorbell, a tad longer that time, made no difference.

Nothing for it. He pressed his thumb to the doorbell, and held it down.

It took Jack over two minutes before he cracked the door open, face red and eyes wild enough to have Gilchrist thinking he was high on drugs.

'What do you think you're playing at?' Jack said.

'I could ask you the same question.'

Jack held onto the door, blocking Gilchrist's view into the flat, then glanced behind him as if to make sure no one could see who he was talking to. Then he pulled at the door and made a move to step outside, onto the landing.

Gilchrist blocked his path. 'Best if we talk inside.'

For a moment, Jack seemed undecided, but another glance behind seemed to deflate him, and he stood back and opened the door wide.

The first thing that struck Gilchrist was the tidy homeliness of the place, a welcoming atmosphere that had him wanting to hang up his jacket, take a seat, and switch on the telly. The second was the Scottish theme. A dark green and blue carpet in the Black Watch tartan pattern, as bold as you like, looked as if it had been laid that week. Tartan throws of yellows, reds, greens, purples, hung over the backs and arms of every chair. Framed pictures of mist-laden lochs and steep-sided valleys did what they could to hide the walls. A double-take at a deflated set of bagpipes lying on a stool in the corner almost brought a smile to his face. And among it all, sitting on the floor, out of place and character, a baby's carrier, one of those modern contraptions that trebled as a pushchair, car seat and cot.

Linna lay on her back, eyes following the lazy movement of a cot-bed mobile. He was surprised at how frail she looked, despite being almost six months old. He kneeled on the carpet, let her tiny hand touch then wrap around his finger. He'd never been one for talking to babies, but surprised himself by whispering sweet nothings and tugging her hand. He gently retrieved his finger, surprised by the strength in Linna's grip, then pushed to his feet.

Jack watched him, half-seated, half-standing, butt on the windowsill, back to Lothian Road. He looked as if he'd been crying, maybe suffering from a hangover, or just struggling to stay sober from the drinks of that day. 'She was sound asleep until you rang the bell.'

Gilchrist glanced down at her. 'She seems happy and content.'

Jack half-smiled. 'She's a nice kid. Easy to live with. Not like . . .' He sighed again, pushed his hand through his hair, then looked hard at Gilchrist. 'How did you find out?'

'Kristen phoned Mo.'

Jack breathed in, let it out in a defeated sigh, and shook his head. 'It's not working.'

Gilchrist didn't want to ask – exactly *what* isn't working? – which could open up a whole other tin of maggots, so he just returned his son's sad gaze in silence.

Jack slid off the windowsill, and walked to the other window where he stood with his back to him. 'I never thought it would come to this. I thought we had a strong relationship, you know? I thought we worked well together.' He shook his head. '*No*. We *did* work well together. Until . . .'

Gilchrist let several beats pass, then said, 'Until you went back to Sweden?'

Jack nodded. 'Until we went back to fucking Sweden.' His body seemed to swell with the intake of a deep breath, then his shoulders shivered as he let it out. He hung his head, and shook it. 'She deserted me,' he said. 'Kristen did. Me and Linna. Can't believe she did that. Just fucked off for the weekend. Not a word. Nothing. Just up and left. I mean . . . what mother would do that?'

Gilchrist thought he saw where this was leading to, but didn't want to interrupt Jack's flow. So he said nothing, just stood watching his son, sharing in his pain, and waiting.

'But I should've known,' Jack said. 'I should've fucking known.'

There could be any number of reasons why Kristen left for the weekend, but he tried the most obvious. 'Drugs?'

'No. She's off these now. We both are.'

Which really left him with the reason he dreaded the most. 'An old boyfriend?'

Jack nodded. 'Hans fucking Dietrich. The *cunt*.'

Jack seldom swore, but when he did it told Gilchrist that he was drunk or angry. The use of that single word warned him that Jack might be both. And who could blame him? Like father, like son, right enough. Maybe being a cuckold ran in their genes. But apathy could take you only so far. Time for a reality check.

'What do you want to do about it?' he said.

'I don't know,' Jack whispered, shaking his head. 'I don't know.' Then he turned from the window, as if a decision had been reached. 'What I *don't* want to do, is lose Linna. I can't lose Linna, Dad. I *won't* lose her. I won't let that happen.'

Gilchrist gave a knowing smile and a slow nod of his head. 'Well . . . in that case, you have to take it one step at a time.'

'What d'you mean?'

'I've managed to hold Kristen off until nine o'clock tonight.'

'You've spoken to her?'

'Mo has.' He watched the meaning of his words filter through Jack's mind, then said, 'If she doesn't hear from you by then, she's going to report you to the police.' He didn't need to mention the word kidnap. Jack was smart enough to know how much trouble he was in.

His eyes narrowed, his lips pressed white, then he nodded. 'That figures.'

Now it was Gilchrist's turn to say, 'What do you mean?'

'Hans fucking Dietrich. He *is* the police. He'll have put Kristen up to it.'

Gilchrist walked to the window, more to hide the turmoil of his own emotions. For crying out loud. Could it be any worse? He watched the stop–start movement of traffic below. Being in the Police Force didn't give you any string-pulling legal advantage over the general public. But he knew how it worked; friends in right places, and a word in the right ear, and particularly a friendly Swedish ear, and Jack could lose Linna forever. If that happened, God only knew what Jack was capable of.

But one step at a time. Wasn't that what he'd said?

He turned to face Jack. 'You need to speak to Kristen right away. You need to let her know that Linna's okay, and that you're going to fly back with her tonight.'

'*What?* What're you saying, man? That's not going to happen. That's the reason I'm here. Kristen's not fit to be her mother.'

'You've no choice.'

'Of course I have a choice. I can stay here.'

'And that would be the wrong choice.' He waited while Jack's rush of anger flushed from his system. 'You have to take her back, Jack. There's no other way. And you have to take her back tonight.'

'Tonight? Fuck sake. How's that going to help me see Linna?'

'It's going to keep you out of prison, is what it's going to do. That's step one. Step two, you do what you can to sort it out between you and Kristen.'

'That's a non-starter, man, now Hans fucking Dietrich's back in the picture.'

'*Back* . . . in the picture?'

'Yeah, that's the problem. They nearly got married years ago. She's already told me it was love at first sight all over again.'

132

Gilchrist felt something turn over in his gut. Once love got in the way, then that really was the end of it. There was no going back for Kristen. Or for Jack. 'Well, that brings you to step three, which is, I'm sorry to say, you have to reach a separation agreement.'

'And get to see my daughter once a year if I'm lucky?' Jack slumped into the nearest chair, and covered his face with his hands.

It took Gilchrist almost ten seconds to realise Jack was crying. He sat beside him, on the arm of the chair, and placed an arm around his shoulder.

'I never wanted this to happen, Dad. I swear, I never wanted it to happen.' The words came out in stuttered bursts, the anguish impossible to hide. 'I come from a broken family, and now my family's broken before it's even started.'

Guilt swamped Gilchrist in a debilitating wave. If he'd paid more attention to his children while they were growing up, or put care and time into his own marriage, rather than being lost to the case of the day, would he and Gail have stayed together? And if so, would Jack's views on marriage and fatherhood have been less brittle?

He squeezed his son's shoulder, wanting to offer some fatherly words of advice.

But all he could say was, 'I'm sorry, Jack. I'm so sorry.'

CHAPTER 24

At the end of the road Jessie did a three-point turn. She never understood why it was called that, for it often took her five tries. That aside, as she tugged the steering wheel right then left, and reversed and braked and changed back into first gear, she managed to clock a dark grey Audi in a row of parked cars. She thought it looked sportier than the others, lower to the ground, with a front grille that hinted of speed and power. But as far as the wheels were concerned, they looked like thousands of others.

She parked outside Green's house, her wee car straddling the pavement, facing the way she'd come. Which meant that when she walked back to the Audi to take photos of its wheels, it couldn't go unnoticed by Green – unless he was as thick as a brick, which she supposed wasn't out of the question.

She stood on the front step, her breath clouding the air. Where was summer when you needed it? She rubbed her hands together, trying to work some heat into her fingers, thinking she should have worn gloves. It was supposed to be the start of spring, for crying out loud. Best just to get on with it. Doorbell pressed good and proper, she stepped back looking for signs of movement at the windows. But the door snapped open before she had time to cup her hands and blow into them, and she thrust out her warrant card.

'Detective Sergeant Janes. St Andrews CID.'

'So?'

'So I want to ask you a few questions.'

'What about?'

'You got a kettle?'

'What?'

'You could put it on and we could have a wee cup of tea inside, rather than stand out here in the cold.'

'Don't do tea. And who says it's cold?'

Standing on the bottom step looking up at Green, who was well over six foot, Jessie was acutely aware of her physical vulnerability. She should have brought Mhairi along with her, but she was up to her ears researching stuff with Jackie. She moved up a step, closer to Green, hoping it would make him feel uncomfortable enough to move back inside and give her some room. But he stood still in T-shirt and shorts, folded his arms, flexed his biceps, and glared down at her, her face no more than six inches from his chest. That close, the smell of stale sweat with a hint of body odour swamped her senses. The thought of having to back down a step entered her mind, then evaporated in an instant.

Not going to happen.

She tilted her head so she could look him squarely in the eye, well, vertically in the eye – hers up, his down. 'Okay, if that's the way you want it.' Without taking her eyes off his, she reached into her pocket and removed her notebook. 'Where were you on Saturday night?'

His lips stretched into a tight smirk.

'I'm waiting.'

Silence.

She looked down at her notebook and printed – RTA – then tilted her head back eye to eye. 'That's *refused to answer*, in case you're wondering. Next. Is there anyone who can corroborate where you were on Saturday night?'

Silence.

Another RTA.

'I have to warn you,' she said, forcing her lips into the tiniest of smiles, and struggling to return his gaze with an unblinking one of her own. 'Three strikes and you're out. Or maybe I should say, three strikes and you're in . . . *jail.*'

'Are you for real or what?'

'Oh, I'm for real all right. You want to do this inside? I can manage without the tea.'

Green worked up a gob from the back of his throat, turned his head, and spat it onto the lawn.

'I'll take that as a no.' She was conscious of Green having eased himself forward so that she now stood with her heels balanced on the edge of the step. 'Right, third and final question.' She gave him her toughest glare, but it was like pointing a torch at the sun. And trying to prevent herself from falling backwards wasn't helping. Nor the tremor in her fingers that threatened to evolve into full-blown shakes. But she'd be buggered if she was going to back down now. She gritted her teeth, then said, 'When did you last see or speak with Nici Johnson?'

Nothing.

'Jennifer Nolan?'

But Green still refused to answer. He stared down at her, lips curling into a smile, eyes creasing with pleasure, as if sensing

Jessie's rising fear. 'That's more than three strikes,' he said. 'Now what?'

Jessie had been raised in a criminal family, with a whore for a mother, and two older brothers who'd spent more time in prison than out. She'd had to fend for herself on many an occasion, but thankfully her family's criminal genes had failed to be passed on to her. Even so, she'd learned a thing or two about looking after number one, and training offered by the Force had made her more than capable of defending herself. In the course of her duty, she'd carried out arrests of men physically stronger than she was. But she wasn't stupid, and knew that with Green, on her own, she had no chance. It didn't matter that resisting arrest was a criminal offence. If Green was a killer – the question was still out there – then adding another body to the pile might not be out of the quesiton.

'You know what I don't like about you?' she said, and reluctantly took the next step down – it was either that, or fall off it. 'You're a bully. And a misogynist. I could look that up in the dictionary for you. But I think you already know what you are.'

Green responded by moving onto the next step down.

Jessie backed up, so that she now stood on the front pathway, still looking up, still physically weaker. But being backed into that position somehow strengthened her resolve. The memory of standing up against her terrifying brothers helped, too. She stepped closer again, and said, 'So, what I'm going to do now, Mr Green, is arrest you for obstructing a murder investigation.'

'Yeah, you and who else?'

'A backup team, if I have to.' She thought she caught the tiniest hint of surprise in his eyes, so pressed home her advantage and started reading him his rights.

'Hold on. What the fuck're you doing?'

But Jessie rattled off his rights, pulled a set of plasticuffs from her belt, and said, 'Turn around, please.'

'You fucking joking, or what?'

'I'm going to ask you one more time, Mr Green, and if you don't do as I ask, you'll be further charged with resisting arrest, which carries a custodial sentence.' She jerked him a cheeky smile. 'That clear?'

Stunned silence.

For a moment, Green looked as if he was going to resist, maybe tell her to fuck off, but she didn't think he would physically strike her – he would have done so by now if he was going to resort to violence. So she kept up the brave facade, and said, 'Turn. Around.'

'What the—'

'Turn around, Mr Green.' Stronger that time. 'I'm not going to ask again.'

'You don't need to put these on.'

'Too late for that, Mr Green. Sorry.' To her surprise, he shuffled around, hands held together, mumbling something indecipherable under his breath, although she thought she caught *bitch* more than once.

For that, she tightened the cuffs to a complaint of, 'Fuck're you doing?'

'Making sure that a big strong lad like you, Mr Green, can't break out of them while I'm driving you in.' She led him down the pathway, to her wee Fiat 500.

He stopped, and stared at it. 'Now you're really fucking joking.'

'No chance.' She opened the passenger door, and put her hand to his head while he squeezed his bulk into her car. She reached for his seatbelt and clipped it on, gripping it tight in an attempt to stop her hands from shaking.

In the driving seat, her wee car's cabin was tight and cramped, and had the two of them sitting shoulder to shoulder. She was conscious of Green's physical presence, but she forced herself to ignore him – after all, he was cuffed. Hoping he hadn't noticed the nervous tremor in her fingers, she fired the ignition, slipped into reverse gear, and said, 'Got to take a couple of photos.'

Green said nothing, just stared out the windscreen as Jessie reversed. She backed off the pavement faster than she should have, and cringed at the sound of metal on stone as the underside scraped the kerb from a heavy side wobble. But she eased back, and took her time parking beyond the Audi, and at an angle such that Green could see what she was doing.

She took her time walking around the Audi, taking the opportunity to snatch a glance at Green. But he sat in the front seat, eyes fixed straight ahead, gaze so strained and focused on nothing that she knew he was struggling to hold in his anger. Attention back to his car, she bent down for a closer look at the front grille. She couldn't resist running her hand over the polished metal. If only she could keep her own car in such good condition. Come to think of it, when had she last changed the oil? She made a mental note to ask Robert to have a look at it for her.

She removed her mobile and kneeled on the ground. From the corner of her eye, she could just make out Green watching her. She moved in closer to the front wheel, not sure what she was supposed to be photographing. But she clicked a couple of shots, then decided it was better if she put her mobile on video mode.

This time, she moved in close and read out the tyre make and number, and holding her mobile as steady as she could, pulled back to take in the entire wheel, showing the alloys – which she had to say looked fancier than others she'd seen – and continuing with the verbal description. Then back a bit farther until first the wheel arch, then the side of the car filled the screen. She watched the playback, feeling chuffed and surprised by the quality, then walked round the front of the car, pretending to inspect every aspect of it, as if she were a potential buyer. But she wasn't sure what she should be looking at, and she risked a glance at Green. But he sat staring out the windscreen, jaw clenched, lips white.

She kept up the charade, taking her time to video record each wheel, and when finally done slipped her mobile into her jacket and returned to the car. Without a word, she clipped on her seat-belt and switched on the ignition.

As she slipped into first gear, Green said, 'I want a lawyer.'

'You can phone from the station,' she said, and inwardly smirked. *Got you by the balls now, you misogynistic bastard.*

CHAPTER 25

6.42 p.m.
North Street Office

Gilchrist entered Interview Room Number 1, which backed onto North Street, the only window a horizontal slot high on the wall so no passersby could see in. Jessie followed, and together they took their seats opposite Green and his solicitor, a matronly woman with small eyes and bitter lips that reminded Gilchrist of his mother trying to contain her domestic rage. A pinched nose added to her severe look. White hair tied back was knotted in a bun so tight it could be patented as a facelift. Beside her, Green sat stiff-backed, trying to look cool and calm. But his white-knuckled grip on his seat's arms told him a different story.

Green's solicitor slid a business card across the table, and introduced herself as Ms Maura Lee, senior partner with Sheridan Acton and Lee Solicitors. He caught her emphasis on the Ms, and noted that her firm was based in Perth.

Jessie switched on the recorder and carried out the formal introductions, noting that Mr John Green was being detained

141

under Section 14 of the Criminal Procedure (Scotland) Act 1995 for questioning in the murder of Ms Nicola Johnson. To which Lee said, 'My client has already been questioned twice in this matter, and on both occasions asserted his innocence—'

'Your client's lying,' Jessie snapped.

'I beg your pardon.'

'Your client's lying. Plain and simple.'

'Well, I can assure you that my client told me—'

'And I can assure *you*, that your client is lying.' Jessie leaned closer, her gaze like a laser between them. 'The second time your client was questioned, he was questioned by me, and he refused to answer any questions at all. Not once did he assert anything, let alone his innocence.' She sat back. 'So . . . you were saying?'

'I would like a few minutes alone with my client, please.'

Jessie noted the time for the record, adding that the interview was being suspended for a few minutes, and without further word, she and Gilchrist exited the room.

Upstairs, in Gilchrist's office, Jessie said, 'I can't stand bitches like that. "My client has asserted his innocence",' she mocked in an upper-class accent. 'Like hell he did. Makes my blood boil.'

'I can see that,' Gilchrist said. 'But it still doesn't make him guilty.'

From his desk, he picked up four separate screenshots from Jessie's video recordings of each wheel, and grimaced. His idea that the alloys on Green's Audi S6 could confirm his connection to the missing Jennifer Nolan had now lost its initial sheen. An enlarged image of the ANPR screenshot of the Audi, which he suspected had picked up Nolan, confirmed only that Green's car had similar alloys, which Jackie had since established were one of the more common set of alloy wheels produced. And to further dowse the flames, the IT department confirmed they were unable to enhance the screenshot any further. What he was looking at was as good as it would ever get. Which was more or less useless.

He threw the screenshots onto his desk and faced Jessie. 'On a scale of one to ten, how would you rate Green for Nici Johnson's murder?'

She puffed out her cheeks, then let it out. 'He's a lying bastard. I know that much. But truthfully . . .? For Nici's murder . . .?' She shook her head. 'Three or four. How about you?'

'Maybe less.'

'It's not looking good, is it?'

'No,' he said, and turned to the window.

Outside, night had fallen, which in an odd way reminded him that he needed to phone Maureen. His visit to Jack's hadn't been a complete waste of time. He'd eventually persuaded him to fly back to Sweden with Linna, but the first flight wasn't until the morning. He'd told Maureen of Jack's decision, and asked her to pass that onto Kristen and to persuade her not to contact the Swedish police – Linna would be with her tomorrow. To tie up that loose end, he needed to hear from Maureen that Kristen had agreed. But for the time being, all that could wait. He needed to figure out what to do about Green.

He faced Jessie again. 'Have you read Jackie's report on Green?'

'I did, yeah. Not a lot there, if I'm being honest. It's hard to say what he's been up to before the Fairmont.'

Gilchrist nodded. 'Well let's find out what he and his solicitor's been up to.'

The atmosphere in the interview room hadn't warmed any. Green sat upright, arms folded, his gaze fixed on the wall opposite, and didn't blink or shift his eyes when Gilchrist and Jessie took their seats. Lee, on the other hand, was leafing through an A4 pad of scribbled notes with an enthusiasm that hinted of some defensive strategy about to be unveiled.

Jessie clicked the recorder, and Gilchrist announced their return to the interview, and noted the time as 6.44. Before he could add anything, Lee said, 'I've instructed my client to answer "No comment" to any and all questions.'

'Oh that'll really assert his innocence,' Jessie quipped.

Lee smirked, but said nothing more.

Gilchrist leaned forward, and waited until Green made eye contact before saying, 'I understand you've already been read your rights, but I think it's worth noting the importance of what the words actually mean.'

Silence.

'So ... for the record ... I'll read them to you once more. Okay?'

Nothing, just a dead-eyed stare in response.

Undeterred, Gilchrist said, 'You do not have to say anything, but anything you do say will be noted and may be used in evidence.' He flickered a smile at Green, but he could have been looking into the eyes of a dead snake. He pressed on. 'It's important to know that you don't have to take your solicitor's advice, that you have a choice. Because answering every question with a "No comment" won't do you any favours if your case goes forward to court. Do you understand?'

'No comment.'

'Well then, there you go.' Gilchrist pushed back from the table, and stood. He stared down at Lee. 'DS Janes will go through a list of prepared questions for the record.'

'After which I will expect my client to be released.'

'That'll be up to DS Janes. But not before your client provides a DNA sample.'

For the first time, Green shifted in his seat. He leaned to the side and whispered in Lee's ear. Lee shook her head, and glared at Jessie. 'Are you intending to charge my client with anything?'

'How about obstruction of a police investigation,' Jessie said.

'That's nonsense, and you know it.'

'How is answering "No comment" not obstruction?'

'My client is not refusing to answer. He's just refusing to give you the answer you're looking for. In legal terms, that's not obstruction, so I hope you have something stronger than that. Furthermore, my client agreed to come to the police station of his own free will, whereas you deemed it necessary to handcuff him like some common criminal. You also refused to let my client call a solicitor immediately, insisting that he do so only at the station.' She sat back as if to let Jessie answer, but said, 'So unless you intend to charge my client with something more legally prescient than obstruction, I have already instructed my client to refuse to give a DNA sample. My client can do so voluntarily, of course, but due to the manner in which you personally have treated him . . .' this aimed at Jessie with a look as severe as her hair, '. . . my client has informed me that he is not willing to volunteer a DNA sample. I will of course be writing a letter of complaint to the chief constable, pointing out your unprofessionalism and lack of common courtesy—'

'Wait a minute,' Jessie said. 'Unprofessionalism? Lack of common courtesy? What're you talking about?'

Lee scowled at the table. 'Do you see a cup of tea? A glass of water? Did you not think to offer my client any refreshment—'

'It's a police interview room,' Jessie snapped. 'Not a bloody Starbucks.'

'Precisely my point,' Lee said.

'Hold on, hold on,' Gilchrist said, putting a hand on Jessie's shoulder. 'Let's lower the temperature a touch.' He let a couple of beats pass. 'Here's what's going to happen,' he said, in a tone that told them who was in charge. 'DS Janes will question Mr Green from her questionnaire, and Mr Green will answer as instructed by his solicitor, or as he deems fit. After which, Mr Green will be asked to provide a DNA sample, which he can agree to, or not. If he declines, a sample will be taken from him by force, if necessary.'

'That's preposterous,' Lee gasped.

'Maybe so,' Gilchrist said. 'But it's within the law.' Without waiting for any further comment, he added, 'DCI Gilchrist leaving the room at eighteen fifty-eight.'

CHAPTER 26

Gilchrist stood at his office window, and eyed a dulling sky. It never failed to amaze him once the clocks were changed how quickly Scotland's nights leaped out of winter mode. Temperatures overnight could still fall below zero, but a later setting sun kept hopes alive that warmer weather really was on its way. He retrieved his mobile, and got through to Maureen on the third try.

'Sorry, Dad, was in the shower. You should've left a message.'

'Didn't want to do that. I'm in and out of meetings.'

'Don't tell me you're still at work.'

'About to leave,' he lied, then changed the topic to the reason for his call. 'Have you spoken with Kristen yet?'

Maureen's heavy sigh sent his hopes on a downward spiral. 'She's not buying it.'

'Not buying what? That Jack's flying back with Linna tomorrow? Or that he's not flying back at all?'

'She doesn't believe him, Dad. She thinks he's just spinning her a yarn.'

'For the purpose of what?'

'To take Linna away from her.'

Gilchrist raked his hair in frustration. This was not what he wanted to hear. He'd spent the best part of an hour persuading Jack to take his daughter back to Sweden. The fact that he couldn't book a flight until the following morning wasn't Jack's fault. Surely Kristen could understand that. But if she didn't believe Jack, and thought he was still going to keep Linna from her, what could he do to prove otherwise?

'Have you spoken to Jack?' he said. 'Does he know about this?'

'Can't get through. He's blocked my number. Remember?'

He whispered a curse. Then the thought that Jack might have changed his mind and blocked his own number, too, surfaced long enough to have him gritting his teeth. If Kristen stood firm with the deadline, then they didn't have much time. He needed to get hold of her, try to talk some sense into her, tell her that Jack would have Linna back in Sweden in the morning. But why would she believe him over Maureen?

'Can you give me Kristen's number, Mo?'

'Don't know if that's a good idea.'

'You have any better ideas?'

Another sigh, followed by a string of numbers, which he assigned to memory.

'Let me get back to you,' he said, and hung up. He had an extraordinary memory for numbers. He couldn't explain why, just always had. Although he was finding that the older he became, the less time these numbers were retained before they evaporated into mental fog. So he opened Contacts and added Kristen's number before it slipped free, then dialled it.

The call went to voicemail, and a recorded message in Swedish. He had no idea what the message said, wasn't even sure if it was

Kristen's voice, just assumed it was the generic recording; *leave a message and I'll get back to you*. Rather than leave his name and number, he hoped Kristen would note the missed call, recognise the UK's international code against the recorded number, and give him a call back.

Another glance at his watch reminded him that time was tight. He thought of calling Kristen again and leaving a message. But somehow, that felt too impersonal, not the best way to persuade anyone to change their mind. What he couldn't understand was why Kristen didn't believe Maureen. She must surely know Maureen wouldn't lie to her. But she would also know that she was just passing on what she'd been told to say. Which had him worrying that maybe Kristen knew Jack better than he did. Was it possible? Could she know something about Jack that he didn't? Would Jack say one thing to him, then do another off his own bat? His relationship with Jack had not always been easy, but he thought he knew his son well enough to know he wouldn't lie about something as serious as Linna. Still, Jack could be sneaky smart when push came to shove.

Nothing for it but to call him.

Jack picked up on the third ring. 'Yeah, man.'

'Tell me you haven't changed your mind.'

'About what?'

'You're still flying back with Linna in the morning, right?'

'Said I would, didn't I?'

'Have you spoken to Kristen?'

'Thought we agreed Mo would do that.' A pause, then, 'She not got hold of her?'

'She has, yes—'

'So what's the problem?'

Thoughts shot through Gilchrist's brain like lightning strikes. He couldn't risk telling Jack what the problem was, because if he did, Jack might change his mind – in fact he would *definitely* change his mind – why fly back to Sweden to be arrested for kidnapping, then hand over his daughter to his bitch-for-a-partner? Christ, he could hear him now. And he couldn't ask Jack to phone Kristen directly, maybe let her hear Linna's voice over the phone, because she might tell him that she's reporting him to the police regardless. Which would make Jack's mind up for him. No return flight to Sweden. Instead, he'd take his chances in court. No, he would have to come up with something else.

'Hey, Andy, you still there?'

'Got distracted for a moment.'

'So what's the problem?'

'No problem. If you send me a copy of your flight itinerary, I'll get it over to Kristen.'

The line fell silent for so long that Gilchrist thought they'd been cut off. Then Jack came back with, 'She's still going to report me to the police, isn't she?'

'No,' he lied. 'She's not. She just wants confirmation of your flight details.'

'So she can have the cops waiting for me.'

'No, Jack, that's not it.'

'I tell you, man, it's him. It's that fuckhead Hans. He's twisted her brain. I knew it. I fucking knew it.'

The line died.

Gilchrist clenched his jaw, and held back a curse. But it was no use. He slammed his mobile onto his desk with a gut clenching, '*Fuck,*' then slumped into his seat. But swearing got you nowhere, and neither did breaking phones. He picked up his mobile, looked at it, then jerked in surprise when a voice at his door said, 'Are you all right, sir?'

'Yes, Mhairi, I'm fine,' he said, conscious of her having overheard his display of anger. He changed the subject. 'I thought you'd gone home for the day.'

'No, sir. Jackie and I have been digging into Timothy Johnson's background, but we can't find a current address for him. We think he's maybe left the country—'

'Recently?'

'No, sir. All records on him appear to fizzle out around two years ago.'

Gilchrist hung his head, and closed his eyes. He squeezed the bridge of his nose with his thumb and forefinger, then squinted up at Mhairi. 'Jesus,' he hissed, then shook his head. 'Don't tell me.'

'Afraid so, sir. Unless Timothy Johnson sneaked into the country and sneaked back out again, he can't have had anything to do with Nici Johnson's murder.'

'Bugger it.' Gilchrist pushed to his feet, and strode to the window. 'So,' he said, not able to keep the disappointment from his tone. 'We're back to square bloody one.'

'Not quite.'

Gilchrist turned. Jessie stood in his office doorway, a hint of a smirk on her lips.

'Green . . .?' he said, more in hope than anything else.

Jessie shook her head. 'Hutton.'

For a moment, the name eluded him. 'But . . . I thought . . .'

'You did. But you underestimated little old Jessie.' She waved a report in front of him. 'DNA results.'

'Hutton killed Nici Johnson?'

'No. Wendy Hyatt.'

Gilchrist frowned, glanced at Mhairi. But she looked just as confused. 'Who on earth is Wendy Hyatt?' he said.

'A young woman whose body was found on an Aberdeen beach twenty years ago.'

'And Hutton killed her?'

'His DNA says he did. Which was why he went out of his way to avoid providing a fresh sample. He probably worried that his DNA was in the system from years ago, and a fresh sample now could connect him to Hyatt's murder.'

'And Green?' It was all he could think to say.

'Don't you worry about Green.' She held up a plastic bag – a DNA kit.

'He volunteered a sample?'

'Of course not. He refused. His solicitor started giving me such a hard time that I told her that if she carried on, I would charge her with obstructing a murder investigation.'

'How did that go down?'

'Doesn't like losing.' She tapped the DNA kit. 'Told you I'd nail that bastard.'

'You certainly did.'

'And talking about nailing bastards.' She twisted her mouth in a grimace. 'We have a bit of a problem with Hutton.'

'In what way?'

'Don't get mad with me, but I obtained a sample of his DNA without him knowing.'

'I'm listening.'

'Well . . . after dropping Robert off at Edinburgh airport, I thought to myself, why not check out Hutton again, and see if he's changed his mind about giving a DNA sample? He wasn't in, so I took the liberty of going through his bins and found a pair of gloves he was wearing the other day. And hey presto, we got a match.'

Gilchrist gave Jessie one of his over-the-top-of-his-specs glares, and said, 'And was the bin just lying about, waiting to be opened?'

'It was outside. I didn't break in. No one was home. And no one saw me. I know we can't charge him on the strength of this DNA sample, but now we know we've got a match, we can use that to our benefit.' She paused for a moment, as if not sure of his response, then said, somewhat sheepishly, 'We can, can't we?'

He nodded slowly. 'So . . . what're you thinking?'

'I'm thinking we arrest him on suspicion of being involved in Nici Johnson's murder. He'll come in willingly, because he knows he's innocent. But once we've got him, we take a fresh sample for DNA analysis.'

'Won't he suspect that?'

'Doesn't matter. The law permits us to take a DNA sample from any suspect, whether they agree to it or not.' Jessie looked as if she was preparing to give a high five, then said, 'So, do you want to arrest Leandro-I-refuse-to-give-a-DNA-sample-Hutton tonight, or first thing in the morning?'

Gilchrist's head was spinning from it all. Although the thought of making an arrest was appealing, albeit related to a different murder, he first needed to get some background on Wendy Hyatt's twenty-year-old cold case, have a debriefing with Jessie, and find out exactly what she'd done, and whether or not it could ever come back to bite them if things went to hell. But it was an extraordinary piece of detective work, and as long as they played it by the book from here on in, he couldn't see how it wouldn't work.

'Let's do it in the morning,' he said.

'Spoilsport. Right,' she said. 'I'll get this over to the lab, then we'll see what Green has to say for himself.'

'We still don't rate him for Nici Johnson's murder, do we?'

'Not sure,' she said. 'But did you see the way he reacted when we mentioned DNA? I swear he was about to shit himself.'

Gilchrist had to agree. Something in the way Green behaved pointed more towards his being guilty than innocent. But if he wasn't guilty of Nici Johnson's murder, what was he guilty of? Could he be another Hutton, a guilty killer in hiding? Only one way to find out.

'Okay,' he said. 'Get on with it. And give me everything you have on Wendy Hyatt.'

CHAPTER 27

On the walk back to Irene's home in South Street, Gilchrist phoned Maureen. She was still living in Glasgow, sharing an apartment with a work associate she'd befriended while settling into her new position with Strathclyde Police. 'It's not good,' he told her. 'Jack hung up on me.'

'Did you speak to Kristen?'

'Couldn't get hold of her. It rang out, and I didn't want to leave a message.'

'You need to phone her again, Dad. She can't dob Jack into the police.' A heavy sigh, then, 'Of course if Jack wasn't such a dipshit, none of this would be happening. Jeez. I'd call her myself if I knew it would help, but I've done all I can.'

Which really left him with only one option. He would need to call Kristen, and this time speak with her. 'Let me give it another shot,' he said, and hung up.

He changed tack on Market Street, veering left, keeping to the middle of the cobbled street, letting cars slide past him while he dialled Kristen's number. He kept walking while the call went through. One car passed, then another, and he caught a gap in the evening traffic and trotted across the road. Again, his call was dumped into voicemail. He ended it, dialled again. Same thing – voicemail. A third time – voicemail. He disconnected, and whispered a curse. Kristen was either ignoring him, or didn't have her mobile on her. But he remembered watching her with Jack, joking and laughing, drinking and eating, walking and talking and holding hands, and all the time her mobile phone was on her person, stuffed into a pocket, always at hand, always close by, ready to take that next call. Like others of her generation, Kristen's mobile phone was as indispensable to her as food and clothing. She would never go anywhere without it. So, he knew she had to have it with her. All he had to do was make her answer. Which was easier said than done. But, like keeping a thumb pressed to a doorbell, eventually someone would give up.

And it wasn't going to be him.

It took three more failed attempts before Kristen picked up. At least he thought it was Kristen, because she never said a word, just made the connection as if to stop it ringing. For a moment, he thought she would hang up, but it took several seconds for him to realise she was at least going to listen to what he had to say.

'Hello?' he tried. 'Kristen?' He let several beats pass, then said, 'Kristen. It's Andy. Jack's father.' He knew he didn't need to say who he was. His number was in her Contacts. But it seemed as good an opening as any. 'I eh . . . I've spoken with Jack, and he's booked a flight to Sweden.' A pause for feedback, but he was on his own. 'It's eh . . . he can't get back before nine o'clock tonight, it's just not possible. He couldn't get a ticket, but he's done the next best thing, which is a flight out of Edinburgh in the morning. Just him and Linna.' He pressed his mobile hard to his ear, searching for the slightest sound, something, anything that might tell him she at least acknowledged what he was saying. But it was like listening for movement inside a coffin.

He pressed on.

'Jack knows he made a mistake taking Linna away from you, and he's filled with regret, *huge* regret.' He had to stop himself there, force himself to keep his message short and to the point, rather than try to explain that Jack loved Linna and didn't want to lose her. And he certainly couldn't mention Kristen's rekindled affair with Hans. It struck him then, that he shouldn't be talking to Kristen at all, that he was overstepping the mark as Jack's father, that it was none of his business, something only Kristen and Jack could resolve. But she was going to set the police on his son, for crying out loud, have him arrested, so he really had to do whatever he could to prevent that from happening.

As he searched his mind for the appropriate words, he feared his silence would cause Kristen to end the call at any moment. So he tried to put some metal into his tone.

'Linna will be with you tomorrow, Kristen. Jack wants to talk. He's her father, and he wants to find a solution to this. One that works for both of you.' He took a deep breath, then said, 'You once told me, Kristen, that you care deeply for Jack. So I'm asking you . . . if you do truly care for Jack . . . please don't report him to the police. He's bringing Linna back to you, so please . . . please just talk to him.'

He kept his mobile to his ear, hoping for a response. But the digital silence seemed to grow into a deafening rush until it ended with the soft click of disconnection.

He let out his breath, surprised to find he'd been holding it. He stared at his mobile, and tried to settle a tremor that seemed to control his fingers. What on earth had he just done? The right thing? Or blown any chance of Kristen and Jack resolving things amicably? And to make matters worse, he had no idea if Jack would still fly back in the morning or, after their earlier heated conversation, simply cancel the tickets and take his chances in court.

Maybe one more lie might help Jack make up his mind.

Well, two more lies. He couldn't let Jack know he'd spoken to Kristen.

He typed out a message – 'Mo says Kristen happy to talk. No police' – and pressed Send.

He walked to Irene's with a heavy heart. How had he let it all come to this?

CHAPTER 28

By the time Gilchrist read all reports on Wendy Hyatt's murder investigation, it was well after nine o'clock. He'd refused to let Jessie arrest Hutton until he'd first gone through the case files in detail with her, and was convinced in his own mind that Hutton was indeed the prime suspect for this cold case.

Wendy Hyatt's naked body had been discovered on a stretch of beach about two miles north of Aberdeen. Two broken wrists and a fractured ulna, bruises on her forearms, hands, thighs and stomach, all confirmed she'd been brutally battered while alive. Her hyoid bone was crushed, and the whites of her eyes bloodshot with petechiae, which confirmed that she'd survived the beating, only to have been strangled to death. The post-mortem also confirmed that she'd been sexually assaulted. Although no trace of semen was found – her killer had worn a condom – severe vaginal tearing, which would have required surgical sutures if she'd survived, was believed to have been done with a broken bottle. No bottles or any sharp-edged glass or plastic items had been found near the scene.

The only evidence the investigation team had found that could link them to her killer was a flake of skin under her right index fingernail, from which a full DNA profile had been developed. And Hutton's DNA sample, sneakily taken by Jessie, matched. The odds of his DNA matching that of some other individual was so infinitesimally small that it was more or less impossible. If not for that small piece of skin, Leandro Hutton would have got away with murder.

Gilchrist said, 'Do we know where Hutton was living at the time of the murder?'

'Already got it,' Jessie said. 'Montrose. Thirty miles south of Aberdeen.' She rattled off the street address, which meant nothing to him.

'Was he employed?'

'Worked as an insurance agent with Scottish Widows.'

'Which probably meant he travelled about a lot.' More statement than question. 'So we have to ask – why wasn't he questioned?'

'Itinerant insurance salesman,' Jessie said. 'Working all over the country. Never long in one place. Always on the move, day in day out. In that case, we might ask – why *would* he be questioned?'

Gilchrist nodded. He looked at his scribbled notes. 'DI Ben Brown was SIO. Might be worth having a chat with him. If he's still around.'

'He is. Retires next year. Here's his number. He's now a chief super, and already knows we have a new suspect for Hyatt's murder.'

Gilchrist raised an eyebrow. 'You *have* been busy.'

'Working with you, you have to be.'

He ignored her quip, and got through to Chief Superintendent Brown, and put him on speaker. Introductions over, Brown said, 'So you've read the reports we sent you?'

'We have, yes.'

A grunt of acknowledgement, or maybe just clearing of the throat. 'Spent countless hours on that case,' he grumbled. 'Sleepless nights, too. Never been able to get her out of my head – that Wendy, the poor lass. Haunted me ever since.' He paused, as if to reflect on the past or wait for Gilchrist to speak, then said, 'Had a suspect for it. Local lad. Johnny-nae-mates. Bit of a loner. And no alibi. He'd been smoking weed and drinking vodka and crashed out at home. That's what he said. Some were convinced it was him. Others weren't.' He grunted again. 'Grilled him for days, the poor bastard.'

He paused again, giving Gilchrist time to say, 'Why poor bastard?'

'Had him in for questioning three times. Couldn't convince the fiscal. DNA wasn't what it is now, back then, and even though we didn't have a match, he couldn't explain the bruises on his hands. In the end, there was eff all we could do. But some here wouldn't let it go.' He grunted again, a hint of anger in it. 'Hounded him every chance they got. Ten months later he was found dead at home. Drug overdose. Accidental or suicide? We'll never know. Anyway. That was it. Case closed. Orders from above.'

Gilchrist sensed the anguish in the man's voice. After having spent months chasing their tails, only for their prime suspect to die on them, effectively closing the case, here he was, with clear evidence – albeit unofficial evidence at this point – that their prime suspect had been innocent all along, and that they might

161

have driven him to take his own life. It didn't bear thinking about. On the positive side, once they'd acquired a legal DNA sample, they would then have irrefutable evidence to finally bring Wendy's killer to justice, and close the investigation once and for all on a high note.

He offered Brown his sympathies, was about to hang up, when Brown said, 'Before you go, this latest suspect you have, he wasn't a local lad back then, was he?'

'From Montrose at the time.'

'That's what I thought. Knew he had to be from out of town.' He grunted again, and said, 'On the rigs?'

'No. Insurance salesman.'

'How did he know Wendy?'

'We don't know that yet,' Gilchrist said. 'But we'll keep you posted.'

The line died.

Jessie grimaced. 'A right bunch of laughs he is.'

Gilchrist nodded, his mind elsewhere. Poor bastard, right enough. An innocent man hounded by the police for a crime he hadn't committed. How many other men and women were currently serving time in prison for crimes of which they were innocent? It had to be your worst nightmare, or if not, certainly in the top two. And how often did the police try to force-fit a suspect to a crime? He would like to think never, but in his own career he'd come across the odd one or two who were known to associate with elements of the criminal world, cruise through life with one foot on the other side of the law. It wouldn't take a huge stretch to imagine them planting incriminating evidence just to get the result they wanted.

He let out his breath, and pushed to his feet. 'I'm going to leave

Hutton to you,' he said to Jessie. 'Don't arrest him on the door-step. Bring him in for questioning. Softly softly. He's got away with this for so long, he won't be willing to confess. We'll probably need to ease it out of him.'

'I'm on my way,' Jessie said, then strode off, almost bumping into Smiler, who'd been standing in the doorway as if eavesdropping.

Gilchrist felt his stomach lurch. Chief Superintendent Diane Smiley – his immediate boss – was smart as a tack, and nobody's fool. How long had she been there? How much had she overheard? If she suspected they'd acquired an illegal DNA sample, the case would be finished, and more than likely his career, too.

'Ma'am?'

'Wendy?' she said. 'I thought the victim's name was Nicola?'

'Yes, ma'am. It is. But we're looking into another suspect who so far has managed to avoid providing a DNA sample.'

'So . . . this . . . Wendy? Where does she come in?'

He tried to keep his tone level, worried that she could read the fluster in his mind, see the panic in his eyes. 'It transpires, ma'am,' he said, 'that this suspect, Leandro Hutton, was one of a number of people questioned twenty years earlier during the investigation into Wendy Hutton's murder.'

'I see.'

Had she seen through his out and out lie? Or was she toying with his bluff? It wouldn't take much effort for her to check the facts. He resisted swallowing a lump that seemed stuck in his throat, as he watched her gaze drift around his room, settle on the corkboard behind his desk for a long moment, then return to him.

'You think this Hutton is good for Nicola's murder?'

'Could be, ma'am.' Another lie. 'But we'll interview him, and obtain a sample of his DNA as a matter of course.'

'Mmhh,' she said. 'You've run up quite the bill with all this DNA sampling.'

'Once we have Hutton's sample, ma'am, I can assure you that will be the end of it.' He tried a smile, but it felt a tad stiff.

'Anything else you'd like to tell me about this Wendy, Andy?'

'Can't think of anything, ma'am.'

She held his gaze for a long five seconds, before saying, 'Good. Keep me posted.'

'Yes, ma'am,' he said, and breathed a heavy sigh of relief when she turned and walked from his office.

CHAPTER 29

Gilchrist tried phoning Jack again, and this time got through. 'Where are you?'

'At the airport, waiting to collect our bags.'

He hid his relief with, 'Thought you always travelled light,' and threw in a chuckle.

'Brought more stuff for Linna than I probably should have. I'm sure you remember what it's like.'

'Indelibly ingrained into my memory banks,' he said, pleased to hear Jack's laugh in response. 'You been in contact with Kristen?'

'Texted her a couple of times. But haven't heard back from her.'

Gilchrist felt his heart sink. Not a good sign. Had Kristen taken any notice of his plea last night? Or was she already there, Hans by her side, waiting to arrest Jack the moment he cleared Customs? 'I'm sure it'll be all right,' he said, with more commitment than he felt.

'Oh, here's our bags. Got to go. Catch you, man.'

'Okay, let me know how—' But Jack had already hung up.

He'd just sat down at his desk to reread one of Jackie's reports, when Mhairi stepped into his office. 'Sir?' The look on her face warned him it was serious, and he was on his feet, grabbing his jacket as she said, 'We think we've found Jennifer Nolan, sir.'

'Where?'

'In a ditch. Out in the wilds. North of Anstruther.'

That almost stopped him. Had he and Jessie been within yards of her body when they inspected her car yesterday? But *north of Anstruther* could put her beyond a mile or two of the place. In reality, she could be in the middle of nowhere. 'You know how to get there?'

'I think so, sir.'

'Right. I'll drive. You give me directions.'

By the time Mhairi directed him to the body, uniformed officers already had the road partially closed, and the crime scene taped off. The SOCOs hadn't arrived yet, but were on their way. As was Sam Kim, the police pathologist.

The body had been found by a young couple out for a jog, who stood tight-legginged and grim-faced, as if they didn't want to be there, being questioned by a police officer. They glanced Gilchrist's way as he drew to a halt and exited the car, and was then escorted by one of the officers across the road.

'She's down there, sir.'

A fence defined the edge of some private property, and a shallow swale that looked as if it had been man-made years ago, ran the length of the fence, and helped prevent water from flooding the field. The edge of the swale was overgrown by long grass thick with thistles and from where they stood, all he could see was a wisp of blonde hair, and the bluish-white of a bare arm in the bottom of the ditch. He realised the joggers must have stepped closer in order to identify the body as that of a young woman. But the grass didn't appear to be disturbed, so maybe they'd taken a peek sufficient enough to confirm they had to report it to the police.

Being first detective on the scene, Gilchrist returned to his car, opened two forensic packages from the boot, pulled on coveralls, gloves, bootees and mask. Mhairi did likewise. He took care not to slip on the damp slope. At the edge of the swale, rather than step into it, he straddled the ditch so he was standing over the body at the head end, looking directly down on it. Mhairi followed, but stopped at the edge of the ditch.

The body was that of a young woman, probably in her twenties, facedown and naked. From where he stood, Gilchrist could see no bruises, tattoos, or marks of any kind, other than freckles that dotted her skin from her shoulders to her ankles. She looked as if she had simply lain down on her stomach, made herself comfortable, and gone to sleep, head resting on one arm, the other by her side. He noted that mud and grass on the bottom of the ditch were tainted red, and a gentle flow of groundwater that trickled from beyond her feet left a pink trail.

He struggled with his thoughts. Jennifer had been missing since Sunday, without a trace, no one knowing where she'd gone. But they'd heard no report of a missing daughter or sister. And it struck him then, that the reason she hadn't been reported missing by her parents or close friends was because she hadn't been missing. She'd been alive and well and ignoring police calls for her to come forward for reasons he couldn't work out at that moment.

And now she was dead. But for how long?

He stepped gingerly into the bottom of the ditch, feet sinking into soft mud which squidged over his feet. He leaned down, pressed a gloved finger to her neck, the skin cold and tinged blue, but soft to the touch. That was about as far as he could go. He couldn't turn the body over, or carry out any physical examination, until the pathologist had first confirmed life had ceased, the body and surrounding area been photographed, and the SOCOs finished, or were at least well into, their forensic examination of the crime scene.

He extracted himself from the ditch, pulled himself up the slope and stood next to Mhairi. 'Two women murdered within a week?' he said to her. 'What are your thoughts?'

Mhairi frowned for a moment, then said, 'Both women were found naked, on their front. No rings, no jewellery, no ID of any kind. But if it's the same killer, there's one big difference, sir.' She grimaced, then said, 'There are no intestines in her hair. And without turning the body over, we don't know if she's been mutilated to the same extent, or not.'

'And we also can't ID her facially,' he said.

Mhairi seemed not to have heard, and said, 'But it's almost as if . . .'

Gilchrist let several beats pass, then said, 'As if what?'

'I'm not sure, sir. It sounds silly. But it's almost as if by leaving the victims face down, that he's trying to hide something.'

'Hide what?'

Mhairi shrugged. 'Don't know, sir. Maybe his own shame?'

Gilchrist felt his eyebrows lift. He hadn't thought of it that way. But who knew what drove someone to cross that line of no return and kill a living person? Certainly not him. But psychoanalysis took you only so far. They still had to ID the victim.

'So, all that aside, do you think we're looking at Jennifer Nolan?'

'I'd say it's very likely her.'

'Okay, let's say it's Jennifer. What do we have? Dead body. Missing since Sunday. Today's Thursday. What do you see?'

'That's five days, sir. If she died on Sunday I would expect the body to show more signs of decomposition. But . . . it looks as if . . . as if she's not been dead that long, sir.'

He nodded. 'Skin's soft, so rigor mortis has come and gone, putting time of death at least twenty-four hours earlier. But Sam Kim'll give a more accurate estimate. Speaking of which . . .' He nodded over Mhairi's shoulder.

In the short time he'd known Sam Kim, it never failed to amaze him how young she looked – like a child doing an adult's job. She stepped out of her car – one of those generic SUVs that all looked the same, but which bore different emblems on the front grille – and strode to the back where she opened the hatchback. She wore her dyed blonde hair tied back so tight that at first glance you could be forgiven for thinking she shaved her head. Black leggings and a fitted top only exaggerated how slender she was, so light and fragile that you might expect a stiff breeze could bowl her over.

Far from it. Sam Kim was nobody's fool, which Gilchrist had quickly learned.

Forensically suited-up, pathologist's case in hand and camera over her shoulder, she faced Gilchrist. 'Where are the SOCOs?'

'Should be here any minute.'

'You had a look at the body?'

He nodded. 'This way.' He escorted her to the edge of the ditch. 'I'm thinking time of death yesterday, maybe the night before.'

'Any chance of it being related to the other one?'

169

'There's every chance, but it's too soon to say.'

'Right,' she said. 'Let me take her body temperature, and see what we've got.'

Gilchrist offered to help her into the ditch, but she shrugged him off, and with an agility that reminded him that she kept herself fit by practising one of the martial arts – he couldn't say which – leaped into the ditch as if it were nothing more than a front doorstep. He watched her remove something from her bag of tricks, then had to turn away as she inserted a thermometer into the dead woman's rectum.

The sound of an approaching vehicle had him clambering up the slope again, and he almost breathed a sigh of relief at the sight of the SOCO Transit van. Once the Incitent was erected, he would be better able to determine how the victim had died.

The bloodied grass, and the downstream trail, warned him that she'd most likely been stabbed in her front. But he dreaded to think her wounds would confirm that she'd been as brutally murdered as Nici Johnson and, God forbid, her stomach sliced open—

'Sir?'

He turned to face Mhairi.

'Looks like we've got some time to kill, sir. If you'd like I could have someone fetch us a couple of coffees.'

A hot cup of coffee was the last thing he needed, and once the SOCOs turned the victim's body over he wasn't sure he would be able to keep it down. But he smiled and reached for his wallet. 'A latte for me, small for a change, and whatever you're having.'

She took his twenty-pound note, and said, 'Would you like anything to go with it, sir? A muffin or a pastry or . . .'

'Not for me,' he said. 'But have one for yourself. Two if you like.'

'Thank you, sir.'

He had to turn away and breathe in clean cold air to stem the rising bile that threatened to claw its way up his gullet.

CHAPTER 30

Jessie eyed the facade of the cottage as PC Brenton pulled to a halt. For a moment she wondered if they'd arrived at the wrong address, because Hutton Cottage looked nothing like any cottage she'd ever seen. Hutton Mansion perhaps, even Hutton Castle, but not Cottage. How on earth did people earn enough money to buy a house like this? she thought. Or more to the point, how big a house did two people need to live in? Because that was the size of Leandro Hutton's family – just him and his wife. She'd had Jackie check it out for her.

'This do here, ma'am?'

'Perfect.' She opened the passenger door and stepped onto the brick-paved driveway. A fully kitted-out Land Rover with metal plates over the front wheels arches – presumably to provide the driver an elevated view of the horse racing while sipping a flute or two of Dom Pérignon – and an exhaust pipe that rose from the bonnet as upright as a chimney stack, sat parked in front of a sleek sports car, the same one she'd seen at Hutton's weekend shag-away. A four-door garage off to the side suggested more exotic cars in hiding.

Brenton came up beside her. 'Looks like someone's home, ma'am.'

'Perfect,' she said again, and strode to the front door. She thought of keying the sport thingy's bonnet as she walked past, but sensibly decided against it – demotion wouldn't look good on her CV. She reached the front door, pressed the bell, and waited.

They didn't have long.

The door opened with a sticky slap to reveal a young woman in a light blue uniform, who stared at Jessie with unsmiling eyes. She had to be the maid or the cleaner or, perhaps in a house this size, the major-domo in charge of an army of staff.

Jessie held up her warrant card. 'Is Mr Hutton at home?'

'One moment.' The door closed.

Jessie turned to Brenton. 'Did you hear her say please?'

Brenton grimaced and shook his head. 'S'always the same with posh folk. Wouldn't give the likes of us the time of day, ma'am.'

'Speak for yourself.'

'Sorry, ma'am.'

'Lighten up, will you?'

'Yes, ma'am.'

She stared at Brenton long enough for a flush to appear on his cheeks. 'How old are you, PC Brenton?'

'Just turned twenty, ma'am.'

'Right. And your first name?'

'James, but I prefer to be called, Jim, ma'am.'

'Okay, Jim, listen. When it's just the two of us, out here on our own on a job, I prefer to be called Jessie. In the Office, when everyone's there, it's ma'am, and you're PC Brenton. That work for you?'

Brenton offered a broad smile. 'Yes, ma'am. I mean, yes, Jessie.'

'Good.' She faced the door.

She wasn't sure if she'd said the right thing or not to Brenton, because familiarity in the workplace, especially in an environment where explicit chains of command provided a strict order and defined who could tell whom to do what and when, could and often did lead to insubordination. But on the drive to Hutton's she'd sensed Brenton's stiffness behind the wheel, as if he were sitting a test, rather than assisting her in bringing Hutton into the Office for questioning.

She'd never forgotten her early days in the Force, where in a man's world the women seemed to have to do three times the work just to stay level. She'd really struggled at the start of it all – the sexist remarks, the leering looks, the comments behind her back, whispered just loud enough to hear, or laughed at when challenged – and wondered if she'd made the correct career choice. But what she did remember, was how high that rare word of encouragement or camaraderie could lift her, and make her feel a valued member of the team at last. So putting Brenton at ease was maybe the right thing to do after all.

Brenton shuffled his stance. 'Someone's coming.'

She felt herself tense at the sound of footfall from within, and pulled her shoulders back in anticipation of the confrontation. 'I've got this, Jim. Okay?'

'Sure thing.'

Hutton opened the door with a confident smile that faded when he recognised Jessie.

She was conscious of Andy's advice to play it safe, keep Hutton in the dark, and held out her warrant card. 'Mr Hutton,' she said, 'I'd like to ask you a few questions with respect to an ongoing murder enquiry.' The fact that the case she was referring to had been closed twenty years ago and only recently reopened didn't need to be mentioned. But it was good to watch the man's thoughts shift from puzzlement to relief then on to annoyed resignation.

He tutted, and said, 'I thought we'd already been through this. But if you must.' He stepped back, opening the door wider, an invitation for the two of them to enter.

'Preferably at the station.'

'Excuse me?'

'I would like you to accompany us to the station please, Mr Hutton.'

'Why?'

'Because I believe you can assist us in our ongoing murder investigation.'

'But why at the station?'

'Standard protocol,' she lied.

'I'm not sure I can spare the time.'

'You have something planned, have you?'

'Well, yes, I've a busy day ahead of me.'

'At the Dundee office?'

'Well . . . yes . . . Zoom calls . . . and the like.'

'It shouldn't take long at the station.' She smiled. 'The sooner we start, the sooner we finish.'

He shook his head, turned away, and mumbled under his breath.

Something flashed through Jessie then; resentment, impatience, anger, or just plain pissed-offness. Her hearing was nowhere near as good as Andy's, but she would swear blind she'd caught the word *bitch*. For tuppence, she could've cuffed Hutton to the car's bumper and dragged him all the way to the station. But the echo of Andy's voice in her ear – *softly softly* – reminded her to tread with care.

But not that carefully. Time to flex some muscle.

'Mr Hutton,' she said. 'Does the name Wendy Hyatt mean anything to you?'

Hutton stiffened, as if his body had lost all power to move, then he turned with slow deliberation until he faced her. 'Who?' he tried.

'Wendy. Hyatt.'

Hutton scrunched his eyes, and grimaced from the force of pure concentration. His lips fluttered as he puffed and pouted his way through his thoughts. If he was trying to look natural, he was fooling no one. It took all of five seconds for his eyes to open and his lips to recover. He shook his head. 'Nope.'

'You sure?'

'Yep.'

'You never heard the name before?'

'Nope.'

'Are you all right, Mr Hutton?'

'Yep.'

'You look pale,' she said, and offered a smile of concern. He tried to smile back, but his lips pressed into a tight line as if he'd forgotten they could show teeth. Jessie could have stopped there, but Hutton's discomfort was a pleasure to watch. 'You sure you don't know Wendy Hyatt?' she said. 'Never heard the name before?'

'Nope.'

'Even when you lived in Montrose?'

That did the trick. As if some neural switch had been thrown, Hutton's eyes blinked in rapid succession, as if he'd been jerked back to life and was trying to figure out where he'd just been. 'I'll tell you what I'm going to do,' he said. 'I'm going to phone my solicitor, and you'll be hearing from him in due course. You won't get away with this. This is harassment. Unadulterated harassment. And a systemic failure in due legal process—'

Jessie raised her hand to interrupt the flow of insulted verbiage. 'I would certainly encourage you to call your solicitor, Mr Hutton. But you can do so from the station.'

'I beg your pardon?'

She nodded to Brenton, who reached to his side and produced a set of plasticuffs.

'Mr Leandro Hutton,' she said, 'I am arresting you on suspicion of the murder of Nici Johnson. You do not have to say anything . . .'

As she read Hutton his rights, she inwardly smirked. For a fleeting moment, he'd looked confused by the caution – Nici Johnson, not Wendy Hyatt. But the mention of Wendy Hyatt clung to him, and as reality set in his demeanour changed from that of outraged citizen threatening legal action to meek and mild arrestee who held out both hands in surrender, lips trembling, a hint of whimpering in his breath, and of all things to behold . . . a solitary tear that leaked from one eye.

As Brenton led him down the driveway and pressed a hand to Hutton's head while he slid onto the back seat, Jessie couldn't resist whispering under her breath, 'Got you now, you bastard.'

CHAPTER 31

Gilchrist entered the Incitent, followed by Mhairi.

The air was redolent of crushed grass and broken thistles, within which the metallic hint of blood tainted the tongue. The forensic tent created a yellowish glow, and the lack of wind and the sound of trickling water added a sense of surrealism to the scene. If you closed your eyes, you could imagine yourself in some bucolic setting about to prepare a picnic.

But Gilchrist's eyes weren't closed. They were wide open as he struggled to study the body with all the professional dispassion he could muster. The SOCO's in situ examination was completed, and the body turned over so that it lay more on its side than on its back, to reveal a stomach cut open. For the purpose of forensic protocol, Sam Kim had confirmed the victim was deceased and, from rectal temperature and the body's limited deterioration, that the estimated time of death to be no earlier than Tuesday. Although cause of death seemed obvious to Gilchrist, Sam Kim would not be drawn until after she'd performed a full post-mortem examination.

As Gilchrist leaned closer, he noted a small love-heart tattooed on her mons veneris, over which a trimmed line of pubic hair stood as short and neat as an exclamation mark. The tattoo alone was not sufficient to ID the victim, and knife wounds to her face made the ID-ing process more difficult. But a photograph downloaded by Jackie, which Mhairi had brought with her, confirmed that the victim was indeed Jennifer Nolan.

Which raised a number of questions for Gilchrist. Jennifer had been missing since Sunday, the day they'd discovered Nici Johnson's body on the Castle Course. But why had she gone missing? Had she known anything at all about Nici's murder? Had the killer made a mistake? Had Nici been killed instead of Jennifer? – because the physical similarities had not gone unnoticed: same height, weight, colour of hair, age, skin tone. Was that even possible? Had Jennifer known she was being hunted for her life and spent the last of her days in fear? Or, as Gilchrist's mind was enticing him to think laterally, had she been involved in Nici's murder, and been subsequently killed by her partner in crime to prevent her from talking to the police? And if any of his thoughts were correct, where did that put the discovery of her Ford Focus, missing since last Saturday? But Jennifer hadn't been murdered until Tuesday at the earliest, per Sam Kim. So where had she been? If he knew that, could that turn out to be the key that solved the crime? But all these questions were not giving him answers.

He took a deep breath and forced these thoughts and others to the back of his mind. Just get on with it. He had to stick with the facts. He let his gaze drift the full length of her body, and found himself gritting his teeth. If he thought Nici Johnson's attack was brutal, Jennifer's was every bit as bad.

Any one of eight stab wounds around the heart were likely to have been fatal, and he prayed that those had been the first wounds inflicted. Surely no one could have been cruel enough to stab her in the face or slice her stomach open while alive. But from the number of open wounds – forty-four at a first count; eight clustered around the heart, three in the vaginal area, random groups of three or four on her inner thighs – he came to realise that this killer wasn't cruel; this killer was enraged with a fury beyond Gilchrist's imagination.

He concentrated on taking steady breaths, and let his gaze return to the open wound on her stomach. No stab wounds grouped together here. Just one long cut, an eighteen-inch slice that ran like a bloodied stripe across her waist. And as he stared at it, his curiosity got the better of him. He leaned closer, let his fingertips touch the edge of the wound. The skin felt strange, a slackness that you might expect to find in an older person. He pressed the skin gently at first, then a tad firmer, then firmer still, until his fingers slipped through the cut flesh and sank into . . .

'Ah *fuck.*'

He pulled his hand free, pushed to his feet, and stumbled from the tent into cold refreshing air that he sucked into his lungs as if his life depended on it. For all he knew at that gut-wrenching moment, it probably did. He spat out a dribble of bile, rubbed a forensic-clad sleeve across his mouth, and sucked in more air. He hissed a string of curses and turned his face to the wind, while his throat muscles did what they could to prevent bile erupting from his mouth. For a moment, he thought he'd lost the battle, but a fresh gust of wind seemed to do the trick, and he let out his breath in a rasping gasp, and tried to steady his breathing—

'Sir?'

He turned as Mhairi emerged from the tent.

'Are you all right, sir?'

No, he wanted to say. I'm not fucking all right. I'm sick to fucking death of looking at mutilated bodies of young girls with their lives cut short because some fucking nutter decided to stab them in the heart and the face . . . and then . . .

He let out a long sigh, and shook his head. 'I'm fine, Mhairi.' Then he stared off into the distance, took a deep breath, and said, 'If the truth be told, I'm far from fine. I'm miles from fine. I'm on the other side of the planet from fine.' He turned to face her then, and felt his gaze being drawn to her eyes. How could anyone destroy the beauty of a young woman's face? Who could be so cruel and enraged? What went through someone's mind when they inflicted so many stab wounds on a woman who must surely have been dead long before the final wound was inflicted? Too many questions, not enough answers. And how was any of this helping his investigation?

'I'm sorry, Mhairi, I didn't mean to swear like that.'

'I didn't hear you swear, sir.'

Ah, he mouthed, and realised he'd only been thinking of swearing. What the hell did that mean? Was he losing his mind? Had it come to that? Had his mental wherewithal come to an end? Had the sight of too many gruesome killings finally done him in? Bloody hell, this job was enough to make anyone lose their mind. He held Mhairi's gaze, jerked his lips into a quick smile to reassure her that he was all right after all, then grimaced as he nodded to the tent. 'He's eh . . . he's removed her intestines.'

'Sir?'

He forced himself to focus on what he was trying to say, get it out so it would make sense not only to Mhairi, but to himself. 'Nici Johnson's intestines were removed, too, then for some depraved reason twisted into her hair. Short lengths of her intestines were missing, which we assume were taken by the killer as some sort of trophy.' He took a deep breath to settle his thoughts, make sure his logic was making sense. 'So . . . what's he done with the intestines this time?'

'Sir?' Mhairi frowned, lips moving in silent confusion.

'Yes,' he said, and nodded. 'They're not in her body. Did he take them away? Or did he . . .?' As his words faded, his thoughts took over, his gaze drifting to the forensic tent and the small burn that ran alongside the boundary fence.

He couldn't say why he felt so sure where to go. All he knew was that some part of his subconscious was leading him back to the stream. He eased his way down the slope, close to the trickling water, then edged downstream. The sides steepened as he moved farther from the tent. At one point he slipped and grasped a handful of tufted grass to prevent himself from sliding into the water. He struggled on for what felt like ages, but in reality was no more than five minutes, until he found what he was looking for: a blueish-pink tangled mess of human intestines in a clumped pile, lying half-in half-out of the stream.

He was no expert in human pathology, but even from that first look he could tell that not all of the intestines were there, that some had been sliced off and removed. He could see that parts had been damaged by wildlife, too, most likely carrion crows; foxes would have run off with the lot. He turned and eyed the way he'd come, his gaze settling on Mhairi's figure, still and silent, a distant silhouette against the grey afternoon sky. He knew he didn't have to tell her what he'd found. He could tell from the way she reached into her pocket and spoke into her mobile that she was calling for assistance, most likely Sam Kim.

He turned away and sat down on the damp grass, his forensic coveralls offering some protection to his jeans. He slipped off his blood-covered gloves, turned them inside out, and tucked them into his pockets. He would sit there until Sam Kim arrived. He would protect the victim's remains as best he could, chase off any wildlife that might turn up.

He felt it was the least he could do.

CHAPTER 32

No sooner had Gilchrist hung his leather jacket over the back of his chair, than Jessie cornered him.

'You look shattered,' she said.

'Well spotted.'

'Want cheering up?'

'Sure. Go ahead.'

'Got Hutton downstairs,' she said. 'With his solicitor. And he's not a happy chappie.'

'Who? Hutton? Or his solicitor?'

'Why do you always have to be so . . .?'

'Precise?'

'Annoying.'

'Aye, right.'

'Anyway. Hutton's chewing nails now. And his solicitor's getting antsy, too. I told them they'd have to wait until you got back.'

Gilchrist nodded. Not that he didn't trust Jessie to carry out an interview by herself; it was better that both of them work on it together, especially because of the thin line on which they were walking. But the downside to delaying the start of the interview was that the clock was already ticking, and they did not have long to interview him, after which they would have to decide to charge him or let him go.

On the positive side, Hutton's DNA effectively nailed him for Wendy Hyatt's murder. But only he and Jessie knew about that, and their interview strategy was to convince Hutton that his refusal to give a DNA sample for Nici Johnson's murder had raised their suspicions high enough to merit pulling him in for questioning. But Hutton's solicitor would challenge this on the basis of his solid alibi. No matter how they worked it, the whole point of arresting Hutton on suspicion of murdering Nici Johnson was to permit them to take a fresh sample of DNA now they had him in custody.

'We ready, then?' he said.

Jessie nodded. 'Ready as ever. Here's your copy,' she said, handing him a bullet-point list of questions she'd prepared from their earlier discussions.

On the short walk to the interview room downstairs, Gilchrist ran his concerns past her – not a word about the DNA sample, and let's focus on Nici Johnson, not Wendy Hyatt – which she took on board with a tight-lipped grimace.

'I'll try my best.'

Hutton's solicitor looked like a white-haired Brad Pitt with Paul Newman eyes, who flashed a perfect set of teeth when he and Jessie took their seats opposite. He slid a business card over to Gilchrist; Ed Jones – what a letdown – senior associate with some law firm in Dundee. Gilchrist noted the office address, but couldn't place it.

Jessie switched on the recorder, noted the time, and introduced herself and Gilchrist, adding, 'Also present are Leandro Hutton and his solicitor, Ed Jones.'

'Gentleman and lady,' Jones said before Jessie could continue. 'My client would like to know why he's been arrested.'

'For suspicion in the murder of Nici Johnson,' Jessie said. 'I told him that, loud and clear, when I read him his rights.'

'You read my client his rights?' A sideways glance warned Gilchrist that Hutton had likely lied to his solicitor – not a wise move. 'That's not what my client says.'

'Well that's why we always have two officers present during a formal arrest. So that lying scumbags like your client don't get away with it.' She paused for a moment, then stared hard at Hutton. 'We'd also like to question your client about his whereabouts on the night Wendy Hyatt was murdered.'

It really was lovely to watch Hutton take a sharp intake of breath, purse his lips, then struggle to control his Adam's apple, which bobbed up and down like a cork in a flood.

Jones on the other hand appeared bemused. 'Who's Wendy Hyatt?' he asked.

'A woman from Aberdeen, whose battered and naked body was found on a beach twenty years ago.'

'And my client's involvement with this is . . .?'

'He lived in Montrose.'

'Excuse me?'

'He lived in Montrose.'

Jones slid a white smile her way, then said, 'So—'

'Stop right there,' Gilchrist said. He leaned forward and raised his hand to keep Jessie out of it. She'd let her emotions run away with her, let herself be pulled under Jones's blue-eyed spell, and in effect lost control of the interview. 'We're here to question your client, not to be questioned by you. Is that clear?'

'I'm only trying to determine—'

'I know what you're trying to do. Now I'll ask you again. Is that clear?'

'My client has the right to—'

'Stop.' Gilchrist leaned closer, his eyes boring into Jones's. 'I know what rights your client has, and I know what rights you have, as you surely do. So for the record . . .' a glance at the recorder to emphasise his point, 'I would remind you that you are here to advise your client only, and not here to question *us*. You can advise your client how to answer any questions *asked* by us. And that's it. Is that clear now?'

Jones sniffed, nodded, and sat back.

Gilchrist reclined in his chair, a signal for Jessie to get on with the interview. Which she did, spending the next thirty minutes grilling Hutton on his movements in and around the Fairmont on the night of Nici Johnson's murder. Gilchrist knew they would uncover nothing new with that line of questioning, but their intention was to avoid the ubiquitous 'No comment' response, and get Hutton talking, let him build his confidence by answering each and every question because he knew he was innocent of that murder, so had nothing to fear. And as Jessie pressed on, Gilchrist found Hutton's mounting sense of anxiety more than a little interesting, as if he knew what was coming, but didn't know how to avoid it.

And when it did, Jessie segued into it beautifully with the non sequitur, 'And how long did you live in Montrose?'

Jones raised his head from its fixed level of boredom, and glanced at Hutton.

'Not long,' Hutton said.

'Months? Years?'

'Months, I think. No more than a year.'

187

'We've got it down as eight months. Would that be about right?'

Jones leaned to the side and whispered into Hutton's ear.

'And how often did you travel to Aberdeen?' Jessie said. 'Once a week? Twice? Maybe more?'

'No comment.'

'Okay,' Jessie said, stringing the word out. 'Are you going to answer the rest of our questions with "No comment", Mr Hutton?'

'No comment.'

Jessie closed her notebook and folder, and smiled at Hutton. 'Well, in that case, I'm going to have to ask you to provide a sample for DNA analysis.'

Hutton sliced a look at Jones as if to say *If you hadn't instructed me to answer with 'No comment', this wouldn't be happening.* But give Jones his due. He tried his best. In his most objectionable court-room voice he pronounced, 'My client is under no obligation to provide a DNA sample.'

Jessie leaned closer, elbows splayed on the table, dagger-eyes at Jones. 'Wrong, sonny Jim. And you know it. Your client can provide a DNA sample willingly, or not. But he is going to provide a sample. Got it?'

'You can't do this,' Hutton said to Jessie, then glanced at Jones. 'Can they?'

Jones pursed his lips, and Hutton sat back and whispered, 'Jesus.'

'Jesus won't help you now,' Jessie said, and reached for the recorder. 'Interview terminated at nineteen thirty-four,' and clicked it off.

CHAPTER 33

Rather than detain Hutton any longer, Gilchrist released him immediately. Jessie had swabbed his mouth and taken hair samples – much rougher than was necessary; out by the roots, and much to Hutton's vociferous complaints. The earliest they could expect expedited DNA results back would be tomorrow, mid-morning. He would have liked to have detained Hutton overnight, but other than an illegally acquired DNA sample, they had nothing to link him to Wendy Hyatt's murder. Assuming the DNA samples came back positive – as he had no doubt they would do – arresting Hutton the next day was the best they could do.

'We should have someone watch his home,' Jessie said, 'in case he does a runner.'

'Which could give the defence something to hang their hat on,' Gilchrist said.

'What do you mean? I don't get that.'

'What reason would we give for putting a team on his home?'

'We don't trust him?'

'Not good enough,' Gilchrist said, and clenched his jaw. 'Listen to me carefully. We have to play this by the book from here on in.

You got that? We arrested Hutton on suspicion of being involved in Nici Johnson's murder. And that was a stretch because his alibi had been confirmed by his golfing buddies. But being detained gave us the opportunity to take DNA samples, which we're legally entitled to do. And, lo and behold, we found a connection to Wendy Hyatt's murder twenty years ago. Pure luck. By chance. Nothing else. *That*, dear Jessie, is how we play this. And no other way.' He lowered his head and eyed her hard, to make his point. 'You shouldn't have mentioned Wendy Hyatt. If you're ever asked in court why her name was brought up before a DNA test confirmed Hutton guilty of her murder, then you're going to have to lie. In court. You got that?'

'I do. I know. I'm sorry.'

He let out his breath in despair. But nothing could be done about that now. 'So, no more illegal searches. We do nothing without first obtaining a warrant. Is that understood?'

'It is. Yes. Mum's the word,' she added.

He thought she seemed cowed by his reprimand. But how often had he bypassed legal process himself in order to obtain a result? Too often, came the answer. And he came to see that Jessie had simply been following his example, that he was responsible for encouraging her to turn a blind eye to protocol, and in doing so had turned her into a maverick detective – just like himself. Somehow, that thought shamed him. He'd been her senior, her leader, the person from whose experience she was supposed to learn. And with that thought he saw how he had failed not only Jessie, but his own children, too.

Maureen, who seemed to have an innate ability to fall in love with the wrong kind of man, and who could drink wine like lemonade when the mood fitted her, which was more often than he dared to admit. Then there was Jack, who'd been lost in artistic isolation for so many years, then found his way, only to revert to vodka shots and child kidnapping when the going got tough. Was this to be his legacy, the creator of dysfunctional children and a maverick cop—?

'Earth to Andy, hello-oh . . .'

He turned to Jessie, who was looking at him wide-eyed, clenched hand raised as if ready to knuckle a door. 'Sorry,' he said. 'Just thinking.'

'I can see that.'

He struggled to recover his thoughts, pick up where he'd dropped them off. 'Okay,' he said. 'In the meantime, we have a double murder to solve.'

'And on that note,' Jessie said, 'Green's DNA's all over Jennifer Nolan's car. I mean *all* over. It's everywhere.'

'As you might expect, if they were in any kind of a relationship.'

'But the point I'm making,' Jessie said, 'is that they've found no one else's DNA in her car. Only hers and his. If she'd been killed by someone else, wouldn't you expect to find another DNA profile?'

'Only if that other person had been in the car with her. She could have driven to that spot by herself, parked her car, then been driven off in another car by her killer-in-waiting.'

'I'm not sure I agree.'

'So what do you think happened?' Which seemed to stump Jessie, for she frowned and slumped into a chair. 'Nici Johnson's killer did what he could to leave no DNA,' he said. 'We struck lucky with the dropped sock. So what I'm saying is, that this killer is forensically savvy. And if John Green's DNA is all over Jennifer Nolan's car, then I don't see him being her killer.'

She looked up at him, her glance askew. 'I hear you. But there's something about that guy that I really don't like.' She paused for a long moment, then said, 'If he is her boyfriend, he wouldn't go to the trouble of wiping all his DNA from her car, would he? Because *that* would look suspicious. So he lives with it. If his DNA is found all over Jennifer's body, so what? He's her boyfriend. Or at least he can claim to be.' She shook her head. 'But I still think the fact that there's no one else's DNA anywhere near the scene is significant.'

Gilchrist had to agree that he saw some merit in Jessie's argument. But even so, there was bugger all they could do about it without more incriminating evidence. 'How are Mhairi and Jackie getting on digging into Timothy Johnson's background?'

'Can't find diddly beyond a couple of years. They think he's living overseas.'

'Any idea where?'

'Not yet.'

'They need to focus on his last known home address, place of work, bank statements, pay cheques, all that sort of stuff.'

'Already done that. And he's gone, Andy. They hit a dead end. Can't remember the exact date, but I can get that for you.'

He shook his head. Some idea was coming to him, some thought that seemed to linger at the periphery of his mind, just out of reach, like some fading shape in a thickening fog. He knew what it was but couldn't quite put a name to it, to him . . . to her. That was it. *Her.* It had to be. He looked away for a moment, to let his logic run through the rationale, and when he turned back to Jessie, he said, 'Forget Timothy Johnson himself. At least for the time being. He's a dead end. You said so yourself.'

'So . . . what're you saying?'

'Get everyone back onto Nici Johnson. Who she worked for, who her friends were, who she spent time with. Look into her social media again; Facebook, Twitter, Instagram, and anything else she might have been on. Go through every single bit of it piece by piece. And focus all efforts around the time she went out with Timothy Johnson. They used to live together for crying out loud. We're missing something. I don't know what yet. But whatever it is, it's important. Nici's the key. She has to be.'

When Jessie left his office, Gilchrist walked to the window and looked out at the cold night. Strong winds had done what they could to clear the sky. A gibbous moon hung low out to the east, wisps of clouds shifting across its face like strips of tattered rags. He couldn't recall what the forecast was, but being Scotland, rain was no doubt in it somewhere.

His thoughts on how to handle his double-murder investigation seemed clearer now, as if Hutton's appearance had been an unwelcome interruption that had simply fogged his path. But Jessie's instincts had turned a cold case on its head. An incredible piece of luck, and an incredible act of detective work if he thought about it. But the trouble with instincts was that you had to trust them and fly with them, not knowing if they were right or wrong until you uncovered the end result – which you had to live with, whether you liked it or not.

And Gilchrist's instincts were alive and kicking at that moment. He'd never been able to explain it, that gut feeling that niggled and nipped at his logic, that sixth sense that seemed to guide him more often than not – an inexplicable feeling that was good enough to uncover a murder weapon in a cemetery when everyone else had lost track and faith; good enough to lead him to a drug-laden garage on the east coast of Scotland, where no one was supposed to be at; good enough to lead him in the right direction time and again, with positive results.

But every now and then, not often mind you, once in a blue moon, maybe less, his instincts failed him. Which wasn't what was troubling him at that moment. His instincts felt solid, strong enough to assure him that Nici Johnson's history had to be the key. They would find what they were looking for there. He was sure of it.

But what he was also sure about, and what worried him more, was the fear that what they would find could prove to be more than any one of them could face, that what they were about to uncover – no, correct that – *who* they were about to uncover, would turn out to be more life-threatening than anyone could be prepared for.

CHAPTER 34

Gilchrist found Irene in the lounge in front of the TV, the sound turned down to little more than a quiet murmur. She put her book aside when he entered, looked up at him and smiled. Which was what he loved about her. He'd been remiss once again not calling earlier to let her know he was running later than planned – so what's new? – and now, even after all those years of Gail no longer being in his life, he still carried a sense of guilt home with him, his feelings burdened from having spent too many hours at work, but which vanished the instant Irene smiled at him.

He leaned down to peck her cheek. 'Sorry I'm late.'

'I'm used to it by now,' she said, and surprised him by taking his head in both hands. 'Don't say sorry. It's who you are. I just worry that you're taking too much out of yourself.'

'At my age?'

'At your age,' she agreed, then said, 'And I've made you a salad, so . . .'

'I'd better eat it before it gets warm.' He laughed with her at their silly one-two joke.

'Do you want me to turn the TV up?' she said.

'No, I'm fine. I'll just have a bite first.' As he walked to the kitchen, he said, 'Can I get you anything?'

'Another glass of water would be lovely, thank you.'

'With some lemon?'

'Yes, please. Oh, and before I forget, Joanne phoned earlier, some muddled message about Maureen being upset. I'm sorry I didn't catch it all, I'd just woken up.'

In the kitchen, he filled a glass with water, cut a fresh slice of lemon, and carried it through to her. 'Did she say why Maureen was upset?'

'She might have, but I was still a bit groggy.' She took a sip. 'I'm sorry. I should've been more attentive, and should've written it down.'

'That's all right. I'll give her a call later.'

Back in the kitchen, Gilchrist was picking at his salad, scrolling through emails from work – none of which told him anything new about the case – when he realised Irene was standing in the lounge, looking at him. 'You're dressed,' he said.

She laughed at his confusion. 'I'm not naked, that's correct, yes.'

'I mean, you're wearing a jacket and scarf.'

'Because it's cold outside.' She nodded to his half-eaten salad. 'Besides, I don't think you're really enjoying that, are you?'

'No it's . . . it's . . .' He flipped his phone face-down on the breakfast bar. 'Sorry. I've not been paying attention.' He pushed his stool back. 'I'll come with you.'

'I think you deserve a pint, and I deserve a glass of wine. And it's my treat.'

He frowned. Other than a glass of Prosecco on Christmas Day, which Irene had more or less played with for two hours over dinner, she hadn't had so much as a sip of alcohol since. 'And what's the occasion?' he said, slipping on his jacket.

'Does there have to be an occasion?'

'I suppose not,' he said, and held out his arm. 'Shall we?'

Outside, she surprised him by turning east on South Street, rather than crossing the road towards the Criterion and the Central beyond. But he said nothing, just held her arm as they settled into their stride together. They exchanged small talk, a bit of this, a piece of that, all the while Gilchrist wondering where she was leading him, what the real reason for this walk was.

When they arrived at the mini-roundabout – left to South Castle Street, right to Abbey Walk – she surprised him once again by continuing on South Street towards the cathedral ruins. But he kept his questions to himself, and walked on. At The Pends he pulled him to the right, another surprise. But he said nothing, and let himself be led down the road towards the inner end of the harbour.

When they reached the end of the cathedral walls and stepped onto the flat of the harbour road, Irene walked to the edge of the harbour wall, and stopped. She released his arm, and for one unsettling moment, he thought she was going to throw herself into the dark water.

'Isn't it beautiful?' she said, raising her gaze to the stars.

The clouds had parted to reveal the moon, which seemed to shine as strongly as he'd ever seen it. 'It's a nice time of year,' he said. 'Past the middle of winter. The summer on the horizon.' He choked a laugh. 'Or what everyone in Scotland accepts as a summer.'

She said nothing, just continued to stare at the sky. At length, she said, 'I've always wondered about it all, about life on Earth, why we're here, and is there any life elsewhere in the universe, or is this it? Are we it?'

'Humans?'

'No. Earth. All life on it.' She lowered her gaze. 'It's so sad, don't you think?'

At that moment, he didn't know what to think, so he played it safe with, 'What's so sad?'

She turned to face him, took hold of his hands. 'Living,' she said. 'And dying. It's the natural rule of things. But that's what's so sad.' She breathed in hard, then let it out as her gaze drifted away, along the length of the pier. 'I should've taken more photographs. Of this. The sea. The stars. The beauty of the night.' She sighed. 'But there's just never enough time, is there?'

He squeezed her hands. 'Irene. Look at me.'

She did.

'You've brought me out here for a reason,' he said. 'But I'm not sure what.'

She moved her lips in imitation of a smile, but said nothing.

He pulled her to him, and hugged her close. 'What are you trying to tell me?' he said, his voice tight with emotion.

'I don't know,' she whispered. 'I'm not sure.'

'You're not sure about what?'

'About what's happening.'

He felt himself tense. 'Happening?'

'To me. To my body.' She sniffed, hugged him tighter. 'I think I'm dying, Andy. I think I don't have long to live now, and there's so much more I want to do with my life, so many more things I want to see, but now . . .'

He pressed his lips to her hair, whispered words of comfort, and held onto her until he felt her sobbing subside. He kept her close, his head against hers, afraid that if they parted she might read the fear in his eyes. 'What's brought this on?' he said, trying to make light of it.

She sniffed again. 'I know my body,' she said, 'and I know something's changed.'

'We'll talk to the consultant tomorrow.'

'No. No more consultations. No more, Andy. I'm tired of talking. I feel as if all I've been doing for the last six months is what everyone has been telling me to do, and I no longer want to do that.' She pushed away from him then, and he could read the determination in the tightness of her jaw, the fire in her eyes.

'Okay,' he said. 'We won't talk to any more consultants.'

Silent, she nodded.

'Then what?' he tried.

'Then I live the remainder of my life on my terms,' she said.

'But . . .'

'But I'm tired, Andy. Please understand that. I'm just tired all the time. I haven't the strength to do the things I want to do.' She let out a gush of despair. 'My goodness, I hardly have the strength to sit around doing nothing all day long.'

'You've managed to walk this far,' he said, and offered her a supportive smile. 'So it can't be all bad.'

She tried a smile in response, but it died on her lips. 'I'm tired, Andy. It's as simple as that. I'm just tired . . . tired of living.'

He was about to remind her of her daughter, Joanne, how she would feel if she knew her mother was thinking of giving up on life, and of plans for more of her photographs to be published, when the echo of her words – *all I've been doing for the last six months is what everyone has been telling me to do* – stopped him short.

He held her gaze, and nodded his understanding.

'I'm sorry, Andy.'

'There's no need to be sorry,' he said. 'But I do have one question.'

'What's that?'

'Are you too tired to buy me that pint?'

CHAPTER 35

6.15 a.m., Friday

On the short walk to the Office, Gilchrist phoned Maureen. He didn't make it a habit of calling at that hour, but since joining Strathclyde Police, Maureen had worked a variety of shifts, so for all he knew she might be heading home after a night on the beat. Besides, by the time he and Irene returned home – after two glasses of wine in the Central, sipped with care and slow deliberation by a determined Irene – then spent some time chatting in front of the TV before she fell asleep, he'd found he was in no mood to return Maureen's call. Best to do it first thing in the morning. So here he was. Despite winter being officially over, frozen puddles dotted the road, streetlights reflected off the frosted pavement like diamonds. His breath clouded the air as he spoke.

'Didn't know if you were awake or not,' he said. 'But sorry I didn't get back to you last night.'

'Didn't matter, Dad. There's nothing you could've done. Jack's in jail.'

'He's been arrested?'

'He was met by police at the airport.'

Gilchrist's thoughts fired off in all directions. Had Kristen not listened to a word he'd said? And with that thought came the worry that it might not have been Kristen he'd spoken with. After all, she hadn't uttered a word during his entire call. Had someone else answered, and listened in silence to his pleas? If so, who? And if Jack had been met by police at the airport, where had they taken him? Were they going to charge him? What with? Kidnapping? Abuse? Or some other crime the Swedish authorities deemed appropriate? What was the legal process in Sweden? Could he be bailed? Or would they hold him in jail until his trial? As a British citizen, he could be deemed a flight risk. And what if they found him guilty? And if so, guilty of what? It all seemed too much too soon for him to rationalise.

'Was Kristen at the airport when he was arrested?' was all he could think to say.

'She said she wasn't.'

'So you've spoken to her?'

'Last night. She called me.'

'Hang on, hang on.' He stopped at the corner of Church Street and Market Street, and pressed the phone hard to his ear. 'I'm struggling to make sense of this. *She* called *you* to say Jack had been arrested.'

'Yes.'

'Had you asked her to call you?'

'No.'

He thought he was beginning to see how it had unfolded. If Kristen hadn't been at the airport to meet Jack, that meant someone else had. And the fact she'd called Maureen to tell her of

Jack's arrest might mean that she hadn't expected Jack to have been arrested. 'So . . .' he said, 'do you think Hans maybe had Jack arrested behind Kristen's back?'

'I'm not sure, Dad. But Kristen didn't sound happy.'

'About what? About Jack being arrested? Or something else?'

'She didn't say, and I didn't ask. She did say she was glad to have Linna back.' A pause, then, 'What's going to happen to Jack, Dad? Will he go to prison?'

Gilchrist didn't want to tell her the obvious, that kidnapping a child was a serious offence no matter in what country it took place, with a custodial sentence being the most likely outcome. But until he knew the details of Jack's arrest, he didn't want to offer a guess. Besides, it could all depend on what Kristen did. If she pressed charges, there would be no let-off for Jack. But if she was pleased to have Linna back, and upset at Jack having been arrested – maybe against her wishes – well . . . who knew what she might do.

'Let me make a few phone calls first,' he said.

'Get back to me, will you?'

'Sure,' he said, and hung up.

He checked the time, not yet 6.30, and thought of phoning later. But like himself, a career's worth of detective work ensured that Dainty had become a habitual early riser.

'Sorry for the early call,' Gilchrist said.

'No problem, Andy. Out walking the dog.' A gravelly cough that could have come from a big man, followed by what sounded like a spit. 'And dog walking these days seems to be mostly waiting for the wee bugger to take a crap, then bagging it while the fucking thing's still warm.' A sniff. 'So what's up?'

'You had dealings with the Swedish police last year, didn't you?'

203

'Did, yeah, sure. Middle of fucking winter. Checking out some paedo ring. Freeze the balls off you that place would.'

'You ever come across a detective by the name of Hans Dietrich?'

'Fuck sake, Andy. Sweden's a big place.'

'I know. Sorry. Just a thought.'

'Why? What's he done?'

Gilchrist spent the next couple of minutes bringing Dainty up to speed, after which Dainty said, 'What's Jack's missus saying about it all?'

'Kristen's not happy he's been arrested. So, I'm thinking Hans might have had Jack arrested behind her back. I'll try calling her later this morning, and get a better feel on what's going on.'

'Let me phone my guy,' Dainty said. 'See what he comes up with.' A pause, then, 'Do you want me to ask if he knows a good lawyer?'

Cold fingers brushed Gilchrist's spine. He hadn't wanted to think along those lines, but it was typical of Dainty to cut through the mire, and go straight to the core. 'Not until I find out what's happening,' he said.

'I'll get back to you.'

And with that, the connection died, leaving Gilchrist to wonder just how deep a pile of shit Jack had waded into.

CHAPTER 36

The bulk of Gilchrist's morning was spent at his desk, reading reports and sifting through downloads and printouts of text messages and social media pages, none of which seemed to be advancing his investigation. He found himself becoming frustrated by the sheer volume of the stuff, as if all Nici Johnson had ever done with her life was to send out useless posts about herself; selfie after selfie of her or with others, clad in cycling outfits with some cloud-smothered hill or woodland or seascape in the background. Others of her bikini-clad figure holding some loaded fruit concoction with the caption *happy hour cocktails* in pubs he'd never heard of – mostly in some sun-soaked spot in the Mediterranean. How on earth youngsters nowadays could afford to go on holiday overseas three or four times a year defied logic. But he'd brought the cause of his frustration upon himself, having insisted on seeing everything Jackie and Mhairi could find on her.

And Jennifer Nolan was just as bad, but without the Mediterranean backdrop, leaving Gilchrist with the impression that she was more of a homegirl – Scotland was where she was born and raised, and proud of it. But so far nothing he considered significant enough to open a new avenue of investigation. It seemed as if all they were doing was producing paperwork.

When Smiler entered his office and closed the door behind her, he wasn't sure if he should be relieved of the break, or worried about what she had to say. She pulled out one of the seats in front of his desk, and sat. 'How did your interview with Hutton go yesterday?'

Gilchrist felt his heart stutter. 'Inconclusive, ma'am, with his solicitor advising him not to comment . . . eh . . . mostly.'

She nodded, as if understanding how difficult the interview process can be with an uncooperative suspect. 'I read the transcript this morning,' she said. 'But I failed to catch the link between the suspect, Hutton, and the victim, Wendy Hyatt.' She flickered a smile that died on her lips. 'Care to enlighten me?'

'It was . . . eh . . . *intuition*, ma'am,' he almost blurted. 'Can't really explain it.'

'Can't really explain it, or don't want to explain it?'

And in that moment he saw with utter clarity that she knew he'd broken the rules. She had him in her perfectly laundered grip, and all she had to do was squeeze, and his career would be over. But she surprised him by pushing her chair back, and standing.

'Intuition,' she said. 'Quantum leap in thinking. A shot in the dark, perhaps.' She seemed to give her words some thought, then added, 'Or something else?'

'Ma'am?' It was all he could think to say.

'I'm not sure I would like to be made privy to the answer. Don't you think?'

'Yes, ma'am. I mean no, ma'am.' Christ, could he fuck it up any worse?

'Let's agree to leave it at that, shall we?' She opened the door and closed it behind her with the gentlest of clicks, leaving Gilchrist to push to his feet, walk to the window, and stare up at a clouded sky.

When Dainty called just before 10.30, Gilchrist was thankful for the break.

'Took a bit of digging, Andy, but Hans Dietrich doesn't have a good record, and not someone you want to mess with. Worked in the drugs squad for six years, but was moved sideways – read that as demoted – on suspicion of being too close to a number of criminals. In other words, he was on the take. Nothing ever proven, of course, but as they say, mud sticks.'

'And where is he now?'

'Still a detective, but mostly investigation of minor violations – domestic disputes, pub fights, vandalism, that sort of stuff.'

'Okay,' Gilchrist said, trying to work out the pros and cons of what Dainty had told him. If Dietrich was a rogue cop, then on one hand it might work better for Jack – who would listen to a discredited police officer? But on the other hand, maybe Dietrich had friends in places you don't want to have friends, which could work against Jack. For the life of him, he couldn't figure it out. 'Did you get any news on Jack?' he asked.

'Being held in a local Police Office, is all I can tell you. If it goes to court, he'll be assigned a duty lawyer, so maybe best to think about getting your own lawyer on board. Got a couple of names for you, if you're interested.'

Gilchrist grunted acknowledgement, and scribbled them down.

When Dainty hung up, Gilchrist pushed to his feet and walked to the window. The skies had cleared, not a cloud in sight, and plants in distant window boxes were doing what they could to announce spring. Overseas visitors could be fooled into thinking it was going to be a good day. He raked his fingers through his hair and whispered a curse at Jack. What the hell had he been thinking about? Why on earth had he taken Linna from her mother and brought her to Scotland with him? He must have known he could never get away with that. And surely his relationship with Kristen hadn't broken down to the point of no return, had it? But Gilchrist knew from past experience that personal relationships could sour in a heartbeat, and what had once promised to be a strong bond could snap like a twig into repetitive abuse.

Is that what had happened to Jack and Kristen?

He glanced at his watch again, and toyed with the idea of giving her another call. Or perhaps one of the solicitors Dainty had given him? But no, he thought, he first needed to hear from Jack—

'You're going to want to see this.'

He turned from the window.

Jessie was standing at the side of his desk, a printout in one hand, her lips pursed tight with a smirk. She flapped the printout at him. 'Nici Johnson and her boyfriend, John Green.'

He took the printout from her – an enlarged selfie of a young couple in tight cycling attire, standing in front of their mountain bikes, bodies slim and tight and fit, faces gleaming, white smiles glistening. Wide cycling sunglasses pushed high on their foreheads to reveal two youngsters, faces pressed close together. But something about the photograph was off. Nici's hair seemed shorter, darker, too. And John Green looked fitter, slimmer.

He looked at Jessie. 'Where is this from?'

'Social media. Where else?'

He returned his gaze to the image. He was missing something. He knew he was. He could tell from the way Jessie seemed to be holding her breath, as if urging him to work it out for himself. The background in the photo could be any one of a hundred Munros in Scotland. Blue skies and thin clouds told him the photo had likely been taken in the summer months. But whatever had Jessie worked up, he couldn't see it.

He looked at her again. 'What am I missing?'

'Check the date.'

He found it on the bottom right-hand corner. July. Three years ago. Okay, he thought. Which meant . . .? Back to Jessie, still somewhat puzzled. 'So this confirms that Nici Johnson knew John Green earlier than we thought. Right?'

Jessie's smirk widened, her eyebrows rose.

Back to the photograph. Which was when he thought he saw it. 'Wasn't Nici living with Timothy Johnson three years ago?' he said.

'Exactly.' She nodded to the printout. 'So who's that?'

And in an instant, he saw where she was going with this. 'Timothy Johnson before he changed his name to John Green?'

'Now you've got it.' She held up her hand for a high five, but after a few seconds let her arm drop when she realised he wasn't going to reciprocate. 'What?' she said.

'Is there any reason why Nici Johnson couldn't be living with Timothy Johnson at the same time as being friends with John Green?'

'Mhairi and I talked about that, before I showed you this. But if you add in the fact that *Jackie* . . . and you know what Jackie's like . . . can't find *anything*, and I mean not a damn thing, absolutely *zilch* on Timothy Johnson after he and Nici split up, then it puts a different perspective on it. Doesn't it?'

There was that smirk again, although he had to say Jessie had a point. Maybe not just any old point, but a bulging nailhead just waiting to be hammered home.

'Let's go,' he said.

CHAPTER 37

The plan had been to bring John Green into the Office for further questioning, but when they arrived at his home, he wasn't in.

'You think he's ignoring us again?' Jessie said.

Gilchrist had stepped onto the front lawn, and was eyeing the upper-floor windows, searching for the slightest signs of movement within. But from what he saw, the house could have been deserted. 'I'll try the back door,' he said, 'and you nip up to the end of the road and see if his car's parked there.'

The back garden appeared more derelict, with last year's uncut lawn sprouting clumps of reeds more suited to a cow pasture than a tended lawn. But no amount of hammering the back door or peering through curtained windows was going to raise Green.

Jessie reappeared at the corner of the house. 'Car's not there.'

'Bugger it.' He retrieved his mobile, and called Mhairi at the Office. 'Get onto the ANPR and find John Green's Audi.' He recited the registration number to her, but had an unsettling sense that he was sending his team on a wild goose chase. It didn't take much effort nowadays to fool the Automatic Number Plate Recognition cameras – a strip of black tape could change the

211

number 1 to the letter T; a couple of strips of white tape could change an E to an F; with any number of variations in between.

Call finished, he said, 'Check with the neighbours. You take this side, and I'll take the side across the street. Maybe someone noticed when he left, or who he was with.'

'If they're anything like the last lot,' Jessie said, 'they couldn't tell the difference between a postie and second-hand car salesman.'

Gilchrist stepped up to the front door of the fourth neighbour, three houses down from John Green's. He couldn't see a doorbell, so rattled the letterbox. He blew into his hands and made a mental promise to wear gloves more often. He glanced at Jessie, who was scurrying from door to door, giving him the impression that she was having as much success as he was, which was close to zero.

The previous three neighbours he'd spoken to hadn't known John Green by name, and had seen him only in the occasional passing. One confessed she didn't like the looks of him – *Widnae trust no one who disnae open his curtains* – which was about as close as he'd come thus far to neighbourly confirmation of Green's presence.

He gave the letterbox another rattle, and stood back at the sound of movement from within. The door opened with a metallic clatter. An overweight woman in tight black leggings that seemed to meet at the knees, and a black sweatshirt stained down the front, stood before him, rocking a baby in her arms. Tails of grey-black hair hung around her face from a badly fitted clasp. The stale smell of cigarette ash wafted off her like body odour.

'Whit?' she said.

Gilchrist held out his warrant card and introduced himself.

She surprised him by stepping back and inviting him inside. 'In youse come. Ah'm in the middle of feeding the weans.'

'I won't take up much of your time,' he said, following her into a small kitchen at the back of the house.

The linoleum floor was littered with toys and clothes, and the room redolent of burnt toast and something more basic, which had him taking care not to tread on any fouled nappies that could be lying around. Two toddlers who looked trapped in small table and chair sets were splashing their food with spoons. A radio DJ was doing what he could to drown out the clatter and indecipherable child-speak.

'Grab a chair if you can find one,' the woman said, and pulled her sweatshirt up and over her baby, to expose for a fleeting moment the expansive aureole of a bulging breast.

'Thanks, but I'll stand,' he said.

'So whit is it?' she said. 'Him across the road?'

Intrigued, Gilchrist frowned. 'Him?'

'Aye, that guy, Green.' She winced for a moment, then juggled her hand under her baby. 'You're supposed tae suck, no bite, ye wee bisom,' she said, then turned back to him.

'So why do you think I'm here to ask about John Green?' he said.

'Seen him coming and going at all hours of the night.'

'He works late hours as a chef, which could explain it.'

'Aye, but no at four in the morning, he disnae.'

'Which morning would that be? Can you remember?'

He almost held his breath as she adjusted her baby again. 'There's nothing wrong wae mah memory,' she said. 'Last Saturday. That's when ah seen him coming hame. Sneakin in and oot he wis. Thought naebody'd notice, but ah noticed.' A clatter to the side had her turning her head and shouting, 'Shut it, you two.' But she could have been talking to the wall for all the difference it made. Then she fixed Gilchrist with a hard glare. 'It's yon girl, isn't it? The one that wis murdered.'

He could have agreed with her, and taken it from there, but instead said, 'You said four in the morning. How accurate is that? Five to? Ten past? Or what?'

'Just efter.' She shrugged. 'Five past, maybe.'

'So you're not exactly sure.' More statement than question.

'The wee yin woke me up screaming, so she did. So ah got up and wandered aboot the hoose trying to shoosh her. Ah noticed the time on the microwave. Right on four, so it wis. Then ah went through to the living room. And when ah looked oot the windie, that's when ah saw him.'

'And you're sure it was him? John Green?'

'Who else wid it be?'

Not quite the answer he wanted to hear. 'Was he driving a car?'

'Ah couldnae say. He parks it at the end of the road. Next to mine. That's how ah know him.'

'Have you spoken to him?'

'Naw. Jist know him tae look at.'

Gilchrist paused for a moment, then said, 'So you knew about the woman's body that was found on Sunday morning?'

'Heard it oan the news.'

'So why didn't you phone the police and report it?'

'And say whit? Ah seen someone coming hame at four in the mornin?'

Well, he supposed it was a bit of a weak question.

He spent another five minutes poking and prodding, but not

really learning anything new. He took a note of her name and phone number, and said, 'Is there a Mr Enderby?'

'Done a runner.'

'I'm sorry to hear that.'

She removed her baby from her breast and pulled her sweat-shirt low to her waist, as if feeling shy about breast feeding all of a sudden. 'Said the twins wis enough. And when this wan came along, that wis it. When the going gets tough, the tough get going. Aye, right oot the door. Useless effin wanker.'

Gilchrist gave a sympathetic smile. 'Thanks for your time. You've been very helpful. I may have someone swing by later today to take a statement from you, if I think it might help.'

'Aye, any time. And make sure he's good-looking.' She chuckled at her own joke, and as he took hold of the door handle, said, 'Have youse spoken tae his bird yet?'

Gilchrist froze, hand on the door handle. He hadn't mentioned anything about having found Jennifer's body, or that she was believed to be John Green's girlfriend. 'Why? Do you know her?'

'No really, naw.'

'So why would you suggest we speak to his girlfriend?'

'Cause she wis wae him.'

'When?'

'Four in the mornin. When he came hame.'

'You sure it was her?'

'Oh aye. It wis her aw right. Couldnae mistake they legs. All the way up to her arse and back doon again.'

Gilchrist had no answer to that, so he thanked her, and set off to catch up with Jessie.

CHAPTER 38

When Gilchrist caught up with Jessie, she said, 'Hope you're having better luck than me. I think these people walk about with their eyes shut all day. Half of them didn't even know who John Green was.'

Gilchrist gave a victory smile, and told her what Mrs Enderby had said. 'Get hold of Jackie and Mhairi. We need to establish if Jennifer Nolan was with Green on Saturday night, or even if she could have been. I mean . . . why are we only finding out about this now?' He pushed his fingers through his hair in frustration. 'And get Jackie to put a post on the PNC for Green's car, with a marker to approach with extreme caution, may be armed.' He didn't know if Green had a gun or not, but if he was the killer they were looking for, he certainly had a knife. Better safe than sorry.

He walked off while Jessie phoned the Office as instructed, and soon found himself at the end of the road, where a number of cars were parked, four in total – no Audi. He walked around the cars like a disinterested buyer, peering in the windows, checking out the tyres, not sure what he was looking for, but in the end concluding that the Peugeot with the scratched paintwork and dented front

216

wing, with two child seats in the back and McDonald wrappers scrunched up in the passenger footwell, had to be Mrs Enderby's.

The space beside it was empty.

He stood back and eyed the houses across the road, trying to figure out which was best positioned for an unrestricted view of the parked cars. One for sure; two maybe. He approached the more obvious of the houses, and rang the doorbell.

He didn't have to wait long.

The door sprung open to a smiling woman in her mid-twenties or thereabouts, who announced in a lilting Welsh accent, 'Whatever it is you're selling, we're not interested.'

Gilchrist held out his warrant card, and introduced himself.

'Oh,' she said, and almost took a step back. 'What've we done?'

'Nothing, I hope.' He added a smile to show he was harmless. 'We're carrying out door-to-door enquiries. What can you tell me about the grey Audi that parks over there?'

'What Audi?'

'It's not there at the moment,' he said, feeling a tad silly from his question. 'We're trying to locate the owner, and—'

'Oh you'd best speak to my husband, love. He knows more about cars than I do.' And before he could respond, she turned and shouted down the hall, '*Ger. Ger.*' She walked along the hall shouting, 'Gerry, love, there's a policeman at the door wanting to know about cars.'

A man appeared from the end of the hall, towelling his hands as he strode towards Gilchrist. 'Out the back,' he said. 'Tidying the garden. So what's this about a car, then?'

'We're trying to locate the owner of the grey Audi that parks across the road there.'

'Oh, aye, well, that'll be John's, like.'

217

'John Green?'

'That's him. Big lad. Fit as a fiddle. And I mean fit. Why? What's he done?'

'So you know John well?'

'Not well. Just have a chat with him now and again, like. But that Audi of his. I tell you. Keeps it immaculate. And I mean sparkling.'

Gilchrist nodded. 'When did you last see John? Or his car?'

'Couldn't really say. A day or so ago. Didn't pay any attention. Why?'

'Was it there this morning?'

Gerry grimaced, wiped his hands on his towel again. 'Sorry. Honestly couldn't say. Was there a couple of days ago. Wednesday. Maybe Tuesday. But that's it.'

Well, if he was looking for a vague answer, he'd just found it. He handed over his business card. 'If you come across John, or his car, can you call this number?'

Gerry looked at the card, then at Gilchrist. 'Which one?'

'Either. The landline's the Office number. The other's my mobile.'

'No. I meant, which car?'

Gilchrist frowned. 'He has another car?'

'Two Audis. Both immaculate.'

A dozen questions sparked through Gilchrist's mind in a burst of possibilities that settled into one question. 'Can you tell me what the other car looks like?'

Gerry grinned. 'Can do better than that. Hang on. Back in a mo.'

Gilchrist removed his mobile, and was about to call Jessie, when Gerry returned, mobile phone in hand.

'Here it is.' He held out his mobile. 'See? Immaculate.'

Gilchrist took the mobile from him, its screen showing a black Audi head on. At first, he was confused, thinking he was looking at the dark grey car they were searching for, until he noticed the number plate was also different. He swiped across the screen to another image of the same car, but from a side view that time. In the background, he recognised the street behind him, the row of houses sweeping round the corner, one of them being Green's. But for all he knew, it could be a photograph of anyone's Audi.

He looked at Gerry. 'Are you certain this is John Green's?'

'Positive. Here.' He retrieved his mobile, tapped the screen, swiped across it, and back. He found what he was looking for, and enlarged the image with thumb and finger, then handed his mobile to Gilchrist.

And there he was. John Green at the front of his Audi, chamois in hand, caught in the act of polishing his car. Gilchrist adjusted the image, shrinking it in size until the car's number plate appeared. Another fiddle with the screen, and he had what he needed – Green facing the camera, car's number plate in full view.

He handed the mobile back to Gerry. 'I need you to send me every photo you have of John Green and his cars.' A pause, then, 'Just the two cars?' he asked, more in hope than anything else.

'Far as I know.' He fiddled with his mobile. 'I'll have these with you in a mo.'

'So what does John do with his cars?' Gilchrist said. 'Change them weekly? Take one out on rainy days only? Or what?'

'Hang on a mo.' He fiddled with his mobile, tapped a button, then said, 'There you go. That's you got them. All twelve.' He chuckled. 'Photos, I mean. Not cars.'

Gilchrist's mobile pinged as the photo files landed. He repeated the question.

'Couldn't really say,' Gerry replied.

'But he only ever parks one across the road, right?'

'That's right.'

'So where does he keep the other one?'

'Has a garage outside of town. Think that's where he keeps it.'

'Do you know where?'

'Now you're asking.' Gerry twisted his mouth for a moment, then said, 'Out towards Cairnsmill Caravan Park, I think.'

Gilchrist's mind pulled up an image of a row of storage units. He'd passed them every now and then, but hadn't paid attention to them. 'You think?' he said.

'Pretty sure. John told me once. A while back, like. Thought nothing of it.'

Gilchrist thanked Gerry, told him to give him a call if anything else came to mind, and had his mobile to his ear by the time he reached the footpath.

Mhairi picked up right away. 'Sir?'

'I'm sending you some images of a car,' he said. 'I need confirmation of ownership. And have Jackie do a search for it on the ANPR. We need to find out where it is.' He ended the call, caught up with Jessie, and told her.

'So you think he's done a runner?'

What could he tell her? That it was all beginning to fall into place? That for the first time he felt as if they had a positive lead? That John Green aka Timothy Johnson was living a double life – sous-chef in the Fairmont one minute, double killer the next? Or was he so far off base he was outside looking in?

Green owned two cars. That's all he knew for sure. And until they found that second car, everything was up in the air, maybe even floating in space. 'Yes, I think he's done a runner,' he said. 'But I think he's done a runner in a swapped car.'

'Right,' Jessie said. 'Let's find it.'

CHAPTER 39

They found Green's car at 4.30 that afternoon, not parked in a garage, but in a storage facility in the back of a housing estate off Cupar Road. Gilchrist had requested CCTV footage of the facility's forecourt for the last three days, and his Office team – led by Mhairi – were in the process of checking it out. Not that he didn't expect to see anyone but Green in the recordings, but for all any of them knew, he could have an accomplice with him.

The vehicle was protected by a dark grey canvas cover, manu-factured to fit to a tee, with inside-out pockets for the wing mirrors, the whole thing shaped to fit the exact make and model, another indication that Green took more care of his cars than his home or garden. The cover was peeled back to reveal an Audi S6, its black paintwork gleaming showroom new. But what surprised Gilchrist was the number plate, not the registration number on the phone images he'd received from Gerry, but the number they had on file for his grey Audi.

'Looks like he's not done a runner in a swapped car after all,' Jessie said.

'No,' he said, troubled by his thoughts. It seemed that Green had simply swapped number plates and was driving his usual car. But why? To make locating him harder, came the simple answer. And as he stared at the black car in front of him, he wondered if he was looking at the car Green drove when he carried out his murders. Commit the crime, then garage the evidence? Or was it not as simple as that?

'Don't touch,' he snapped at a young officer who looked set to try a door handle.

'You all right, Andy?' Jessie said.

'Cordon off this unit,' he said, 'and get Colin and his team here tonight. I want this car forensically examined from top to bottom. And don't miss a thing.' His mobile rang at that moment, and he stepped away to answer the call.

'Ben Brown here.'

For a moment, the name didn't register. Then he had it. Chief Superintendent Brown from Grampian Police. 'Yes, Ben. How can I help?'

'I'm in St Andrews, and wondered if we could meet up.'

'Eh . . . sure . . . but it might have to wait a while.'

'I heard you'd got a hit on Hutton's DNA, and I'd like to be there when you arrest the bastard. If you don't object, that is.'

Gilchrist frowned. How had Brown known about Hutton's DNA results?

'Sam Kim used to work with us during summer holiday breaks,' Brown said, as if in answer to his unspoken question. 'Asked her to keep me posted. Sorry if I've stepped on anyone's toes. Didn't mean to. But this case has been eating at me for years.'

'I'll get back to you in five minutes,' Gilchrist said, and hung up. He then phoned Sam Kim. 'Just been on the phone with Chief

Superintendent Brown,' he said to her. 'And he tells me we have a match on Hutton's DNA.'

'That's right, yes.'

'You are aware that we have a chain of command, and that all reports and results on this case have to go through my Office in the first instance.'

'Yes, I am.'

'And?' he said, struggling to control his rising temper.

'And I've already sent them to you. Let me see.' A series of clicks at her end. 'Sent them over to you this afternoon by email at . . . here we are . . . three twenty-four and seventeen seconds.'

He held onto his mobile in confused silence. What had he been doing when she'd sent him that email? Driving to the lock-ups came the answer. But why hadn't he heard his mobile ping? A quick glance at the volume control told him he'd turned it down by accident. He then tapped his email icon, and said, 'Sorry. Got it now.'

'Before you go, Andy, I've ordered a mitochondrial DNA test on that sock we found.'

'That's a more sensitive test,' he said. 'Isn't it?'

'It is, yes. I ordered it because I heard you were having difficulty finding anything on your prime suspect, Timothy Johnson.'

'What do you mean?'

'A mitochondrial DNA test can identify familial connections, which might enable you to track down a family member, which might in turn help you locate Timothy Johnson, or at the very least, provide more information on him.' She paused for a moment, and when he didn't respond, said, 'It's a bit of a long-shot, I know.'

'No, that's great work, Sam. Well done.' He thought of telling her they might have a whole car-load of samples for DNA analysis, but that would come only after Colin and his team had completed their forensic examination of Green's car. 'Let me know what you find,' he said, then added, 'Any luck on Jennifer Nolan's case?'

'Still waiting for DNA results, but the wounds to her stomach and groin area and the missing lengths of small and large intestines, make it a no-brainer. Same MO. Same killer.'

'Get back to me as soon as you find anything,' he said, and ended the call. He made several more calls before he went looking for Jessie.

He found her outside Green's lock-up, pointing this way and that, fussing with the uniforms setting up the crime scene tape.

'Colin and his SOCOs should be here shortly,' he said.

'That's good to know.' She shook her head in despair. 'Trying to get this lot to do as they're told is like herding cats. What's wrong with everyone nowadays?'

'Well, I've got some good news for you.' He raised his eyebrows. 'Just in. Hot off the press. And it's official. Hutton's DNA's a match.'

Jessie high-fived him with, 'You beauty. Right, that's it. We'll drive straight to his office and cuff that bastard. Hopefully in front of his employees.'

'Just one minor detail.'

She froze, her eyes fixed on his. 'Don't tell me he's gone and died on us.'

'No, but I've just phoned his office, and he's not there.'

'We'll have to arrest him at home then, hopefully in front of the wife and kids.'

225

'He's not there, either.'

'So where is he?'

'That's for you to find out.' He could tell from the way Jessie frowned that she was working out the odds of Hutton having done a runner or not. He didn't want to share his own concerns with her, that Hutton might already be halfway to Europe, so instead said, 'I spoke to his wife, who told me he'd just popped out to the petrol station, and would be back soon.'

'But you don't believe her, do you?'

'Can't say that I do.'

'That's it,' she said. 'He's getting ready to do a runner, if he's not already on his way. I wouldn't trust that bastard one inch.' She removed her mobile from her pocket. 'I'll have Jackie run his car's number through the ANPR. Did she say which car he's driving?'

'No.'

'I'll get her to run both numbers through ANPR then.'

It took Jessie less than two minutes to sort it out with Jackie, and no more than fifteen minutes for Jackie to get back to her with a positive sighting. 'His number was captured on the A90 heading north,' she said. 'Six miles out of Dundee.'

Gilchrist frowned. 'Where's he going?'

'I know exactly where's he going. Come on. You drive. And you can flex your foot on that accelerator pedal as much as you like.'

'Pedal to the metal, you mean?'

'That'll work,' she said, and headed towards his car.

For a moment, he thought of telling her to hold off, that they should go through the formal process of applying for, and securing, an arrest warrant. But the fact that Hutton had told his wife that he was popping out – her exact words – to fill his car with petrol, but was already on his way out of St Andrews, warned Gilchrist that the man had to be treated as a flight risk. And with more money than he knew what to do with, for all anyone knew, he could be on his way to one of any number of small airfields along the east coast.

Long story short, they couldn't fool around, and needed to arrest him.

Right away.

CHAPTER 40

Gilchrist stopped off at Greyfriars Inn where Chief Superintendent Bill Brown had checked in for the night. He'd already phoned ahead to update Brown, and to ask if he was still interested in witnessing Hutton's arrest, albeit someplace north of Dundee.

'I've waited twenty years for this moment,' he said. 'I would've chased that bugger to the other side of the world given half a chance back then. So, yes, count me in.'

Jessie tapped the address for Hutton's holiday home into the car's satnav system, and forty minutes later, Gilchrist pulled into the expansive driveway.

'I told you he'd be here,' she said, nodding to a sleek James Bond-like car that sat abandoned at the front entrance with the driver's door wide open.

'Don't like the looks of this,' Brown said, and stepped onto the brick driveway.

He was mounting the front steps, Gilchrist only a few feet behind him, when Jessie shouted, 'Round the back.'

Gilchrist and Brown followed her along the side of the house and into a back garden that was lit up like some druid's party.

Spotlights under the eaves – too many for comfort was Gilchrist's first thought – shone onto a concrete area overflowing with patio furniture – two tables, twelve chairs, a gleaming barbecue as big as a storage cabinet. Three gas heaters, as red as hot pokers, gave out heat that could be felt face-on. The side of the house seemed to consist of mostly glass, which had opened like a concertina to create an entrance wide enough to drive a herd of elephants through. From within, discordant music could be heard, a hard beating of piano keys that sounded as if they were being thumped in anger.

Hutton didn't notice them when they entered. He was sitting in the corner half-hidden by a grand piano, and continued to thud the keys like a manic concert pianist more interested in making noise than music. A bottle of vodka – Grey Goose with the top off – stood on the piano like some frosted phallus. Another bottle, either spilled or emptied by choice, lay on the floor by the piano legs.

Without a word, Gilchrist reached for a bank of light switches on the back wall, and pressed a couple. The patio lights went out, as did a row along the garden fence. The outside flickered into blackness, and burst alight again at his click of a switch.

The noise seemed to stumble as Hutton glanced up, eyes wild and confused, searching the space around him. Then the place fell into silence as he realised he was not alone.

On the drive through Dundee, at Brown's insistence Gilchrist had relented, and agreed that Brown could make the formal arrest. After all, this was his murder investigation. Brown stepped forward, cuffs at the ready. 'Leandro Hutton,' his voice boomed. 'I am arresting you on suspicion of the murder of Wendy Hyatt. You do not have to say—'

Which was when Hutton reached to his side, then swayed to his feet, arms swinging upwards and forwards, shotgun in hand, as he struggled to level his aim.

Gilchrist shouted, '*Down,*' and slapped his palm at the light switches.

The room snapped into darkness.

Brown roared, '*Don't,*' as Jessie screamed.

An explosion of light like a stroboscopic flash exposed the room for a blinding static moment, enough for Gilchrist to catch the stumbling bodies of Jessie and Brown, and enough for him to fix his bearings. He rushed forward to that last point of light, and in the darkness thudded into Hutton hard, as another flash blinded him, and a deafening roar almost blew his eardrums out.

He lay there in the darkness on his back, momentarily stunned, instinctively patting his body, searching for the spot that felt warm and damp. Then found it. His left biceps. For a few confusing seconds, he couldn't work out why he could move his arm, why he felt no pain, then realised it must be Hutton's blood.

Movement by his side told him Hutton was still alive, as a sour stench filtered into his senses. The floorboards shivered from the weight of someone moving towards him, and he winced as the room exploded into brightness. Then Brown stood over him, looking down, face flushed, eyes dancing. 'Are you hurt?' he demanded.

Gilchrist was aware of Hutton by his side, mumbling words in slurring moans. He pulled himself upright. 'Jessie?' he said to Brown. 'Where's Jessie?'

'Don't worry. I'm fine,' she shouted.

He frowned at a stream of blood that smeared her left cheek and dripped from her chin. 'You're bleeding.'

'Stuck the head on a table lamp.'

Gilchrist took in the mess before him, plants scattered on the floor, tables upturned, a table lamp on its side, its cover crushed, presumably when Jessie and Brown had dived out of Hutton's line of sight. Another glance at Jessie, and he thought she seemed confused as she dabbed a handkerchief to the side of her head and hissed whispered curses.

Brown kicked the shotgun to the side, where it slid under the piano. Then he reached down for Hutton, rolled him onto his front, and read him his rights. Hutton grunted, spasmed, then spewed onto the wooden floor. Gilchrist glanced at his biceps, rubbed a hand over his arm, and realised he'd mistaken Hutton's vomit for blood.

'Ah, shit,' he said, and pushed himself to his feet.

Brown was doing his best to pull Hutton upright, but he was so beyond drunk it was as good as lifting a dead weight. Brown grunted, released his grip, and let Hutton's body thud back onto the floor. 'He needs a paramedic,' he said, and strode from the room to call it in.

Gilchrist eyed the shotgun under the piano, slipped on his latex gloves, and picked it up. Then he carried it to a table on the other side of the room, well out of Hutton's reach. You never could tell what the man was desperate enough to do. Then Jessie stood by his side, hankie to her head to stem the blood.

'You going to shoot him with that?' she said.

'Just making sure he doesn't have any other ideas.' He reached for her hand, eased it from the side of her head. 'You've got quite a gash there. You'll need a few stitches at least. And a check for concussion.'

'I'm fine,' she said. 'But the table lamp isn't.'

A glance at Hutton lying on the floor, hands cuffed behind his back, told him the man was going nowhere soon. He thought he understood what Hutton had been intending to do: down two bottles of Grey Goose, maybe more, then position the shotgun under his chin and pull the trigger. He'd known what was about to happen, that his DNA would connect him to Wendy Hyatt's murder, and when it did, and the inevitable happened, his life of wealth and luxury was over for good, something he could clearly not do without.

The mention of Wendy Hyatt's name during his recent interview, and the gloating way in which Jessie swabbed his mouth for DNA samples, had told Hutton the writing was on the wall, and that it was only a matter of time.

It never failed to amaze him the lengths some people would go to avoid being sent to prison. For those destitute souls with no hope of any decent future, prison could be a home from home, a safe refuge, somewhere they could live for free and receive three square meals a day. For others, people whose definition of success in life was to be wealthy enough to be able to surround themselves with all the accoutrements of luxury, all the toys they could buy in the world, prison was worse than death.

Back to Jessie, who was still fussing with her head.

'Kitchen,' he said, and led her by the arm.

He pulled out several pieces of kitchen roll, soaked them under the tap, then squeezed them dry. He dabbed at the wound on her head, trying to stem the flow, but she had an open gash well into her hairline above her left ear.

She squirmed under his touch. 'Anybody tell you your bedside manner sucks?'

'Not in so many words.' He dabbed some more. 'When the paramedics get here, we'll have them look at you first.'

'Yes, doctor.' She glanced to the side as Brown entered the kitchen.

'You should see the mess of the roof,' he said. 'Missed us both by a mile, thank God.' He nodded to Gilchrist's sleeve. 'I see he got you good and proper with his mouth.'

Gilchrist ripped off another piece of kitchen roll and dabbed at his sleeve, which was when he saw them, small white lumps in the vomit, crushed and partially digested.

'Shit,' he said. 'He's taken some pills as well.'

Ben Brown was first to move. 'I've not waited this long for that bastard to die on me now.'

When Gilchrist returned to the living room, Brown had Hutton over the back of a chair, almost upside down, fingers stuffed down the back of his throat. A spasm jerked Hutton's body, once, twice, to the sound of him emptying his stomach.

CHAPTER 41

3.43 a.m., Saturday

Gilchrist woke from a troubled sleep with a mumbled groan. Whatever nightmare he'd been having was doing what it could to recede out of reach before he could recover it, leaving wisps of itself behind – a naked body in a river, entrails swirling in the flowing water like pink ribbons, her white face unrecognisable, a dizzying sense of falling as he struggled to resist being drawn towards her, a woman he knew, but couldn't put a name to . . .

He took a deep breath to free his mind of the image, and slid from bed, taking care not to waken Irene. He pulled himself upright and took a few seconds to let his heart settle. Then he reached for his phone in the mid-morning darkness, and walked towards the bathroom.

A glance in the mirror told him he was becoming far too old for all those late nights and long days, although yesterday had been productive in the end, a real shot in the arm of his investigation, and a solid lead that *might* – emphasis on the might – lead to an arrest. John Green's car had been picked up on the ANPR meandering through the streets of Edinburgh and Glasgow, which confirmed he hadn't made his escape south, or further to Europe, but instead seemed to have holed up somewhere in Craigend, a seventies council development on the eastern outskirts of Glasgow. Within the housing estate, CCTV cameras were uncommon, but Gilchrist instructed Mhairi and Jackie to search the area for other databases to determine an address. He'd then phoned Dainty in Strathclyde Police late last night, to ask for local assistance.

'Needs to be for a good cause, Andy,' he'd said, 'because the bean counters down here go off their fucking heads when budgets get blown.'

'This man's our prime suspect in a double murder up here.'

'How prime a suspect?'

'Hundred per cent, I'd say.'

'You sure?'

'Positive.'

'Right. Leave it with me. I'll get back to you later in the morning.'

Even though he had Mhairi and Jackie working on it, Gilchrist needed all the help he could get. And what better way than to have local presence? 'Any chance of having someone work on it right now?' he said. 'Maybe locate his car, and put an address to it?'

'Fuck sake, Andy, you trying to get me into trouble?'

'When did that ever bother you?'

A pause, then, 'How soon can you get here in the morning?'

'Any time. You name it.'

'Okay, send me what you've got, and I'll get somebody started on it. Let's meet up at eight. My office. That good enough for you?'

When Gilchrist hung up, he phoned Jessie and arranged to collect her from home at six that morning, in plenty of time to drive to Glasgow to meet Dainty. Now, in the bathroom, he checked his phone and read several messages, none of which offered anything, until he opened a text from Sam Kim – Emailed DNA report. It's a match. For one confusing moment, he hissed a curse – he needed more information than that – before realising it would be in the email she'd sent. It took him no more than a couple of minutes to open that email using his mobile, and read the report, which he then forwarded to Dainty, copied to Jessie, with the message – 110 per cent now. Green's DNA is a match. Game on.

He thought of returning to bed to try to squeeze in an hour or so of sleep, but his mind was too wide awake, thoughts of finding and arresting Green in Glasgow rattling around like a loose pinball. Instead, he decided to stay up, and went downstairs to make himself a cup of tea, then set the ball rolling for an arrest warrant.

He'd just filled up the kettle, when his mobile rang – ID Jessie.

'You're up early,' he said.

'Couldn't sleep. Had to take some pills for a headache.'

Her wound had required three stitches, well, some glue and a few staples after A & E shaved her hair around the gash. But for some reason he couldn't understand, she'd refused to have a scan. 'I'm telling you, Jessie, you need to have that head of yours checked out.'

'I'm fine, Andy. It's just a sore head—'

'Which could be caused by a bleed in the brain.'

'I'm fine, Andy. Okay?'

He couldn't fail to catch the nip in her tone, and thought it best not to push. 'So you got my text,' he said.

'I knew we'd nail that bastard. And talking about bastards, I don't suppose you've heard that Hutton's in Intensive Care.'

'I thought the paramedics had it all under control.'

'That's what they thought, too, until he took a heart attack. According to Mhairi, who has family contacts in Ninewells, his father died from a heart attack, and his father before him, so a weak heart runs in the family. Couldn't have happened to a nicer arsehole.'

'Does Ben Brown know yet?'

'Don't have the heart to tell him, excuse the pun.'

And neither had Gilchrist, when he thought about it. Brown had spent the best part of his career chasing down Wendy Hyatt's killer, and now, with her killer in his grip, he would not want to miss his day in court. Still, the man needed to be told. 'We'll get an update on Hutton's condition later this morning, and I'll keep Brown posted.'

'Thanks, Andy. So why are you up so early?'

He didn't want to tell her about his nightmares, which seemed to be more prevalent the older he became. It seemed as if his mind could no longer handle the gruesome nature of his profession, that it had filed away enough horrific images to fill his brain, and one more horrific image would simply overload it, or be regurgitated in the form of a nightmare.

Instead, he said, 'Couldn't sleep.'

'Hungover?'

'Not yet.'

Jessie chortled at his comment. 'Yeah, once we've got Green cuffed and jailed in the morning, we'll all be nursing hangovers tomorrow.'

'We have to find him first.'

'Craigend, you said. I know it well. Out past Hogganfield Loch. Not too many places to hide, if memory serves me. So it shouldn't be too difficult, especially now you've got Dainty involved. He'll be champing at the bit.'

Gilchrist didn't want to dampen Jessie's enthusiasm with the reality of the situation. They'd both seen Green and knew how fit he was, how strong, too. Well over six foot, with shoulders out to here and biceps that spoke of long hours in the gym. And handy with a knife, too, another worry that niggled at the back of his mind. He couldn't see Green giving himself up easily. Too cocky for that. They would all need to be prepared. Himself included. And they would need to locate him first, before any arrest could be made. Which was why he'd instructed Mhairi and Jackie to monitor the situation. Even so, for all any of them knew, Green could have abandoned his car in Craigend and simply walked off.

'You might want to try and grab an hour's kip,' he said, 'and I'll pick you up at six.'

'I'm too fired up now. We can leave earlier if you want, grab a coffee on route. A muffin, too, if you're up for it.'

'Six is soon enough,' he said.

'Spoilsport.' And with that, she hung up.

Gilchrist laid his mobile on the kitchen counter top, and turned his attention back to making a pot of tea. Despite the likelihood of an imminent arrest and the resolution of his investigation, try as he might, he couldn't shift a dark sense of failure that seemed to hang around him like a shadow, as if it were an omen of things to come. Or maybe it was just the lingering afterthoughts of his nightmare.

The kettle switched off with a hard click that seemed to echo around the walls in the silence of the night. Hair on the nape of his neck rose, and an involuntary shiver left him with the oddest sense of being watched. His gaze shifted around the kitchen and beyond, his eyes searching for, and settling on, deeper shadows in the blue-hour gloom of the adjacent room.

A floorboard creaked, and he froze, breath locked, senses on high alert.

But it was only the old house preparing itself for a new dawn.

He released his breath, and forced his thoughts to focus on the day ahead.

CHAPTER 42

7.50 a.m., Saturday
Strathclyde Police HQ, Glasgow

'We've located his car,' Dainty said, and rattled off an address.

Jessie, who'd started her career with Strathclyde Police before being transferred to Fife Constabulary, had been born and raised in Glasgow, and had a sound knowledge of the streets of the inner city and its surrounding housing schemes.

'That's close to the Queenslie Industrial Estate,' she said.

'And Garthamlock,' Dainty quipped. 'An old haunt of yours.'

Jessie grimaced at the reference. Garthamlock was close to Easterhouse where she'd been raised, and where her bitch-for-a-mother once lived with Jessie's brothers, Tommy and Terry – all of them dead now, thank God – a part of her life she'd rather not remember.

'Got one of ours watching the place,' Dainty pressed on. 'No movement reported, so the bastard's probably sleeping off a hangover. Not the uniform. The target.' He coughed a laugh. 'But some of those dozy bastards of ours could sleep for Scotland.'

Gilchrist said nothing as he listened to Dainty rattle off his plans for an arrest, while Jessie seemed strangely subdued, he thought. A search and arrest warrant had already been applied for and signed off early that morning, and by 8.30, with every last-minute detail finalised, they were ready to set off to make the arrest.

'You drive,' Dainty said to Gilchrist. 'That way I'm hands-free to liaise with the team leader, Alpha Charlie One.'

Without a word, Jessie clambered into the back, while Dainty took the passenger seat next to Gilchrist, and strapped himself in. No one said a word as Gilchrist followed the police cars and vans ahead, a trail of black cars as ominous as a funeral cortege. Dainty's hand-held radio whispered and hissed with the background crackle of static.

Once on the M8, they travelled at a fair pace, never less than ten miles an hour over the speed limit, but no blue lights, which somehow conveyed the seriousness of what they were about to do. Within a few minutes, the cavalcade took the sliproad onto Avenue End Road, quickly followed by a right-hand onto Glenraith Road.

'We're nearly there,' Dainty said, then pressed his radio to his ear. 'This is Alpha Charlie Two. Give us an update, Alpha Charlie One?'

It took all of eight seconds for the team leader to respond, by which time Dainty was on the verge of speaking again. 'This is Alpha Charlie One. Uh . . . suspect appears to have left the area.'

'What the fuck do you mean – appears to have left the area?'

'The car's no longer there.'

'Where the fuck is it, then?'

'We're looking into that. Alpha Charlie One, out.'

All of a sudden, the cars in front of Gilchrist accelerated, blue lights flashing, sirens blaring. Gilchrist said, 'When did they last have a visual?'

'This is Alpha Charlie Two. Alpha Charlie One, when did you last have a visual on the suspect?'

'About a minute ago.'

Gilchrist thought that was an exaggeration, but said, 'Split the team up. He must still be in the estate,' then slammed on his brakes. As his car slithered almost to a halt, he pulled the wheel hard right and did a hard U-turn, tyres spinning as he powered back the way they'd come.

'How well do you know this area, Jessie?'

'It's been a while. Why?'

'Where would you go if you were trying to flee the police?'

'The back streets of Garthamlock,' she said. 'Then through Easterhouse and onto the Edinburgh Road.'

'Not the motorway?'

'No, you'd have to cross the motorway to get to the Edinburgh Road.'

'Where would you cross?'

'Jeez, Andy, I don't know. Just turn left up here, and follow the road.'

Dainty's radio had taken on a life of its own. Commands and responses bombarded the cabin as Gilchrist veered left and raced along a two-lane road, per Jessie's directions.

'Anyone got a sighting of the bastard yet?' Dainty shouted into the radio.

'Negative,' followed by a series of indecipherable comments.

At that moment the car phone rang – ID Mhairi. Gilchrist took it on speaker.

'Green's car's on the move, sir.'

'Has Jackie got it on screen?'

'We're following it on ANPR, sir. It's just turned onto Cumbernauld Road, heading east.'

Gilchrist glanced at Dainty. 'Where's that?'

'Behind us.'

'Shit.' Gilchrist slammed on the brakes again, and skidded into another U-turn. 'Stay on the phone, Mhairi. Get Jackie to follow that car. Give me a running commentary.'

'Yes, sir.'

Dainty roared into his radio, giving directions, swearing out instructions.

Gilchrist wasn't familiar with the road layout, but Cumbernauld hit a memory chord. 'Get onto the Cumbernauld Office, Jessie, and alert them to what's going on. If he's headed that way, they might be able to set up a roadblock.'

Mhairi interrupted with, 'Still on Cumbernauld Road heading east, sir.'

Another glance at Dainty. 'Where's he going? Any idea?'

'Christ, now you're asking. Once he connects with the M80, he could pick up the M73 south onto the M74 and head for England. Or he could pick up the M8 to Edinburgh. We'll know which way he's going soon enough.'

'How about air assistance?'

'Would take too long. Best bet is for our boys to catch up with him.' He spoke into his radio again, then back to Gilchrist. 'Don't have him in sight yet, but it won't be long.'

Gilchrist didn't feel as confident as Dainty, but kept his thoughts to himself.

'Turn right here,' Dainty said.

Gilchrist braked sharply, then accelerated onto Cumbernauld Road. Motorway construction had all but diverted traffic away from what had once been one of the busiest commuter roads in and out of Glasgow. Now, bicycle lanes and parking bumps and painted lines here, there, seemingly everywhere, had reduced it to not much more than a two-lane road devoid of heavy traffic. Speed signs prominently placed ensured what little traffic did use the road now, did so at a sedate speed.

'Still heading east, sir. Been picked up on a speed camera through Muirhead.'

Dainty grumbled, 'Could be heading to Edinburgh. But still too soon to say.'

Gilchrist shouted over his shoulder, 'Any luck, Jessie?'

She shook her head. 'Still trying to sort it out.'

Dainty had the radio to his ear again, nodding. Then he slapped the radio on his thigh, and turned to Gilchrist. 'Got the bastard in their sights. He's just made it onto the M80. They'll follow him for a bit, then pull him over in the next minute or so.'

'He could be armed,' Gilchrist warned.

'Don't worry. These guys know what they're doing.'

Gilchrist nodded. But again, he didn't share Dainty's confidence. That sixth sense of his was niggling, warning him that something wasn't right. Despite Green having fooled the surveillance team outside his Craigend bolthole, only to lead them on a wild goose chase on the outskirts of Glasgow, in the end his capture seemed far too easy. If he was trying to make an escape, why be caught on a speed camera outside, where was it . . . Muirhead? And why do all of this in broad daylight? Why not wait until the dark of night? And why spend the night in Craigend? He'd left Fife, so why not continue on his way to wherever he was going? But on the flip side of that coin, maybe he didn't know the police were on to him. If not, though, why run in the first place? Or was he not running at all, but heading out of town to take care of one more victim? He had to have had suspicions, surely, because he must have known his DNA would link him to both murders. Or maybe he believed he was smarter than the police, but hadn't realised he'd dropped a sock on that first murder. Too many questions, and not enough answers. But all his thoughts and worries were about to be resolved.

Five minutes later, they arrived at the scene.

Two police vans had been set up, straddling the inside lanes of the M80, with a string of cones already being laid out around a lone Audi that sat parked on the hard shoulder, doors wide open, and a prone figure on the grass verge, hands cuffed behind his back, two uniforms with radios to their ears, standing by him. Traffic had backed up on the motorway, not only from two lanes shut down, but from rubber-neckers slowing down as they passed, intrigued by the intense police activity.

Gilchrist pulled up in front of the first van. Dainty jumped out, flashed his warrant card and stomped towards the cuffed figure with long strides more suited to a tall man. Gilchrist almost struggled to keep up with him.

'Right,' Dainty said to the uniforms, 'what the fuck've we got?'

'John Green, sir.'

'His ID check out?'

'Driving licence, sir, yes.'

'Anything else on him?'

'A number of credit cards, sir, all in his name.'

'Good. Let's have a fucking look at him.'

And Gilchrist knew, even before they turned Green over onto his back and he looked up at them with a smug smile, he just knew they'd stopped the wrong man.

'Fucking hell,' Dainty said.

But Gilchrist had turned away, mobile to his ear. Mhairi picked up on the first ring. 'Do you and Jackie still have eyes on that house in Craigend?' he said.

'Not on it, sir, but close by. Maybe sixty or seventy metres, sir.'

Which was close enough to pick up anybody leaving. 'Green's not in the car,' he said. 'He's sent a decoy. Check CCTV footage again, and follow anyone who left that address in the last fifteen minutes or so, just before you picked up his car on Cumbernauld Road.'

'On it, sir.'

CHAPTER 43

For a small man, Dainty had a six-foot-six temper. If he had a bucket of nails close by, he would have chewed the lot and spat them out in the shape of a hammer. Which was what he needed right now, he thought, a fucking hammer to batter some sense into that lot of his, the useless fucking wankers.

'And as for you, sonny Jim,' he snarled, as a uniformed officer helped the John Green decoy to his feet. 'You're in so much deep fucking shit, you'll be choking on the stuff for the next twenty fucking years.'

'I didn't know—'

'Don't make it worse,' Dainty roared. 'Don't try and tell me you never fucking knew a thing.' He narrowed the gap between them, and tilted his head to look up at him. Nowhere near eye to eye, but somehow Dainty made it work just as well. 'How much?' he growled. 'Eh? How much did he give you?'

'What?'

'How much did he fucking pay you to drive his car? And be careful how you answer this, sonny Jim, because the next words out of that lying fucking mouth of yours could be the difference between being charged for wasting police time or spending the next twenty years inside for being an accomplice in a double murder.'

That did the trick.

The man's eyes widened, and his mouth formed a silent 'What?'

'That's right,' Dainty said. 'You've just helped the prime suspect in a double-murder investigation avoid being arrested.'

'But . . .'

'So how much did he pay you?'

'I . . . I didn't—'

'That's it,' Dainty snapped. 'Book him,' then turned away in search of Gilchrist. 'What've you got?' he said, when he found him by his car, mobile to his ear.

Gilchrist cupped his mobile. 'We might have eyes on Green leaving the house in Craigend.'

'On foot?'

Gilchrist nodded, turned his attention back to his mobile. 'Then where does he go?'

'Not sure of the street names, sir. I can get these, of course,' Mhairi said. 'But he's just walking.'

Gilchrist signalled Dainty to join him in his car, but Dainty declined.

'Need to stay here to sort out this lot. But what d'you need?'

Gilchrist held up his hand, while Mhairi gave him a couple of street names. He assigned them to memory, then faced Dainty. 'Team of four to make an arrest.'

Dainty's eyes widened. 'You got him?'

'Not yet. He's on foot. Don't know where he's going, but I'll need a couple of your guys who know the area well.'

Dainty nodded, then put two fingers to his mouth and let out a shrill whistle.

One of the detectives looked Dainty's way.

'Matt,' Dainty shouted. 'I need you and Finlay. Plus two. Right away.'

Without a word, Matt strode towards another detective, said something, then jogged towards Dainty. 'Sir?'

'DCI Gilchrist. DS Matt Brennan.' As good an introduction as any. 'DCI Gilchrist has eyes on our suspect back in Craigend. I need you to lead the arrest team, Matt. DCI Gilchrist will give directions. Our suspect's on foot.'

'For the time being,' Gilchrist added, just to keep the pressure on. They couldn't hang about. Who knew where Green was heading? He turned to Jessie, who seemed to have been on the periphery of events – not like her, he thought. 'I want you to set up comms with Matt here. I'll get directions from Mhairi, and you pass them to Matt. At the moment he's on foot.' He repeated the street names, then looked at Matt. 'That work for you?'

'Yes, sir.'

'Right. Let's go.'

'I'll let you know how I get on with this waste of space,' Dainty said, and grimaced at the John Green decoy, who was being escorted to a waiting car, but putting up a struggle, as if that would convince them of his innocence. 'And good luck.'

Gilchrist nodded, then slid behind the wheel. With Jessie beside him, strapped into the passenger seat, he eased forward and worked his way past the scene of the arrest. 'What's the best way to Craigend?' he said.

She pressed a switch on her hand-held radio. 'Matt, you there?'

'Not far behind you.'

'Don't wait for us. Show us the way.'

A few seconds later, an unmarked police car, lights flashing, siren wailing, powered past them. Jessie smirked, as if pleased with herself. 'Better than any old satnav,' she said.

Gilchrist put his foot to the floor and followed the police team. He turned up the volume on his car's speaker system. 'You still have him on CCTV, Mhairi?'

'Yes, sir. He's still on foot, but he's cutting through open space and making it more difficult to follow. We're about two minutes behind him, as best I can work out. I've put a call into Glenrothes HQ for assistance. I hope that's all right, sir.'

'It is,' he said, pleased that she had the sense and the where-withal to work off her own initiative. Glenrothes HQ was where the police CCTV hub was located, with a full-time staff who spent every day and night reviewing banks of monitors that could connect to any CCTV camera in the Kingdom of Fife. It was a fairly simple job to have the connection extended on a temporary basis to other counties. In the meantime, he had Jackie and Mhairi doing what they could to keep Green's whereabouts current. 'We're heading for Craigend right now,' he said. 'ETA five minutes, give or take.'

'One second, sir. Jackie's pulling him up crossing a main road, Mossvale Road, sir, and he's now walking in front of a row of shops. Got better CCTV coverage here, sir.'

Jessie relayed the latest location to the arrest team in the car ahead, which seemed to increase its speed, as if DS Brennan couldn't wait to make the arrest. Despite a light drizzle that had begun to fall, Gilchrist followed in close pursuit, both cars speeding past traffic that pulled to the side of the road at the sight of blue and white flashing lights. Hard braking and a sharp left turn had tyres skidding on the damp road surface, and Jessie slapping her hands on the dashboard. Another burst of speed, and cars on the inside lanes zipped past them as if driving backwards.

'Where does he think he is?' Jessie said. 'Silverstone?'

But Gilchrist was too busy concentrating on the road ahead to respond. The rain had worsened, one of those localised showers that seemed common only to Scotland – you could be running for cover while your neighbour was enjoying a sunny fag in the back garden.

Mhairi said, 'We've lost him, sir. Looks like he's gone into one of the shops.'

'Which one?' he said, and had to brake hard as a car ahead threatened to pull out in front of Brennan, its driver oblivious to the lights and sirens. Brennan swerved past the offending vehicle, Gilchrist hard on his tail, then they were off again.

'Don't know yet, sir.' She spoke off-speaker, her voice low and mumbling in the background, then came back with, 'Looks like he's stepped into the bookies, sir.'

'Keep an eye on him, Mhairi. If he reappears, let us know.'

DS Brennan's voice crackled over the radio. 'I know exactly where he is. We should be there in less than a minute. I've already called for backup from the Shettleston Office, but we should have him done and dusted by the time they arrive.'

Again, Gilchrist found it difficult to share his enthusiasm. From experience, nothing was ever certain when you were dealing with criminals, and was never more true than with criminals who had killed and believed they had nothing to lose. John Green was of that ilk, a killer on the run, who knew his luck had run out, and that it was only a matter of time before he was caught.

Then what?

Hands behind his back, cuffed like some docile animal to be led to the cells to suffer the harsh injustices of the Scottish legal system, which would no doubt put him behind bars in some high-security prison for twenty-plus years with little or no chance of parole? Or, with nothing to lose – at least to Green's way of thinking – make one final stand for freedom and go down fighting, come hell or high water?

Gilchrist was no betting man, but even with John Green trapped in a bookies he felt the odds were still against him. But if you asked yourself – why go into a bookies now, when you must surely know your decoy had been uncovered, and the police were hot on your trail once more? – the only logical answer had to be: it was a means of escape.

But how?

He took hold of Jessie's radio. 'How well do you know that bookies, Matt?'

'Never been in it, but I'm familiar with the area, particularly the chippy.'

'I'm assuming there's a back door to the bookies.'

'Every shop has a back door. Parking and deliveries to the rear.'

Mhairi interrupted with, 'He's just come out the front, sir, and he's running across an open space.'

Brennan overheard Mhairi on speaker, and said, 'ETA fifteen seconds. We've got the bastard this time.'

Up ahead, Gilchrist saw the outline of a row of shops to the right. Pedestrians turned and stared as both cars powered along the road. Brennan had to veer wide of some idiot who pretended he was about to cross the road in front of him. All of a sudden, brake lights flashed as Brennan's car skidded to a halt. To Gilchrist's surprise, the car sped up again, took a sharp right, and mounted the pavement with a heavy thump that rocked the car sideways and had the back-end swinging wide for an awkward moment.

Jessie gasped in shock, then said, 'Has he crashed?'

'He's going to run him down across the open space.'

And sure enough, as Gilchrist's car slithered to a halt at the side of the kerb, he stared in disbelief as Brennan's car beelined for a distant running figure, spinning tyres spitting up clods of dirt and grass and splashes of water as it swept across the field in front of him, then skidded sideways as it tried to pull up on the damp grass. Doors were flung open before the car had fully stopped, and three officers spilled out, one landing on all fours, the other two on their feet, chasing the fleeing figure.

Then one of them shouted and fired a taser. Green fell to the ground as if he'd been shot, his body spasming as the officers caught up with him, turned him over, and cuffed him with much more force than Gilchrist thought necessary. But on the other hand, they were arresting a double-murder suspect who could be armed to the hilt. So you couldn't be blamed for trying to play it safe.

By the time Gilchrist stepped from his car, the officers had Green upright and were marching him across the open space. Green's clothes were dirtied with mud, and every now and then he would make a weak attempt to break free, which had the officers tightening their grip and struggling to keep their balance on the wintry grass.

Spectators had appeared as if from nowhere, and stood in groups of twos and fours as they watched Green's arrest being played out. Then chanting began, low at first, but gaining in strength, swear words that mocked the police, and pulled a half-smile to Green's face. As the group neared, it struck Gilchrist that Green seemed much smaller than he remembered, and skinnier, too. Which was when he pulled out his mobile, pressed it hard against his ear and strode with grim resignation to the back of the shops, knowing with absolute certainty what he was going to find. And sure enough, there it was, a dry spot on the tarmac in the rectangular shape of a vehicle that had only recently been moved.

'Ah, *fuck* it,' he said.

CHAPTER 44

Gilchrist struggled to keep his voice level. 'He's done it again, Mhairi. Taken another car from the back of the shops. Get Jackie onto it right away. We've no time to waste.' Then he slipped his mobile into his pocket and ran along the back of the shops, and knew as soon as he arrived at it which shop Green had escaped from, for the rear door lay half ajar.

He walked up to it, pulled it open, and stepped inside.

He was in an office of sorts, with two desks and chairs that had seen better times. The air was redolent of cigarette smoke and alcohol and the stale fug of something gone off. The walls were papered with pages of racing sections from a variety of newspapers – not that he knew which ones were which – and three darts grouped together stuck out from a headline, as if thrown there for revenge at a lost bet. A door to his side – with a toilet sign pinned to it – creaked open, and a women with dyed blonde hair and botoxed lips stepped out, tugging down the hem of a black skirt that was six inches shorter than decent. She stopped when she caught sight of him, but recovered quickly.

'You're no allowed in here.'

255

Gilchrist flashed his warrant card. 'Yes, I am.'

At that, a man stepped from the same toilet, fiddling with his zip, and froze when he noticed Gilchrist. From the look on his face, he hadn't been relieving himself – well, not in a urinary sense, that is.

'Who came through here?' Gilchrist asked him.

'When?'

'A few minutes ago.'

'Never seen a thing. Was otherwise engaged.' A smirk at the woman told Gilchrist he was wasting his time talking to him.

Gilchrist faced the woman. 'Where do you keep your car keys?'

'Why?'

'Whoever came through here, stole a car.'

He followed her gaze to a row of hooks on the wall, as she reached up and grabbed a set. She tinkled her way through them, then said, 'Naw, he didnae take mine.'

'So whose keys did he take?' He faced the man. 'Yours?'

The man tapped his pockets. 'Naw. Mine are here.'

Gilchrist struggled to control his frustration, then realised he'd got it wrong. The car didn't belong to any of the bookies' employees, or shaggers-on, but likely belonged to the man Brennan's team had just arrested. He cursed under his breath, gave both the man and the woman his hardest glare, and strode to the back of the office where he wrenched a door open.

From behind him, the woman shouted, 'Hey, you cannae go in there.' But he bullied his way through the mid-morning bustle of the main shop floor and out through the entrance to the front of the shops. About thirty yards away, near Mossvale Road, whoever Brennan's team had just arrested was making it difficult for them, wrestling left and right to the cheers of a small crowd egging him on. Down onto the grass again, and one of the team put a knee on the man's back in an attempt to stop him thrashing about.

Gilchrist jogged across the grass, and when he reached the group, said, 'Has he been read his rights?'

'You bet.'

He kneeled down on the grass, ignoring the dampness soaking through his jeans. He flashed his warrant card out of habit, and introduced himself. 'You can do yourself a huge favour by answering a few questions,' he said.

'Piss off.'

He ignored the remark, and said, 'What car do you drive?'

'No comment.'

'I want make, model and registration number.'

'No comment.'

'Do you know how much trouble you're in?'

'No comment.'

'I suspect you don't realise that by not cooperating you're making yourself fully complicit in a double murder.'

'What?'

'That's right,' Gilchrist said, knowing he now had the man's attention. 'The guy you're pretending to be is wanted in connection with two murders. And every minute you delay telling me what car you gave him to drive is going to add a year onto your sentence. And believe me, pal, I'll make sure the judge knows that.'

'But I didnae—'

'Make model and registration number.'

'It's a van. I don't know the make and number. A big van. It's my brother's. He lent it to me.'

'Colour?'

'White. Youse cannae miss it. He's an electrician. Got his business name all along the side, so it has.'

'And your brother's business name is . . .?'

'Home Electrics, I think.'

'You think?'

'Naw, that's it. Home Electrics. But I'd nae idea whit big Tamson done. Honest. If I'd've known I widnae have . . .'

But Gilchrist was already walking away, mobile to his ear. 'Mhairi, get Jackie onto this right away.' He rattled off the business name, and a quick description of the van. 'Last seen at the shops on Mossvale Road, Craigend.' He thought for a moment, trying to recall what, if anything, he'd noticed in the background as they'd rushed to arrest Green, or the man impersonating him. But his mind pulled up a blank. As he ran to his car, signalling for Jessie to join him, he was sure of one thing – Green wouldn't have turned right when he drove the van from the car park at the back of the shops. Doing so would have put him in the sightline of the police chasing him. The only way out of that car park was Mossvale Road – and Green would have turned left. He knew he would have turned left.

Because that's what he would have done.

He'd just stabbed his key into the ignition and switched the engine on, when he said, 'Shit,' and switched the engine off again. 'Bloody hell,' he said.

'What is it, Andy?'

He opened the door, and stepped out. 'Stay here. Liaise with Mhairi. We're looking for a white van. Owner: Home Electrics. And coordinate with the others.' He looked up, and shouted to Brennan's team. The man, whoever he was, was now cuffed and seated in the back of Brennan's car, looking at the small crowd, no longer so sure of himself. Gilchrist reached the car and opened the door. One of the officers looked up in surprise, as if ready to defend himself against an unprovoked attack.

'You,' he said to the young man.

'Whit?'

'What's your name?'

'Teddy Feehan.'

'You mentioned Tamson?'

'Whit about him?'

'You said you didn't know what big Tamson had done.'

'Aye. I didnae. Honest. I wouldnae've got myself messed up with him if I'd've known. I'll tell you everything. I'm no wanting nothing to dae with that mad cunt any mare.'

'Well, start off by telling me who big Tamson is.'

'Big Tamson?'

'That's what you said.'

'Big John Tamson's one of my brother's mates, so he is. I don't really know him.'

'Tamson? You mean Thompson?'

'Aye.'

'How do you spell Thompson? With or without a P?'

'Donno? Without I think.'

'So, big John Thomson, one of your brother's mates, told you to do what, exactly?'

'Meet him in the bookies, and hand over the keys for the van.'

'Your brother have anything to do with this?'

A look that slid to the left and back again, told Gilchrist that the next words out of his mouth would be a lie. 'Naw,' he said.

'What's your brother's name?'

'Look, he's got nothing to dae wi this. Aw right?'

259

'I know he hasn't,' Gilchrist lied. 'Name?'

It took all of five seconds, and one of Gilchrist's hard looks before he said, 'Tony Feehan.'

Without a word, Gilchrist strode back to his car, mobile to his ear.

'Mhairi,' he said. 'Get Jackie to look into two more names for me. John Thomson, aka John Green. And Tony Feehan.'

'I'm on it, sir.'

Next Gilchrist called Dainty.

'You catch the bastard?' Dainty said without introduction.

Rather than go into the details – Dainty would hear it from his own side – Gilchrist said, 'Two more names. John Thomson and Tony Feehan. Know them?' he said, and slid in behind the steering wheel.

'Thomson could be any one of a dozen Thomsons. But Tony Feehan I know. A small-time player in some gang involved in minor thefts, assault and robbery, that sort of thing, but preparing to graduate to something bigger. Rumour has it he stabbed some punter's balls to bits with a screwdriver, just because he disagreed with him. So you wouldn't want to meet him in a dark alley. Why?'

Gilchrist did a U-turn, tyres spinning on the wet asphalt. 'Green slipped us again.'

'He *what*?' For a small man, Dainty had a big voice.

Gilchrist put his foot to the floor. 'John Green, aka John Thomson, escaped by driving off in Tony Feehan's van. I've got a team trying to locate it on ANPR, but we could do with support, maybe by air. Can you organise that?'

'Could take a while for air support, but the way this bugger keeps giving us the slip, we could still be chasing him at Christmas.'

A hard cough, followed by a spit that sounded like it could crack concrete. 'Right. Leave it with me.'

'You might want to ask your perp if he knows Feehan or big Tamson.'

'Do I get to pull the bastard's toenails out?'

'Go easy on him, Dainty.'

'Aye, that'll be fucking right.'

The line died.

Jessie said, 'Jeez, Dainty's hot to trot.'

'One thing I can say about Dainty . . . he hates to be made to look like a fool.'

'Like us, you mean?'

Gilchrist grimaced, and nodded in defeated agreement. 'Call Mhairi. See if Jackie's come up with anything yet,' he growled, then gritted his teeth, and drove on.

CHAPTER 45

At Cumbernauld Road, Gilchrist turned west, heading back to Glasgow. They hadn't heard from Jackie or Mhairi yet, but that sixth sense of his, that gut-niggling feeling, told him that Green wouldn't have turned east, because that would be heading in the same direction as his first decoy had led the police. So, until he heard to the contrary from Mhairi, the opposite direction seemed like a good choice.

With Hogganfield Loch on his left, and the road about to split, he had to make another choice – stay left on Cumbernauld Road, or branch right onto Royston Road. He let his sixth sense guide him left.

'Where does this lead to?' he asked Jessie.

'Alexandra Parade and into Dennistoun,' she said.

He'd heard the names before, but they meant nothing to him. 'Check with Mhairi again, will you? She has to have something for us.'

A few seconds later, Jessie had Mhairi on the car's speaker system. 'You got anything for us?' Jessie said.

'We can't find anything live on the van, so we think it's already parked somewhere. I've asked CCTV Control for assistance.'

'How about Home Electrics?' Jessie said. 'Any luck with that?'

'It's not registered with Companies House, so we're thinking it's a fake business. But Jackie's found an address for another company in Birkenshaw Street in Glasgow, which is worth checking out—'

'Why?' Gilchrist interrupted, his frustration mounting at their inability to locate Green or Thomson or Johnson or whoever the hell he was.

'Sorry, sir, it's the address for Home *Electronics*, which *is* registered with Companies House, and the sole director is Anthony Patrick Feehan.'

Now they were onto something. Had Teddy got the name of his brother's company wrong? Or had he been trying to mislead them, keep them guessing? 'Where's Birkenshaw Street?' he said.

'Dennistoun, sir.'

Jessie added, 'We're almost there,' and tapped the address into the satnav.

'Get back to me if you find anything else,' he said to Mhairi, and tightened his grip on the steering wheel. 'What do you think?' he said to Jessie.

'I think we could be on a winner.'

'Keep Dainty up to speed,' he said. 'And Brennan, too. We might need backup.'

While Jessie communicated with the others, Gilchrist focused on the road ahead, taking visual directions from the satnav. As he drove through a set of lights at an awkward junction, veering right onto what he assumed was Alexandra Parade, he worried that he had it all wrong, that he really was just setting everyone up for a pointless chase. He slowed down, kept to the inside lane as much as possible, and noted a street sign ahead – left to the

City Centre which according to his satnav took him past Birkenshaw Street. For a moment, he felt disoriented when he saw he was still on Cumbernauld Road, but it split left at the sign, with Alexandra Parade straight ahead, and he recovered from his momentary confusion.

'We're nearly there,' Jessie said. 'It should be up ahead on the left.'

Gilchrist slowed down almost to a halt as they approached Birkenshaw Street, which branched off Cumbernauld Road at a fine angle as shallow as a sliproad. A row of tenement buildings lined the left side, with derelict ground and the occasional fenced-off lot bounding the right. He eased down the gentle decline, eyes scanning properties on the right, searching for the address, but also for a white van with Home Electronics on the side panels.

On the left, the end of the tenement flats opened up to another fenced-off lot behind which a few well-travelled company vehicles sat in a worn grass area that doubled as a car park – but no sign of Home Electronics on the side panels, or on the adjacent rundown shed that Gilchrist presumed doubled as an office. Beyond that, Birkenshaw Street came to an end, the tarmac road tailing off to a grassy wasteland.

'What are we missing?' he said.

'Don't know, Andy. This is the street, so it should be here, but it isn't.'

'Is there another Birkenshaw Street?'

'Not in Dennistoun.'

'Check with Mhairi.'

'Just did.' She looked out the side window. 'I'm afraid this is it.'

He whispered a curse under his breath, and had just begun a three-point turn when he noticed tyre tracks, more like worn

ruts, that ran through the grass at the end of the street. 'See that?'
he said.

'Is that a dirt track?'

'Don't know, but let's find out.'

He completed his U-turn, and nuzzled his car half-on half-off
the pavement, then stepped into a cold Glasgow morning. The air
felt moist, nowhere near as icy as it did on the east coast. He
breathed it in and looked around him, as if surprised to find an
open area that close to the city centre.

Jessie was waiting for him at the end of the road. 'Okay,
Kemosabe. After you.'

Gilchrist eyed the ruts at his feet, if they could be called that:
little more than flattened grass that would, after considerable
use, form a perfectly rutted track – bare soil over which tyres ran,
tall grass in between to scrape the underside of the chassis. He
lifted his gaze, and let it follow the tracks, but only so far, as they
thinned out and rounded the end of a metal fence. His gaze
settled on what appeared to be an extension to the fence, as if it
had been added as an afterthought.

'Over there,' he said, and stepped off the road surface.

'Don't you think we should wait for backup?' Jessie said.

'We need to find out if he's here or not. Then we'll make a
decision on what to do.'

'We?' she said, and followed him along the lines of flattened
grass.

Twenty yards in, he stopped. 'It takes a turn there. You see it?
Round the fence?'

'I don't like this, Andy. It's too quiet.'

He cocked his head. 'No, I hear something. Someone speaking. Maybe on a mobile.'

'Anyone tell you you've got bat ears?'

'Shh . . .' He held his arm out, a sign for her to keep quiet and still, then eased closer to the corner of the fence. As he neared it, the back of a white van came into view, the sound of someone on the phone grew louder. He crouched down and jiggled forward on bent knees, all the while keeping his gaze on the van, while his periphery vision searched for the man on the phone.

He stopped again, arm out. 'This is it,' he said. 'Home Electronics.' The van was parked at an angle that let him confirm the name on the side panel, beneath which a mobile number had been added. 'Take a note of the phone number,' he whispered over his shoulder, 'and forward the registration number to Mhairi. I'm going to try to get closer.'

He edged forward on bent knees, and crept no more than a few feet when a muffled sound from behind stopped him. He turned in time to see Jessie stumble, then crumple to the ground like a puppet with its strings cut. Behind her stood the six-foot-three gym-fit figure of John Green, looking every bit as mean and muscled as the name big Tamson suggested. A baseball bat gripped in one hand slapped menacingly into the palm of the other, its smooth finish roughened with ugly-looking nails.

'You are one persistent fucker,' he said, lips curling in a psychopathic grimace.

'*Don't*,' Gilchrist shouted, as Green stepped forward and swung the bat at him.

CHAPTER 46

Gilchrist had time only to duck as the bat skimmed the top of his head and thudded into the fence with a force that should have torn it down. He was too stunned to know if it had split his head open or not. All he knew was that he was still conscious, and that Green was doing what he could to disentangle the bat from the fence, where it had jammed in the metal palings from the strength of the hit.

Then Green had the bat free and was coming at him, both hands high, eyes wild, lips tight and determined, as if preparing for the coup de grâce. All Gilchrist could do was fall on his back and roll to the side as the bat thudded into the grass beside his head with an impact that could have started an earthquake.

Another roll to the side, followed by another thunderous thud. One more roll, and he realised with horror that he'd jammed himself against the fence, with nowhere else to roll to.

'Got you now, you wee fucker.'

Gilchrist barely had time to twist the opposite way as the bat came down at him and landed with a hard smack against the concrete footing of one of the fence's stanchions. The wood splintered to the sound of Green cursing. Gilchrist pulled himself onto unsteady feet, and watched Green toss the bat aside, the madness in his eyes letting him know he was going to enjoy tearing him limb from bloodied limb.

The obvious move was to run off, try to stay ahead of Green somehow. But the sight of Jessie's stilled body lying by the fence, blood pooling on the grass, somehow warned him against that. He'd always thought it strange how the mind works in times of extreme stress, and he found his peripheral gaze searching for the other man, the man on the phone, and wondering if he was Tony Feehan, and who he'd been speaking to. But he could no longer hear him, and a high-pitched ringing in his ears told him that the skimmed blow to his head might be worse than he first thought.

He felt his body sway for an awkward moment, his vision darken, and he stumbled to the side. As his confused mind struggled to make sense of what was happening, it stuttered through the possibilities, the odds, the options, in a lightning strike of panicked thought. And in one of those instances of clarity that can occur in a fight-or-flight life-threatening event, he saw that his only hope of surviving Green's attack was not to run, but to somehow make his way closer to the fence. That way, he could support himself, stay upright, because he knew with absolute certainty that if he landed on his back again, it was lights out, and thank you very much for being a good detective.

All those thoughts had fired through his mind in the space of a millisecond, as some sketchy plan began to manifest itself from the burgeoning fug of his mind out of nowhere, it seemed. But all that aside, Green appeared to have closed the gap between them in no time at all, arms outstretched to strangle him, or worse, tear his head from his neck and punt it over the fence. In an attempt to escape the onslaught, Gilchrist staggered back, feet stumbling in the grass, heels catching, until his back thudded hard against the fence.

Shit. He'd miscalculated. Got it wrong.

This was it. He'd just trapped himself.

And Green had him cold.

Euphemistically it is known as a Glasgow kiss, but in real terms a head-butt to the face can cause catastrophic damage to the skull. Gilchrist could do little to protect himself as Green's hands gripped the lapels of his leather jacket. All he could think of was to try to time the lowering of his head to the split second as Green pulled back to launch a full-bloodied head-butt.

It worked, in a sense. Green's attempt to butt Gilchrist's face and flatten his nose, maybe even crack open an eye socket or two, failed, his forehead smacking onto the top of Gilchrist's down-turned head. To Gilchrist, it felt as if he'd been hit by a sledge-hammer, but the pain from the mistimed head-butt worked both ways, and Green grunted with surprise, stunned for a pained moment.

But only for a moment, for he snarled in anger as he drew his head back again, and Gilchrist knew he would get it right this time.

On instinct, he jerked both knees upright, not in an attempt to knee Green in the balls, but to cause his body to slump to the ground – having no legs will do that to you. He landed with a thud on his coccyx, back to the fence, face at Green's waist. It took Green all of half a second to adjust his position and swing a kick Gilchrist's way, and another half second for Gilchrist to catch Green's leg, hold it, and slap a pair of cuffs around his ankle.

Another click, and Green was cuffed to the fence.

Green roared in anger as he tried to free his leg, rattling the fence in maddened rage, hopping up and down like a maniac. He gripped the metal with both hands and roared like a caged lion as he tried to break it loose. But it was no use. He shook the fence and kicked it with his free leg, which caused him to fall to the ground. And as he fell, Gilchrist twisted his body away, and made sure he rolled out of reach. Just as well, for the look on Green's face as their eyes met, told him he would tear his body to pieces if only he could reach him.

Gilchrist staggered to his feet, but his legs weren't working the way they should. He fell sideways, grappling the air like a drunk off a stool. He landed with a grunt that took his breath away for a muddled second, then he pulled himself into a sitting position, ran a hand over his head. His fingers came away sticky with blood. He fingered the spot again, searching for the cut, and felt a loose flap of skin where the nail-jagged baseball bat had skimmed the top of his head. Another fraction of an inch, he thought, and it could have been his brains spilling out, not blood.

He pushed himself to his feet, and half-crouched half-staggered towards Jessie, who was lying on her stomach, head to the side, facing away from him. She seemed deathly still, no signs of movement, maybe not even of life. He reached her and sank to the ground beside her. He couldn't see the bleeding wound, which was on the other side of her head, then he placed a finger to her neck, checking for a pulse.

But he found nothing. He tried again, but still nothing.

'No,' he said. 'No, Jessie, no.'

He felt the burn of tears sting his eyes, and he leaned down and pressed his lips to the side of her face, his tears spilling onto her cheek. 'Oh, Jessie, please, no, Jessie.' He swept a finger over her cheek to dry it of his tears, pressed his lips to her neck, and whispered, 'Oh, Jessie, dear God, no.'

Which was when he thought he felt it.

He pulled back, stared at her neck, pressed his finger to her skin again, harder that time, searching for the vaguest signs of a pulse, praying he hadn't imagined it.

Had he? Had it been his own pulse he'd felt?

He moved his fingers over her neck, behind her ear – no pulse – and back again, hoping to find some other spot that might provide him with a pulse.

And, yes, there it was. The faintest of faint beats.

Jessie was alive. But barely.

She needed help. And quickly.

He pushed to his feet, mobile in his hand, worried for a moment that he was about to lose consciousness. But the moment passed, and he was about to call for an ambulance when he realised the fence was no longer rattling from Green's attempt to free himself. He looked over at him, saw he was still cuffed by his ankle to the fence, but no longer enraged, just staring at him with cold calculation as he spoke into his mobile phone with a grim smile.

CHAPTER 47

Over Green's shoulder, beyond the end of the fence, Gilchrist heard movement, and caught the back door of the van opening. Someone – presumably the other man, the man on the phone, and at a guess, Tony Feehan – was leaning into the back of the van as if searching for something inside.

Then the man pulled back, slammed the van door shut, and turned to Gilchrist.

Gilchrist's first thought was – where were all of Scotland's short arses these days? This guy had to be every bit as tall as Green, and just as muscled. His second thought was to remove Jessie's handcuffs from her. That trick worked once, and might work again. But his third thought was – no chance – as the man advanced towards him like a lion to its prey. But where lions only have claws and teeth, Feehan, if that's who he was, had a metal jemmy in one hand and a look in his eyes that told Gilchrist he knew how to use it, and into which part of his body he was going to implant it.

Gilchrist pushed to his feet, using the fence as support, and held out his warrant card. 'Police,' he shouted. 'You're under arrest.'

'You're gonnie have to dae better than that.'

Well, it had been a silly idea, he supposed. 'Don't make it worse for yourself,' he tried. 'You haven't broken any laws so far. We only want to question you.' Nowhere near the truth, but worth a try.

In response, Feehan gritted his teeth in a hardman's gesture, turned his head to the side, and spat a gob of phlegm that clung to the fence like a strip of glue. Then he looked at Gilchrist and smiled. 'I'm gonnie fuckin enjoy this.'

Feehan was no more than fifteen yards away, and closing the distance with every step. Gilchrist would have run for it if he could, but his head was splitting, his ears were ringing, and he had the strangest sensation of half-floating instead of standing. He worried that if he tried to move he would topple over and never get up. On the other hand, he couldn't just stand there and let Feehan bury the jemmy in his head.

He slipped his hand inside his jacket. 'I'm armed,' he shouted.

But still Feehan approached. 'Go for it, then.'

Shit. This really was it. A glance to the side caught Green watching on with gleeful delight, like a gambler who'd bet a fortune on a surefire winner and couldn't wait to get it over with and collect his winnings. Gilchrist narrowed his gaze, and eyed Feehan.

Nothing for it, but to take him on.

He took one step towards Feehan, and stopped. For a moment his world tilted, and he struggled to stay upright. Feehan was no more than six steps from him, eyebrows raised as if surprised by how easy it was going to be to hammer Gilchrist's brain out his ears. But all Gilchrist could do was sink to the ground on all fours, and look up at Feehan glaring down at him. He thought of trying to time his move again, roll to the side when the blow came. But his peripheral vision was failing, and darkness seemed to be creeping in from all sides.

But he couldn't just let it happen. He had to fight.

He struggled to his feet, spread his legs wide to keep his balance, while his world rocked as if on a boat. He couldn't work out the look of puzzlement on Feehan's face. Not that the man was gloating at him. Rather his gaze was somewhere over Gilchrist's shoulder, at something behind him.

Then Feehan dropped the jemmy and turned and ran back to the van.

On instinct, Gilchrist chased after him. Well, chase was the wrong word, more like stumbled and fell, picked himself up again, only to stumble forward. But this time he picked up Feehan's abandoned jemmy and somehow found enough balance for eight or nine steps before falling once more. He gasped from the effort, grunted from the pain, pulled himself to his feet, just in time to hear the high-pitched sound of a motorbike's engine power alive.

The door in the shed burst open and Feehan exploded out, narrowly missing the van as he skidded to the side. He wore no helmet, no gloves, no protective gear, just a fierce look of criminal defiance as he hunched over the handlebars, twisted the handle-grip and powered out of the compound. For a moment Gilchrist thought Feehan was going to run him over, but his escape route wasn't up Birkenshaw Street, instead it was down through the grass and out some exit only he knew about. Which was all good and well, and he might have got away with it if Gilchrist hadn't thrown the jemmy at his bike in the passing, and by pure luck hit the front wheel.

Caught in the spokes, the jemmy whipped up to the main fork, jammed the wheel, and the bike stopped dead. Feehan flew over the handlebars, arms flailing wildly as he performed a slow-motion somersault that ended with him landing on his back at an awkward angle. Gilchrist heard a bone snap and Feehan's pained squeal at the same time as his hearing cleared and the sound of sirens wailing and shouts of, '*Police, stop, you're under arrest,*' flooded his senses.

Someone rushed past him, then others followed, booted feet thudding the ground like a Serengeti stampede. Gilchrist turned to say something, but his world tilted again, one way, then the next, and the grass came up to hit him in the chest. He grunted in surprise, and tried to roll over onto his back, but for the life of him he had no strength.

'Sir? Sir?' Soft hands were by his face, then his side, turning him over.

He thought the policewoman looked attractive, smooth skin, ethnic tan, same dark eyes as his daughter, Maureen, and oh so young, too young to be in the Force, to his mind.

'Sir? You have a cut on your head.' Fingers dabbed the top of his head, and he winced from a sharp stab of pain. 'Are you hurt anywhere else?'

'Jessie . . .' he said, and tried to pull himself upright.

'Sir. Don't move. We'll have you in an ambulance shortly.'

'Jessie . . .' He gripped the young woman's arm, and managed to lift his back from the ground for a short moment, but long enough to see a team of three police officers working on Jessie. Four others were grouped around Green, who kicked and spat like a cornered cat.

Then Dainty stood above him.

'Fuck sake, Andy, you gave yourself a right doing!'

'Jessie . . .'

Dainty grimaced. 'Too early to say, but she's breathing, which is all I can tell you at the moment.' He glanced in Green's direction. 'As for that bastard, I'm going to have his fucking balls on a plate.'

But Gilchrist could only say, 'Jessie . . . is she . . .?' as he slipped into unconsciousness.

CHAPTER 48

Gilchrist opened his eyes, and took several bleary seconds to work out that he was in a moving vehicle, and a few more to realise he was in an ambulance.

'Where . . .?' he tried, but the effort of speaking was too much.

'You've an open cut on your head,' the paramedic said, 'which'll need stitched. But all your vital signs are good – blood pressure, heart rate. A few bruises on your back and arms. A lump on your forehead. Some cuts and grazes. Other than that, you appear to be in good health. But we'll need to check for concussion. Sit still.'

He flinched at a bright light that blinded his right eye, then his left.

'Where are we going?' he asked, as he followed the light of the pencil torch left, right, left, right.

'The Royal. Should be there in a few.'

'What about Jessie?'

'Who?'

'The other detective. She was beaten unconscious.'

'All I can tell you, mate, is that she's in good hands. How do you feel? Headaches, dizziness, nausea?'

'No,' he lied.

'Can you try sitting up?'

Strong hands gripped his arm, but as he eased himself up, the ambulance swayed to the side, as if entering a roundabout too fast, and he turned his head to the side and felt his insides spasm. He would have thrown up if he'd anything in his stomach, but he hadn't eaten that day.

'This should help,' the paramedic said, and took his time filling a syringe from a vial of clear liquid. 'Sleeve up.'

Gilchrist obliged, and winced when the needle pierced his biceps.

Neither of them spoke while the ambulance took a sharp left, slowed down, shuffled over a bump, then drew to a halt. When the door opened, Gilchrist was already on his feet and waiting.

'I'll take it from here,' he said.

But the paramedic took hold of his arm with a grip that said he wouldn't take 'No' for an answer. 'It's my responsibility to see you into triage.'

Gilchrist let himself be led through a reception area that seemed far too crowded for that hour, but Glasgow on a Saturday at any time of day was more or less guaranteed to fill any A & E room. The paramedic bypassed reception and led him into a small room that was closed off with a sliding curtain.

A smiling nurse glanced at him, and frowned. 'Head wound?'

'He's all yours,' the paramedic said, and proceeded to bring the nurse up to date with a list of tests he'd carried out on the drive in.

When the paramedic left, Gilchrist said, 'I need to go to the toilet.'

'I'll have someone help you.'

'I'll manage on my own.'

'Do you know where it is?'

He raised his hand in a dismissive wave and pushed through the curtain, only to find that he was nowhere near as steady on his feet as he thought he was. The corridors seemed too bright for his eyes, and he had to reach for the wall when he felt the floor move.

In the reception area, he showed his warrant card at the desk. 'A female detective was brought in here with a head injury. DS Jessica Janes,' he said. 'I was with her when the incident happened. Can you tell me where she is?'

The receptionist studied her monitor, clicked the mouse a couple of times, then said, 'She's being prepped for theatre. Suspected brain bleed.' She looked at him, and frowned. 'Are you all right?'

He shook his head. 'I . . . eh . . . I need to see her.'

'You can't. Not until after her operation.'

Gilchrist had been in enough hospitals in his career to know you don't argue with the medical profession. You let them get on with their job, and hope it works out well in the end. But he handed over his business card. 'When she's out of theatre, can someone call me on that number?'

The receptionist gave a non-committal shrug as she took his card. But he thanked her, and made his way back to the triage room.

'You were quick,' the nurse said. 'Find it all right, did you?'

He nodded, and took his seat while she asked him to roll up his sleeve as she reached for a blood pressure armband.

'Just had that done in the ambulance,' he said.

'That means they're doing their job. Relax your arm for me. There you go.'

As the armband tightened, he watched his blood pressure readings rise and fall, rise and fall, then settle at a steady number.

'One forty over eighty,' the nurse said, peeling the armband free. 'Perfect.'

'Told you.' He said nothing more while she went about her tasks – lights in his eyes, questions about headaches, dizziness, nausea, tiredness. Then she stood behind him, her fingers playing with his hair, pulling it one way then the other.

'Nasty cut you've given yourself,' she said. 'Looks superficial, but we'll have to have it X-rayed, and give you a CAT scan to make sure there's nothing more going on.'

'I don't have time for that,' he said. 'Just stitch it up, then I'll get going.'

'I can't recommend that.'

'I wouldn't expect you to. But I really need to get going.'

'You're suffering from concussion. You realise that, don't you?'

'It'll pass.'

She tutted and shook her head. 'Wait here,' she said, and pulled the curtain back.

Ten minutes later, she returned with a doctor in tow, a fresh-faced man who looked young enough to be her son. 'You'll need to sign this disclaimer form,' he said, 'once your wound's been stitched.'

Gilchrist nodded, then bent forward to give the nurse an unrestricted view of his head.

'This local anaesthetic will sting,' she said, 'but only for a moment.'

And she was right. He gritted his teeth as a needle stabbed the top of his skull in three separate spots. But after a few minutes he couldn't tell if she was shaving his hair around the wound, or stitching it.

'Head wounds often bleed heavily,' she said, and he felt his head move as she gave the needle a tug. 'You've got a tear in the skin. How did that happen?'

He really couldn't be bothered explaining it all, and didn't want to start any kind of conversation. But he said, 'Someone resisting arrest,' and hoped that would cover it.

'It's a dangerous line of work you're in.'

He felt a tug on his crown, and said, 'Are you stitching or darning?'

'Stitching.' Another tug.

'Go easy there. I've got a date tonight,' he said, then realised he should have phoned Irene, told her what had happened and that he was all right, rather than have her hear about his injury from someone else.

'I wouldn't recommend you go out on any date,' she said. 'You'll be on painkillers for a few days. So plenty of rest, no driving, and certainly no drinking.'

'But it's the weekend.'

Another tug with the needle warned him that she didn't find his joking funny, and a few minutes later, she was all done. 'That's you,' she said, and handed him the pen and form.

He scribbled his name without so much as a glance at what the disclaimer form said, then pushed to his feet. For a moment, his world shifted on its axis, and she frowned at him as she took hold of his arm.

'Not a good idea to do things quickly,' she said.

'Noted,' he said, gathering his jacket from the back of a chair.

He took his time walking along the corridor, mobile in hand, finding that his sense of direction wasn't as good as he thought it was. He took a wrong turn, then with deliberation read the signs on the walls and corridor openings. He waited until he'd exited reception and was back in the damp cold of a Glasgow spring day before he phoned Dainty.

'You okay, Andy?'

'A few stitches. Other than that, I'm ready to go.' A pause, then, 'Have you heard anything about Jessie?'

A sharp intake of breath warned him to expect bad news. 'I hear she's in a bad way.'

Gilchrist felt his breath leave him. 'Define bad,' he said.

One beat, two beats, then Dainty said, 'She's in a coma, Andy. Don't know if it's induced or not, but she's likely going to be out of it for several days, maybe longer. Been advised that they won't be able to tell if there's any permanent brain damage until then. It's a fucking travesty, is what it is.'

Gilchrist felt his world shift, and for a fleeting moment thought he was going to throw up. He didn't like the sounds of *out of it*, but couldn't find the words to challenge Dainty. The thought that Jessie might have suffered permanent brain damage just didn't compute, and he took a deep breath to steady himself.

'I'm sorry, Andy, but we could use your help here. If you're up for it, that is.'

'Yeah. Sure. Yeah. Where are you?' He felt as if time had slowed down, his thoughts churning through treacle.

'Pitt Street. I've already sent one of our boys to pick you up.'

'Okay, good, I'll look out for him.' The words sounded heavy, and his tongue felt thick, as if it had forgotten how to enunciate clearly. 'Is there . . .?' he tried, but the question seemed to have floated out of reach.

'It's John Green,' Dainty said. 'We've got him in the interview

282

room. Seated next to his solicitor, some plonker who fancies himself as the next Johnnie fucking Cochran.' A heavy sigh, followed with, 'Problem is, Andy, the bastard's refusing to talk.'

'So what's new?' Gilchrist tried to joke.

'Oh he wants to talk, all right. Gives the impression he's got something to brag about. But he's not going to talk to anyone as lowly as me.'

Gilchrist frowned, struggling to comprehend. 'I don't follow.'

'The only person he says he's going to talk to, is you. Wouldn't explain why. Just said that's how it has to be. So that's us properly fucked.'

'Not necessarily.'

A pause, then, 'I'm not going to condone you having a one-on-one interview with this guy behind the scenes, Andy. If that gets out, it'll blow our chances of getting a conviction.'

'Maybe that's what he's after,' Gilchrist said. 'Looking to set up a loophole for his defence.'

'Well, if he does, like I said, that's us properly fucked, because there's no way you can interview the bastard, being a victim of his assault.'

'Yes there is.'

It took Dainty all of three seconds to say, 'Are you losing your mind?'

'Not last time I checked.' On instinct, he found his fingers searching for the stitches on his head, which felt jagged. Was he losing his mind? But if you asked the question – how often were sentences for assault served concurrently? – the answer provided the solution. If Green was found guilty of his and Jessie's assault, it was more than likely that his sentence for each would run concurrently, which had always been a bone of contention of

Gilchrist's. It seemed to him to diminish the result of a conviction. Well, now he had a chance to use that perceived failing in the legal system to his own benefit. 'I'm not going to press charges,' he said. 'So as the SIO, I'll take the lead in interviewing Green for his assault on Jessie. Attempted murder.'

Dainty let out a chuckle. 'Can't wait to see the bastard's face when you do.'

Just then, a police car pulled up to the kerb.

'Looks like my taxi's arrived,' Gilchrist said. 'I'm on my way.'

CHAPTER 49

By the time Gilchrist entered the interview room, Dainty had arranged for Green to be cuffed, leg restraints around his ankles, and two police officers – the biggest he could find – to stand guard behind him. He'd also confirmed that Tony Feehan was in the Royal's A & E being treated for a broken arm and shoulder and suspected broken ribs, and under guarded protection. All attempts to interview Feehan so far had him answering every question with 'No comment'. So if Green was willing to talk, but only to Gilchrist, then Dainty was happy to go along with that. Despite his earlier attempts to interview Green, Dainty decided to sit in on Gilchrist's interview, and chip in his penny's worth if given the opportunity.

As Gilchrist took his seat, he was conscious of Green studying him. But he never so much as glanced at the man, choosing instead to focus his attention on his notes before him. He switched on the recorder, introduced himself, and noted the date and time for the record. Dainty did likewise, then waited for Green's solicitor to introduce himself – James McTear of some legal firm that didn't bear his name, with an address in the south side of Glasgow

– then his client; simply John Green, and adding, 'Of no fixed address.'

Gilchrist ignored the question of Green's address – he could come back to that later if necessary – and looked hard at Green for the first time. Green returned the firm look with one of his own, more smirk than smile, which twisted his lips in a couldn't-care-less hardman attitude, and creased the edges of his eyes.

'Nice haircut,' Green said.

Gilchrist knew he looked a mess. His hair was shorn around the wound on his crown, and the stitches looked black and wicked. Although the A & E nurse had cleaned what blood she could from his hair, he'd had no time to change his shirt with its bloodstained collar. But if Green was trying to rile him, he was failing. Gilchrist had interviewed loads of criminals who'd acted tough as nails at the start of their interview, only to fall silent, or crumble in despair, as the reality of their situation sunk in.

Meanwhile, he could almost feel the anger shimmer off Dainty like heat off molten rock. He kept his face deadpan, placed both hands palm down on the table, and said in as level a tone as he could, 'John Green, you are being charged with the murders of Jennifer Nolan and Nicola Johnson, and also for the attempted murder of Detective Sergeant Jessica Janes. You do not have to say anything, but anything you do say will be noted and may be used in evidence. Do you understand?'

Green narrowed his eyes. 'Is that it?'

'Is that no fucking enough?' Dainty said.

Gilchrist raised his hand to keep Dainty out of it, and said, 'Is what it?'

'Just her? No you?'

'That's right. Just her, Detective Sergeant Janes is alive, but in a coma in the Royal Infirmary, being operated on even as we speak.' He struggled to keep his emotions in control. 'If she doesn't pull through, we can always amend the charge from attempted murder to one of murder. As for me . . .' He raised his hand to his head, tapped the stitches. 'Occupational hazard. That's all.' He flickered a smile. 'Happy?'

Green's lips tightened to a white line.

'So, moving forward,' Gilchrist said. 'For the avoidance of confusion, which name do you prefer to be known by? John Green? Timothy Johnson? Or John Thomson, also known as big Tamson?'

'You choose.'

'Okay. Why don't we go with John Green?' he said. 'For the time being.'

McTear frowned, as if puzzled by the reference to *for the time being*. He glanced at Green, who seemed more interested in his fingernails.

'Are you a gambler, Mr Green?' Gilchrist said.

Green looked up. 'What?'

'The question's simple enough. Do you gamble?'

'What the fuck's that got to do with anything?'

'Just wondering why you went into the bookies.'

'Who said I did?'

'CCTV. And a number of other witnesses.' Gilchrist didn't know if anyone had come forward as a witness or not, but it was good to watch mounting doubt clear the smirk from the man's face. He flashed a quick smile, then said, 'How well do you know Tony Feehan?'

'Who said I knew him?'

287

'So you don't know him? Just drive his van around, do you?'

Green shrugged, almost as good as 'No comment'.

'For the record,' Gilchrist said, 'Mr Green shrugged in response.' Then he leaned forward, and said, 'I understand you wouldn't talk to anyone, and that you asked for me specifically. Is that correct?'

'I might be changing my mind.'

'Want me to leave?'

'S'up to you.'

Gilchrist held his gaze, then said, 'No. I think I'll stay a while. So . . . what's with all the name changes?'

'I like being anonymous, you know? Being somewhere, and no one really knows who the fuck I am. I like that.'

'Why?'

'Just the way I like to live. That's why.'

'It's nothing to do with the fact that you murder someone under one name, then move somewhere else to murder someone else under a different name?'

'Who said I murdered anyone?' He flexed his muscles, rocked his head from side to side. 'That's fucking crap, so it is.'

'Is it?'

'Fucking bet it is.'

'I don't believe you.'

'You're going to have to prove it then, aren't you?'

'We'll come to that soon enough.' A glance at his notes, flicking over a page or two, then back to Green. 'Jennifer Nolan. How well did you know her?'

'Hardly at all.'

'Weren't you and her in a relationship for a while?'

'Who told you that?'

'Yes or no.'

'No.'

'How about Nici Johnson?'

'Yeah, I knew her. For a while.'

'For how long?'

'Difficult to say. Years ago. Didn't last long.'

'Fall out, did you?'

'Got fed up with her, more like. You know what I mean? Don't like poking the same hole too often. Gets boring after a while. Not that you would know much about that.'

Gilchrist ignored the taunt, and decided to try some shock tactics. 'Seeing as how you seem to think you're a man of the world when it comes to women, what do you do with the body parts?'

'What body parts?'

'Nipples,' he said, then added, 'And intestines.'

McTear leaned forward. 'Excuse me, are you suggesting that my client . . .?' He stopped then, as if lost for words.

From his folder, Gilchrist removed two photographs of Jennifer Nolan's and Nici Johnson's naked bodies, each with gaping stomach wounds, and breasts tipped with bloodied flesh rather than aureoles. He slid them to McTear who placed a hand over his mouth as his eyes widened in horror. 'This is what we're charging your client with. The murder of Jennifer Nolan.' He tapped one of the photos. 'And the murder of Nici Johnson.' He tapped another. 'The forensic pathologist confirmed in both cases that not all intestines were present. Some had been cut off and removed.' He pulled another couple of photos from the folder, the open wound on the stomach yawning like a mad joker's toothless smile. He slid them to McTear. 'In addition to that, each

289

victim had her nipples sliced off.' Two more photos showed the flesh of breast wounds as red as raw meat.

McTear stared at the images in shocked disgust for several beats, then turned to his side, cupped his hand to Green's face, and whispered ferociously into his ear. But Green smiled, and pushed him away. 'No fucking way.'

'For the record,' McTear blurted, 'I've advised my client not to answer any questions, other than to say "No comment".'

'Noted,' Gilchrist said, and retrieved the photographs from McTear. Then he slid them over to Green. 'Former girlfriends of yours?' he said.

'If you say so.'

'Don't you recognise them?'

'Well, now you mention it, they don't have any clothes on, so, yeah . . .' He pulled the photographs closer, his lips working up a smile as he studied the images. 'Yeah, I think I do recognise them. Although last time I saw that pussy, it was shaved. And this one here, she liked a Brazilian cut. Kept it nice and trim for me.' He coughed out a laugh, then sat back smiling.

Gilchrist kept his gaze on Green. He'd come across many a cold-hearted killer before, but Green was pushing the envelope. By his side, he could sense Dainty shuffling in his seat, struggling to contain his anger, ready to explode. Which wasn't what Gilchrist wanted. Not at that stage of the interview anyway.

'When did you last see Jennifer Nolan?'

'Months ago, I think.'

'That's not what her neighbours say.'

'What do they say?'

'And when did you last see Nici Johnson?'

'Couldn't tell you. Ages ago, like I said.'

Gilchrist reached inside his folder again, and removed another photograph, this one a printout from a CCTV camera. He turned it around for McTear and Green. 'Recognise that?'

Green looked closer at an image of Jennifer Nolan's white Ford Focus abandoned at the side of the road. 'It's a car,' he said, then chuckled.

'Do you know whose car?'

'Go on. Surprise me.'

'And this one?' he said, shoving another photograph across the table.

'Another car.'

'Not just any car. But your car.'

Green frowned, then leaned closer. He shook his head. 'Not sure it is.'

Gilchrist retrieved the photos, and took his time slipping them back into his folder. Then he stared hard at Green. 'Every time I came across you, you were wearing black. Black jeans, black top, black sweater.' He flickered a smile. 'Black in fashion, is it?'

'Helps show off the muscle tone, yeah.' He flexed his pecs as if to prove a point.

'Your underwear black, too, is it?'

'What the fuck? Are you for real, or what?'

'Oh I'm for real all right don't you worry about that.' He paused for a moment, then said, 'How about your socks? They black, too?'

'As you said, black's in fashion.'

'Did you lose a sock?'

'What? Lose a sock?' Not quite so sure of himself.

'A black sock with a red Pringle logo on the ankle.' He opened the folder again, and slid a photo of a single sock across to Green, the material damp where it had lain outside in the rain all night, the stitched logo clear. 'This one.' He let five beats pass, then said, 'We found it on the golf course, close to the Fairmont Hotel, and not far from Nici's body. You must've dropped it after you murdered her.'

Green tried to keep a straight face, but he was fooling no one. 'Never seen it before in my life. Nope. Not one of mine.'

'You sure?'

'Positive.'

'That's strange,' Gilchrist said. 'Because we lifted your DNA off it.'

Green's face twisted. 'You're fucking lying,' he said. 'You're trying to set me up.' He slammed both fists onto the table with a force that had Dainty out of his seat and reaching for the man's throat. But both police officers beat him to it, and thudded their hands onto Green's shoulders and crushed him back into his seat.

Dainty let out his breath in an angry, 'Fuck sake,' then ran his fingers through his hair, and said, 'Interview suspended at . . .' He glanced at the recorder, read out the time, and stomped from the room.

CHAPTER 50

Throughout the fracas, Gilchrist had remained seated, like a spectator watching a hard arrest from afar. McTear on the other hand was on his feet, back to the wall, eyes wide, face drained of blood, as if stunned by the animal ferocity of Green's outburst. Without a word, Gilchrist gathered his notes with careful deliberation, closed his folder, and followed Dainty from the room.

He found him by the coffee machine, lips white, face flushed, jaw ruminating in anger as he crushed his teeth. He handed Gilchrist a cardboard cup of coffee then stuffed another one under the nozzle. 'I'm getting far too old for all this fucking shite,' he snarled. 'That bastard needs to have his balls cut off and stuffed down his fucking throat.'

'Before we do that,' Gilchrist said, 'we need to find out where he keeps the body parts.' He opened his mobile, and pulled up a text from Mhairi. 'You might find this interesting,' he said.

Dainty lifted his coffee cup from the machine, took a sip, then scowled. 'My office,' he said, then stomped off.

Gilchrist followed him along a corridor, up a flight of stairs, surprised by the speed and agility of the man. Dainty might be small, but Gilchrist found himself walking hard just to keep up with him, through a door and into an office redolent of fresh aftershave and warm dust. Dainty slumped into his seat, opened a drawer, and removed what looked like a slender bottle wrapped in brown paper. He poured a measure – a small one, right enough – into the cardboard cup and returned the bottle to the drawer without offering Gilchrist any.

'Medication for my heart condition,' he said, and took a sip.

'Didn't know you had a heart condition,' Gilchrist said, as he took a seat facing Dainty's desk.

'That's what I tell anyone who dares to ask.' He sat back, took a sip, and from the change that shifted over his face like clouds uncovering the sun, Gilchrist knew it wasn't heart medication he was taking.

'Listen to what Mhairi's come up with,' he said, and while Dainty sipped from the cardboard cup, he read out Mhairi's text. 'Mitochondrial DNA confirms familial connection to Matt Duffy.'

Dainty frowned. 'Duffy? Duffy? Matt Duffy? He sounds familiar. But he's not from Glasgow, I don't think. Edinburgh, maybe? And that bastard downstairs is related to him? Is that what she's saying?'

'Let me give her a call.'

A few seconds later, he had Mhairi on speaker.

'Got your text, Mhairi. What've you found?'

'Jackie's still looking into it, sir, but Sam Kim carried out a mitochondrial DNA test on a sample from that sock we found, and the result confirms a familial connection. It turns out that John Green's father is the convicted killer Matt Duffy.'

'You have anything on him?'

'Yes, sir. Fifteen years ago he killed his wife and her two sisters, then fled to Spain. It took several years before he was located and extradited.'

'Where is he now?'

'HMP Shotts. High security. He won't be considered for parole for another ten years. And he's been involved in a number of violent incidents in prison, so it's not likely he'll ever be released.'

Gilchrist thought Dainty was about to say something, but he took another sip from his cup and glared at the phone. 'Does Duffy have any other children?' Gilchrist asked.

'He has a daughter, Siobhan, and two sons, Patrick and James.'

'No John?'

'No, sir.'

'So is John Green the result of an extramarital affair?' Gilchrist said, 'Or has he gone and changed his name again? And if he has, which one is he? Patrick or James?'

'From their birth certificates, James Duffy is the older brother. But he was stabbed to death in a bar in Edinburgh seven years ago, sir.'

Dainty said, 'Edinburgh. I knew that's where I'd heard the name.'

'Keep going,' Gilchrist said.

'And the younger brother, Patrick, he'll be thirty-one now, sir, which fits in well with John Green's age. So, we're thinking maybe that's him.'

'Okay, I need you to find out what you can on Patrick Duffy. Check DVLA's records, HMRC, PNC, the lot.'

'Already got Jackie working on it, sir.'

'Well done, Mhairi. Let me know what she comes up with.'

'One other thing, sir. Both Siobhan and Patrick share the same birthday.'

'So they're twins.' He paused for a moment, thinking it might be worth having a word with Siobhan. Or maybe not. But you never could tell. 'Can we find an address for her?'

'Yes, sir, she lives in Glasgow. Nothing on the PNC, sir. She doesn't have a driving licence, and by all accounts lives an honest life.'

'She married?'

'Yes, sir, to a Blair Dougal. But from what we know, they're separated, but not divorced.'

Dainty said, 'Is that Blair *Cameron* Dougal?'

'Yes, sir.'

Dainty ran a hand over his face, then said, 'Bammie Cammie. Another low-lifer. Right nasty son of a bitch. Used to do collections for big Jock Shepherd when he was alive. You might miss one payment, but with Bammie Cammie on your case you never missed another, if you get my drift.'

Gilchrist said, 'And what does this Bammie Cammie do now?'

'Still out there ducking and diving. But no longer with Shepherd's family.'

'Is he worth talking to?'

Dainty grimaced. 'Shouldn't think so.'

Gilchrist nodded, then said to Mhairi, 'Does Siobhan have any children?'

'None that we can find, sir.'

'Well, that's good to hear,' Dainty said. 'Hopefully the end of the fucking line.'

'Text me Siobhan's address,' Gilchrist said.

'Will do, sir.' A pause, then, 'Sir?'

'Yes, Mhairi.'

'Do you know how Jessie is?'

Gilchrist gritted his teeth. He glanced at Dainty, who seemed to have found something of interest in his cup. 'She's in the Royal Infirmary in Glasgow. All I know is, that she's . . .' he was about to say *in a coma*, but instead said, '. . . she's still unconscious, and they're operating on her to release pressure on her brain.'

'If she . . . if . . . if you get a chance, sir, can you please tell her we're praying for her?'

'Of course, Mhairi. We're all praying for her.'

'Thank you, sir.'

The line died.

Dainty crushed his coffee cup and threw it into the bin. 'So that murdering bastard downstairs is the son of another murdering bastard. Fuck sake. You couldn't make it up.'

'What do you know about Matt Duffy?'

'Not as much as we're about to find out.' Dainty lifted the handset on his desk, and rattled off a string of commands that brooked no questions and would have you believing he was six-foot-two. He clattered the handset back down, pulled himself to his feet, and said, 'Right. Let's nail this bastard once and for all.'

CHAPTER 51

Gilchrist followed Dainty into the interview room, and couldn't fail to catch a sense of heightened tension. One police officer stood with his back to the wall, facing Green, while the other stood a couple of feet behind Green, as if to make sure he was within easy striking distance.

McTear had returned to his seat, and undone his tie at the neck, but his body language told Gilchrist that he was keen to distance himself from Green, who glared at Gilchrist as he and Dainty took their seats opposite. Still aware that Green might not yet be prepared to talk to anyone other than himself, Gilchrist restarted the interview.

'Right,' he said, leaning towards Green. 'Do you know Matt Duffy?'

Green's lips tightened, and he shook his head.

'For the record,' Gilchrist said, 'Mr Green shook his head, which for the sake of this interview will be taken as a negative answer.' He sat back and stared at Green, as if willing him to look him in the eye. 'How about James Duffy?' he tried.

McTear said, 'Excuse me, but what do any of these people have to do with my client?'

'Why don't you ask your client?' Dainty snapped.

McTear turned to Green, but said nothing.

'So I'll ask again,' Gilchrist said. 'How about James Duffy? Do you know him?'

Green's lips pressed tighter, and Gilchrist sensed the police officer standing behind him was on the verge of stepping in to thwart another outburst. But the moment passed, and Gilchrist said, 'Mr Green has once again refused to answer.' He opened his folder, flipped over a couple of pages, then looked at Green. 'How about *Patrick* Duffy?' He paused for a reaction. 'That name ring a bell?'

Nothing.

'Again, for the record, Mr Green has refused to answer.' He closed his folder, reclined in his seat, and sensed, rather than saw, a relaxing in Green's demeanour.

'If I may?' McTear said, and referred to his own scribbled notes. 'Once again, I have to ask. What do the names Matt Duffy, James Duffy, and Patrick Duffy, have to do with my client?'

'All in good time,' Gilchrist said. He pressed closer to the table, focused his gaze on Green, and tried to soften his tone. 'You must surely know by now,' he said, 'that we have your full DNA profile from that sock you left at the scene of Nici Johnson's murder. You must have left it accidentally, I'll grant you that, but you left it behind just the same.'

Green offered no reaction.

'How else would we know about your father, Matt Duffy, now in Shotts high security prison? And your brother, James, too? Killed in a knife attack in a pub in Edinburgh, almost a decade ago. That must have been hard to take. How did that make you feel when you heard your brother was murdered? Did you want revenge? Did you feel helpless? Go on, tell me. What did his murder make you want to do?'

Again, nothing.

'And then we come to *your* name. Not John Green. Not Timothy Johnson. Not even John Thomson. But Patrick Delaney Duffy, born in Edinburgh Royal Maternity Hospital on . . .' He read out the date, and once again sensed the tiniest change in Green's demeanour, an almost imperceptible flaring of his nostrils, as if he was preparing himself for something else he didn't want to hear.

But they had his birth date, so surely he must know they knew.

'Can you confirm that we have your details correct, and that your name is indeed Patrick Delaney Duffy?'

Green shrugged. 'If you say so. You seem to have everything in order.'

'Ah, he speaks,' Dainty said.

But Gilchrist said nothing, just tried to work out why something in the tone of Green's voice, and the manner in which he'd spoken, had his sixth sense niggling. Not a denial. And not quite a confirmation. But something else, relief – perhaps – that his aliases had been found out? Or perhaps because he thought something more troubling had been missed.

Gilchrist said, 'For the purposes of this interview, and for the avoidance of any doubt, I am going to read Mr Duffy his rights again, this time in his own name.' Overkill to the point of pedantry, he knew, but these days you could be forgiven for trying to fill in the tiniest of loopholes that could be argued against by any competent defence attorney.

Once done, Gilchrist sat back in his seat. 'So, Mr Duffy, is there anything you'd like to say in response to the charges?'

'Not guilty,' he said. 'That good enough for you?'

'It's a start. When did you last see your father, Matt Duffy?'

McTear leaned forward again. 'For the record, I am advising my client once again to answer all questions with "No comment".'

Dainty smirked. 'Making sure you're covering your legal arse?'

McTear diverted his gaze as if ashamed, and Gilchrist repeated the question.

'Can't remember,' Duffy said.

'Did you ever visit him in prison?'

'You've got to be joking.'

'No joke.' He paused for a moment, then said, 'Do you think Siobhan visits him in prison?'

McTear said, 'Who on earth is Siobhan?'

But Gilchrist wasn't listening to McTear. He had his full attention on Duffy, who'd narrowed his eyes at the mention of his sister, and seemed to be having difficulty controlling his emotions.

But Gilchrist pressed on. 'What do you think Siobhan would say if I asked her?'

'You keep Siobhan out of this,' Duffy snarled. 'You hear?'

'Out of what?' Another pause. 'You've done nothing but side-step my questions and deny all knowledge of anything and everything.'

Duffy gritted his teeth. Anger shimmered across his face in waves.

'Keep Siobhan out of what?' Gilchrist repeated. 'Did she help you kill—'

'No.' Duffy's cry was so sharp, so sudden, that McTear jerked in his seat. 'She had fuck all to do with it,' he shouted. 'So leave her the fuck out of it.'

Gilchrist raised his hand to prevent the officer behind him from clamping a hand on his shoulder. Then he leaned forward, focused all his attention on Duffy. 'Keep her the fuck out of what, Patrick?' One beat, two beats, then, 'If she didn't assist you in the murders, what did she assist you in?'

Green's mouth twisted in an ugly grimace, his eyes darted left right left right, as if he was searching for an escape route he knew didn't exist. Then the moment passed, and he sank into his seat, as if all of a sudden deflated of energy. Then he breathed in hard, gave Gilchrist one of his hardman looks, and said, 'She didn't assist me in anything, because I'm innocent of all charges.'

'Christ on a stick,' Dainty said. 'I've heard it all now.'

'We have your DNA on a sock at the scene of the—'

'I must've lost it when I was out for a walk on the golf course.'

'When?'

'Two weeks ago.'

'Why?'

'Looking for golf balls.'

'Why take off your sock?'

'I like the feel of grass on my bare feet.'

Gilchrist sat back, knowing he'd lost the impetus of the interview. Duffy's quickfire explanations were feeble, nothing more than lies to muddy the water, unlikely to stand up to the full legal force of a Scottish prosecutor. On the other hand, Gilchrist thought he saw them for what they were: misdirection, like a magician's attempts to pull off a trick by having the audience focus on something other than the heart of the matter. And if you worked through the rationale, it seemed clear to him that the way forward was through his sister, Siobhan.

But how? That was the troubling question.

Only one way to find out.

'DCI Gilchrist excusing himself from the interview at two forty-three.'

Then he pushed away from his chair and walked from the room, conscious of Duffy's hateful gaze following him all the way.

CHAPTER 52

The Royal Infirmary, Glasgow

Gilchrist noted the name tag – Ellen Moir – on the nurse's uniform, and held out his warrant card. 'Thanks for agreeing to meet me,' he said, all of a sudden feeling it was wrong to present himself as a police detective in a hospital ward. Slipping his warrant card out of sight, he said, 'Let's keep this informal. I'm Andy. Do you mind if I call you Ellen?'

She shook her head, a tad unsure.

'So how is . . . how is Jessie?'

'She suffered an acute subdural haematoma, and was unconscious when admitted. Mr Marsh performed an emergency craniotomy to remove blood clotting, and I'm happy to say the operation was a success, although it's still early days. Jessie's in an induced coma and heavily sedated. But the fact that she underwent surgery within an hour of the incident, went a long way to minimising brain damage.'

Gilchrist didn't like the sound of *brain damage*, but felt he had to ask the question, if only to better explain her injury to the rest of his team, but also to Robert. 'Will she fully recover?' he said. 'All her faculties, I mean.'

'As I said, it's too soon to say. But you should know that a craniotomy is a serious operation, which in itself can cause her to have a seizure or a stroke and . . .' She grimaced for a long beat, then said, 'And keep her in a coma. Not to mention the potential problems with speech, memory, or movement, sustained from the injury.' She paused for a moment, and offered him a grim smile. 'I see from the look on your face that you understand the seriousness of the situation.'

He nodded. 'Can I see her?'

'She's still under sedation.'

'I won't stay long, if that's all right.'

She frowned, and stared over his shoulder into the depths of the ward.

'I just . . . I just need to see her, Ellen. Please?'

It took her a couple of seconds before she relented, and said, 'Follow me.'

She led him past a double row of beds, some curtained off, others with patients who watched in silence as they walked by. At the end of the ward, she pushed through a door into a small room that contained only one bed. Gilchrist was struck by the quietness, a library stillness broken only by the digital beeping of medical machinery and the soft sound of their own footfall.

If he hadn't been shown to Jessie, he would never have recognised her. Her head had been shaved, her eyes closed and swollen. A painful-looking row of stapled stitches stretched from behind her right ear to the top of her crown. A plastic tube was taped to her nose, and two other tubes led from a cannula in her arm to bags of clear fluid attached to a moveable apparatus by the side of her bed.

He stood quietly while Ellen checked the monitors and pulled the sheets up a touch before saying in a whispered tone, 'Just a couple of minutes, then. Okay?'

He nodded, and waited until she left the room before pulling up a chair.

Her hand felt cool to the touch, her skin soft, and as he ran his thumb over her fingers he found himself smiling at the memory of her complaining about some cheap moisturiser she'd once been given as a present – *would be better using butter.* He'd never taken notice of her hands before, how small they were, with slim fingers and tidy nails she seldom polished – *never seem to have the time; besides, it's cheaper.*

He lifted her hand, raised it off the bedsheet, and clasped it in both of his. 'I don't know if you can hear me or not,' he whispered, 'but Mhairi and Jackie wanted me to let you know that they're praying for you, and hoping you get well soon.' He closed his eyes for a long moment, surprised to feel the nip of tears, and when he opened them, said, 'We're all praying for you. Dainty, too. Now there's a surprise. I bet you never knew he had it in him.' He chuckled, trying to make light of his comment, and gave her hand a gentle squeeze, then returned it to the bed. He'd read somewhere that the fingers of comatose patients tend to curl inwards, as if searching for something to grip, so he took care to straighten Jessie's, pressing them flat against the palm of his hand.

He said nothing more for a minute or so, just stroked her hand, his eyes searching her face for any hint of awareness, the tiniest acknowledgement that she knew he was present. But he saw no movement, only the gentle rise and fall of the sheets from her breathing.

After a few more minutes of silence, he pushed his chair back, and stood. Then he leaned forward, his face only inches from hers, and whispered, 'We're all praying for you, Jessie. You have to get well. Robert needs you. He loves you. He loves his wee mum.' He felt his voice waver, and he had to take a couple of breaths before he could say, 'And I love you, too, Jessie.'

He dabbed a hand at his eyes, gave her hand a gentle squeeze, then left the room.

It took until seven o'clock that night for Mhairi to get back to Gilchrist.

'You were right, sir. Jackie picked up Duffy's Audi on the ANPR in the vicinity of Siobhan's home on the day following Jennifer Nolan's murder, and again following Nici Johnson's murder, too.'

Which was all he needed to put his and Dainty's plan into action.

In anticipation of having a positive response from Mhairi, Gilchrist had convinced Dainty to apply in advance for a search warrant for Siobhan's home on the outskirts of Glasgow.

'You could be wrong,' Dainty had said.

'But I'm not,' Gilchrist replied, sounding more confident than he felt.

'I'm sticking my neck out. You know that, don't you?'

'But not for the chop, I'm sure. You saw how Duffy reacted when I mentioned his sister's name. He's hiding something. He has to be. I'm sure of it. And whatever he's hiding, it has to be at Siobhan's.'

307

Dainty grimaced, as if not fully convinced. 'Fuck sake, Andy, I'm already in the chief super's bad books.'

'Look on the bright side, then. This could get you into his good books.'

'Or kicked out the Force good and proper.'

Back in Pitt Street HQ, Gilchrist stood back while Dainty took charge of the raid on Siobhan's home. He thought it odd how positive news could change a person's outlook, how Dainty had sprung into vociferous action the moment he'd learned that Duffy's car had been sighted on the ANPR in the vicinity of his sister's home. And for a small man, Dainty was a force to be reckoned with. But now the search warrant was in hand, Gilchrist found himself worrying about the outcome. What if he had it wrong? What if there was nothing to be found at the address? What if . . .?

He gritted his teeth, and followed Dainty from his office.

CHAPTER 53

Siobhan's home was off Weirwood Avenue in Garrowhill in the east end of Glasgow, one of the older housing estates that now consisted mostly of renovated homes bought from the council years ago for a song. Gilchrist noted that Garrowhill was south of Barlanark and not far from Craigend, which worked in well with Duffy's knowledge of the surrounding area and roads network.

Dainty wasted no time in implementing the warrant. He was out of the car almost before it drew to a halt, and first up the path, hammering the door like a demon by the time Gilchrist stood beside him.

The door cracked open to a grossly overweight woman with grey hair and a smoker's pallor, which had Gilchrist thinking they must be at the wrong address.

'Siobhan Duffy?' Dainty said.

'Ah've been expecting youse,' she said, and stood back while Dainty barged past her, followed by a conga line of officers wearing bulletproof vests, two of them armed with sub-machine guns.

Gilchrist was one of the last to enter, and followed Siobhan into the front room, where she flopped into a well-worn armchair in front of a TV with a screen that had to be all of sixty inches. As he faced her, she said, 'Ah've no idea what youse're expecting to find,' she said, and lifted a cigarette packet from the side table.

'Why did you say you were expecting us, then?' he said.

She glared at him, as if seeing him for the first time, then turned her attention to her cigarette, which she sparked to life with a cheap lighter, then sucked in for all she was worth. Then, as if Gilchrist didn't exist, she picked up the remote and switched on the TV, followed by an exhalation of smoke that threatened to cloud her from view.

Gilchrist tried again. 'You were expecting us, you said. Why?'

'Youse no heard of mobile phones?'

'Someone give you a call, did they?'

'Aye, that's how it works.'

'Who called?'

'Cannae remember. Memory's shot these days, so it is.' She scowled at something behind Gilchrist, then shouted, 'Mind they plants. Ah'll be charging youse for everything that's broken, so ah will. And if ah have to get cleaners in to clear up your mess, youse'll be getting the bill for that and aw.'

Gilchrist stepped closer, and waited a few seconds until he had her attention again; well, as close to having her attention as she would let him. 'And what did this person say when he or she called?' he said.

She coughed then, a hard rattling in the chest that produced a mouthful of phlegm which vanished with a quick bobble of her Adam's apple. Another suck of her cigarette to kill the taste, he supposed, then she clicked the remote and changed the channel.

'Do you mind?' He pulled the remote control from her grip, and clicked the TV off.

'Ah was watching that, so ah was.' Another long pull on her cigarette had her cheeks drawing in; not a pretty sight.

He thought he would try another tack, toughen up his approach a tad. 'We can do this the hard way, or the easy way.'

'Do what?'

'Interview you.'

'Is that whit this is? Youse barging into mah hoose wi yer hobnail boots leaving mud all over the place? Youse call that an interview? Mare like effing ransacking, so it is.'

He ignored her complaint, and tried again. 'When someone called you on their mobile phone, what did they say?'

'That youse've arrested big Tamson.'

'Don't you mean Patrick? Your twin brother?'

Something shifted behind her eyes at that, some dark thought that surfaced like a crocodile's eyes from a waterhole for a fleeting moment, only to sink from view again.

'Patrick? Mah twin brother?' She sucked her cigarette, twisted her lips and exhaled a burst of smoke, then shook her head. 'It's no mah Patrick. Mah Patrick's deid, so he is.'

'Do you ever visit your father in prison?' he said, just to change the tempo.

'Whit?'

'Your father. Matt Duffy. HMP Shotts. Have you ever visited him?'

'That'll be effin right.'

So, no denial that she was Matt Duffy's daughter. Just the ludicrous statement that her brother, Patrick, was dead. 'We'll need to take a DNA sample from you,' he said.

'Whit for?'

311

'To rule you out as a suspect.'

'Suspect for whit?'

'For murder.'

She sneered at that, but he wasn't put off. In fact, he felt encouraged. It's not what she was saying that was giving him answers, but what she wasn't saying. No question as to which murder. No question as to why they would suspect her for murder in the first place. Nothing that would tie her into any kind of relationship with her brother, Patrick.

'And once we have your DNA profile,' he said, 'it'll confirm that the man you call big Tamson is in fact your brother, Patrick, despite him being . . . dead, as you say.'

She narrowed her eyes as she drew her cigarette down a good half-inch in one hit, then let it out in an angry burst. Just then, Dainty returned from the kitchen, and stood in front of her. 'We need the key to a cupboard,' he said to her.

'Whit for?'

'So we don't have to batter it in.'

'Ah don't have it.'

'Suit yourself,' Dainty said, then strode off.

A few seconds later, the sound of wood splintering erupted in a sharp crack, which pulled a twisted smile from her lips, and told Gilchrist that whatever cupboard Dainty was breaking into, she knew he was wasting his time.

'You look pleased,' he said, which changed her hint of a smile to a scowl.

'Ah wis needing a new cupboard door, so ah wis. Ah'll just add it tae the list.' She stubbed out her cigarette on an ash-laden plate on the side table, and fired up another one. 'Youse can batter the whole place doon to the ground, for all ah care. Cause youse are gonnie end up paying for it. Mah solicitor's gonnie have a field day with youse lot, so she is.'

Something about her demeanour, her couldn't-care-less attitude, wasn't sitting right with Gilchrist. He felt that she was just too . . . what was the word he was looking for? Too . . . *confident*, that was it. She was just too confident, too self-assured they would find nothing in her home, whatever that nothing they were looking for was. Which brought him to the only logical conclusion he could make – that no matter how hard they searched her premises, or how many cupboard doors they broke down, they would find nothing – and told him that he needed to find some other angle of attack.

'The call from this friend of yours,' he said. 'Did you take it on your landline?'

'Don't have one.'

'On your mobile, then?'

She shrugged.

'We'll have to confiscate it,' he said. 'Have our IT guys go through it with a fine-toothed comb. Just to make sure you're not telling any fibs.'

'Suit yourself. But ah don't have it.'

'Where is it?'

'Who the eff knows? Lost it a couple of days ago.'

'I thought your friend told you that big Tamson had been arrested.' He held her gaze. 'That was earlier today.'

She tightened her lips, as if embarrassed by being caught out in such a simple lie. But that didn't trouble Gilchrist. He pulled out his own mobile and dialled the number Jackie had found for him.

It took a few seconds for the connection to be made, by which time Siobhan had picked up the TV remote and switched it back on. She then adjusted herself in her armchair, as if to watch the TV in greater comfort, which was when he thought he heard it, the dulled buzz of a mobile on vibrate.

He snatched the remote from her, powered off the TV, then held his mobile away from his ear. He'd always had superb hearing, but twenty stone of flesh on top of a well-worn armchair cushion made for good soundproofing. He thought he saw what had happened – an unexpected knock at the door, the hard hammering loud enough to convince her it was the police paying her a surprise visit; no time to do anything other than to stuff her mobile under her seat; thinking they had come only to ask her questions, not to search her home . . .

He held her gaze and watched it turn to defeated anger.

Then he turned to the nearest officer. 'There's a mobile phone under that seat,' he said. 'Bag it.'

CHAPTER 54

By the time Dainty and his team had cautioned Siobhan and huckled her from her home under loud protest for questioning at the Pitt Street Office, Gilchrist had slipped on a pair of latex gloves and done some IT work of his own. He'd calculated the approximate time when a call to Siobhan's mobile would most likely have been made after Patrick Duffy had been arrested, and the local gossip had begun to transmit the news down through the criminal jungle. It also helped that her mobile had the simplest of passwords, which he'd guessed correctly first time – her and her brother's common birth date.

Without that lucky break, he wouldn't have had such a head start. While Dainty and his team continued to hammer their way through Siobhan's home, Gilchrist – despite his lack of IT nous – identified three incoming calls that matched his approximate timeline, of which two calls were from the same number. Interestingly, or so he thought, one outgoing call had been made to that same number.

Using his own mobile, he dialled that number first, but it failed after two rings: most likely a declined call from an unknown number. Rather than try again, he dialled the other number, but it rang out. Rather than use Siobhan's phone to call again – which might give the person a heads-up or a head start – he called Mhairi and asked her to locate the addresses to which each number was registered. If they were burner mobiles, then not only was he barking up the wrong tree, he was pissing in the wrong forest. Still, it was worth a shot, and while he waited for her response, he caught up with Dainty.

'Anything?' he asked.

Dainty gritted his teeth. 'Cheap laptop and an iPad, which we'll get our IT lads to tear apart. Might show us something. But . . . other than that . . .' He blew out a long breath. 'Not a lot so far, I'm afraid.'

'You know you're not going to find anything here, don't you?'

Dainty whispered a curse, then said, 'It's beginning to look like it, aye.'

Gilchrist held up Siobhan's mobile phone.

'Where did you find that?' Dainty growled. 'Was she hiding it up her arse?'

'Almost.'

'Right, hand it in, and we'll have our guys take a look through it.'

'Before we do that . . .' Gilchrist spent the next minute bringing Dainty up to speed, so that when the call came in from Mhairi, with the address for the single call on the south side of Glasgow, and the address for the double call just around the corner, they were both ready.

No search warrant that time, just the usual Dainty-thuds against the door and a curse under his breath as he stepped back to wait. The lights were on upstairs and downstairs, and Gilchrist could hear the staccato sound of some movie on the TV in the living room. A quick background check had confirmed that Erin Tweedie was a single mum, with three girls – twelve, ten and nine. Not much of a criminal record: drunk and disorderly, shoplifting and an eighteen-month ban for drink driving – which explained the empty driveway – and twenty hours outstanding on a community service term.

When the door opened to a small woman in a dressing gown, jet black hair awry with rollers, Gilchrist held out his warrant card and introduced himself and Dainty. 'We're sorry to disturb you,' he said, 'but we'd like to ask you a few questions.'

'Ah was about to go to mah bed.'

Gilchrist cracked a smile. 'We won't take long.'

She pressed her lips into a tight line, and glanced along the street. 'Is this to dae with that Siobhan?'

Gilchrist felt his heart leap. 'Why do you say that?'

As if realising she'd slipped up, she shrugged. 'Just the polis cars and that. All the fuss. I mean . . . whit the eff's goin on?'

'Can we talk inside?'

Another glance along the street, then she stood aside. 'Through the back. The weans are watching the telly. They don't need to know youse're here.'

'Thought you were going to bed,' Dainty grumbled as he stepped inside.

Nothing more was said, until Gilchrist stepped into a tidy kitchen, and the door closed behind him with a firm click.

'Right. Whit is it?' she said, and pressed her fingers and thumb hard to her mouth.

Silent, Gilchrist held her gaze, watched it dart to Dainty and back again.

'Whit?' she said. 'Whit dae youse want?'

'The truth,' Gilchrist said.

'About whit?'

He gave her one of his firm looks that told her he was going to stand for no nonsense, and certainly no lies. 'Do you let your girls see their father?' he said.

'Whit?'

'Just answer the man's questions,' Dainty said. 'We've not got all night.'

'Naw. We've nuthin to dae with that bastard, excuse mah French.'

Gilchrist nodded. 'So . . . what do you think would happen to them if their mum was suddenly taken away?'

'Whit? Whit d'you mean? Oh mah God. Whit. Naw. Youse cannae dae that—'

'Settle down,' Dainty said. 'You're not going anywhere. Not just yet . . . anyway.'

Gilchrist said, 'We know you have a record. Nothing serious, but with that in mind, it wouldn't take much to . . .' he searched for the right word, but ended up with, '. . . to put you away.'

She gasped, pressed her hand hard to her mouth.

'But if you answer a few questions truthfully, then we'll be on our way and out of your hair, and nobody will be any the wiser. Okay?' He offered a smile. 'So why don't you take a seat, and let us get on with this.' A statement, not a question.

She swallowed once, twice, then slumped into the kitchen chair that Dainty held out for her. Tears swelled in her eyes, and a trail of snot dribbled from her nose. A quick scan of the kitchen, and Gilchrist pulled a strip of kitchen roll from a holder by the sink.

She grabbed it from him, and pressed it under her nose.

'Can you confirm your mobile number?' he asked.

'Whit? Aye, sure.' She reached into her dressing gown pocket and removed a phone. A few clicks while she worked into Settings, then read out the number.

'I called that number earlier,' he said. 'But you didn't answer.'

'Ah don't take calls frae numbers ah don't know.'

He'd been correct in his assumption, so pressed on. 'We know you spoke to Siobhan today,' he said.

She sniffed, and nodded. 'Aye. We're always on the phone. So whit?'

'Do you know her brother?'

'Who? Naw. She disnae have a brother.'

'Big Tamson?'

'That's no her brother.' A pause, then, 'Is it? Naw. He cannae be.'

'So you know big Tamson, do you?'

'Jist to look at. That's aw.'

Gilchrist pulled out a chair, and sat opposite her. He breathed in, held her gaze, and nodded to her. 'So you know him, this big Tamson. But you don't know him too well. You're not friends. You don't go out for a drink with him. Is that correct?'

'Aye.' She pressed the paper towel to her nose, but couldn't prevent tears from spilling down her cheeks.

'That's good,' he said. 'That's good that you don't know him well. Because that way, you might not be implicated.'

'Implicated?' She let out a gasp. 'Impli . . .' But it seemed too much for her to take in, and she buried her face in the towel. Her sobbing turned to shudders, and Gilchrist gave her a few minutes to settle herself down. When she next looked at him, eyes

319

swollen and red, he could tell she was broken. 'I didnae dae nuthin,' she said. 'I jist . . . I jist . . .'

'You just what?' Gilchrist asked in as kind a tone as he could muster.

'I jist took whit Siobhan handed me. I havenae looked at it or nuthin. Jist . . . jist kept it for her. Jist for a wee while, she said. That's aw.'

'And what did she give you?'

'A wee suitcase. Nuthin more. Honest.'

He had one more question to ask. 'When did Siobhan give you the wee suitcase?'

'This efternoon.'

Gilchrist pushed to his feet. 'Can you show me the suitcase?'

CHAPTER 55

The suitcase turned out to be a hardshell Samsonite, small enough for cabin storage, with four wheels and an extendable handle. It had a number-protected padlock, and a blue nylon rope that ran around the outside twice, crossed-over and tied in a Gordian-like knot that was also double padlocked to a side handle.

Whatever it contained was meant for Patrick Duffy's eyes only.

When Gilchrist lifted it off the top of the bedroom wardrobe with latex-gloved hands, it felt lighter than he'd expected. Despite Dainty's demands to *Get our lads to cut the locks and just open the fucking thing*, he carried it to the back seat of Dainty's car, where he sat next to it all the way to Pitt Street.

When they entered Dainty's office, the SOCOs were already waiting. They set to work on it right away, taking DNA samples from the handles and the nylon rope, including in and around the knot. They took photographs of it from every conceivable angle, and dusted it for fingerprints. They also checked it for drugs, then explosives – just to be safe.

'Is that us finally ready, then?' Dainty said.

The lead SOCO, a woman in her thirties, pulled her mask down in agreement.

Dainty nodded to a man called Danny whose face was so lined and haggard that he looked as if he hadn't slept for a couple of months, maybe longer. But he was reputed to be able to open any lock on the planet. He'd arrived twenty minutes earlier, smiling and rubbing his hands and announcing to anyone who could be bothered to listen that he was on time and a half until midnight, after which he was on double time. With forty minutes to go before the midnight hour, he looked disappointed when Dainty told him to get on with it.

The nylon rope was cut around the knot, freed from the double padlocks, then bagged for further DNA tests on the exposed lengths of knot, and the suitcase photographed again. In less than three minutes Danny had both padlocks snecked open, and the number-protected padlock cracked. He was about to click the suitcase locks when Dainty shouted, 'Don't. We'll take it from here.'

They waited while Danny gathered his tools together and left the room, before Dainty sprung the locks, and opened the lid.

Gilchrist hadn't known what to expect, but certainly not padded foam that filled the inside, and cut into rectangular shapes that housed plastic bags – five of them in total.

'What the fuck . . .?' Dainty said, and stepped back while the police photographer took some more photos.

Gilchrist leaned closer, and as carefully as he could, took hold of one of the plastic bags and pulled it free from its slot. He felt his breath leave him as he read the name written neatly on the outside in indelible ink – **Nici** – as if that single name made the bag's contents all the more personal for him.

By his side, Dainty hissed a curse, and said, 'Is that pubic hair?'

Gilchrist couldn't say for sure, but nodded and said, 'And both nipples.' Then he eyed the other cut-outs. 'There's four more,' he said, and read them off, one at a time, holding up each plastic bag as he did so. 'Jen,' he said, 'could be Jennifer Nolan.'

Dainty reached in. 'So who's this?' He held it up. 'Ana. Another pair of nipples, and a right batch of pubes. And he could do with a lesson in spelling.'

'What do you mean?'

'Ana. With one n.'

As a teenager, Gilchrist had spent a summer in Spain, working in the bars then beach-bumming for six weeks before returning home. He'd loved the experience, which he'd known would be his final youthful fling before settling down to a career in the Police Force. He'd done what most youngsters did back then, which was to indulge in too many drunken parties and late-night discos, and the inevitable free-loving affairs. One Spanish beauty he'd become particularly besotted with was the daughter of a local restauranteur. With glossy black hair, and smooth skin the colour of caramel, she stood out from the others. He'd kept in contact with her for six months, but the airmail letters dwindled to none as the day-to-day reality of focusing on a new career took over, and his memories of his summer romance faded. But he never forgot the way she'd smiled as she'd introduced herself to him in her broken English – *My name is Anabela*, she'd said, her husky whisper stirring his emotions. *But everyone calls me Ana.* And as was the Spanish norm, Ana was spelled with one n.

He removed another plastic bag. 'Maya,' he whispered, then lifted out the fifth and final one. 'Lucia.' Well, there he had his answer. He looked at Dainty, and shook his head. 'He hasn't misspelled her name at all,' he said. 'Ana, Maya and Lucia are first names of Spanish women.'

'Spanish?' Dainty said, as if the word was filthy. 'Why Spanish?'

'Maybe he lived there. Who knows?' Dainty took the plastic bags from him, holding each up for a better look, then shaking his head in disgust. Meanwhile, Gilchrist had turned his attention back to the suitcase, and in particular, the cut-out foam padding. With all five plastic bags removed, he saw that the depth of each cut-out space was shallow, no more than an inch or so deep. He pressed his fingers into one of the spaces, and realised it wasn't solid all the way through, but a layer of shallow padding that sat on top of another foam pad. He slipped his hand under the top layer, and lifted it out to expose more foam padding, but with no cut-outs in it. He thought the foam pad appeared to be a loose fit, and when he touched it, he came to see that it was another thin layer of padding, which he removed and set aside.

Dainty was first to reach in and remove the contents. 'Ah for fuck sake,' he hissed. 'How many's this bastard killed?'

But Gilchrist could see the other cut-outs were smaller in size, but much deeper, and contained what appeared to be shrink-wrapped meat product. He eased one of the plastic bags out with care, noted the name, **Lucia**, printed with indelible ink on the bag's surface, and held it up to the light.

And there they were, Lucia's intestines, still pink and glistening in whatever fluid Duffy had chosen to pickle them in. A quick count confirmed five deeper cut-outs, with each name on removal being paired with one of the other five in the top layer – a serial killer's gruesome mementoes of the five women he'd murdered.

Gilchrist turned to Dainty. 'We need to run these names through HOLMES and the PNC to see if they link up with any other missing person or unsolved murder,' he said. 'And also contact the Spanish authorities, and Interpol, find out if they've any missing persons or unsolved murders that match these names, too.'

'Leave it with me,' Dainty said. 'I'll start the ball rolling, but by the looks of you, you need to be in your bed.'

It hadn't struck Gilchrist until Dainty said it, but with the discovery of fresh evidence that indisputably linked Patrick Delaney Duffy – or whoever the hell he liked to call himself – to five brutal murders, all of a sudden he felt drained. Exhaustion swept through him in a debilitating wave, and he had to steady himself by holding onto the edge of Dainty's desk.

'You okay, Andy?' Dainty said.

'Fine. Yeah. Just tired.'

'I'll have someone drive you home.'

'I'll manage.'

'Anybody ever tell you you're a stubborn bastard?'

'I can think of a few,' Gilchrist said, and tried a smile as he turned and left the room.

CHAPTER 56

Outside, the cold air seemed to revive him. He took several deep breaths before clicking his key fob and sliding in behind the wheel. He thought of calling Irene to tell her he was on his way, but she would likely be asleep, and he could be home in an hour and a half, so he decided against that. Instead, he eased his way through Glasgow traffic and stopped off at the Royal Infirmary intent on an update on Jessie.

Her ward was in darkness, and stirred with the night-time sounds of light snoring, bedsheets shuffling, machines beeping. He spoke with the night sister, only to be told that Jessie was still in an induced coma, but that her vital signs were stable. He was pleased to learn that a family liaison officer, with competent signing skills, had been despatched by Strathclyde Police to quote unquote *speak* with Robert, at home in person. So there really was nothing more he felt he could do. He left his business card, and asked the sister to have someone call him when Jessie recovered consciousness.

He was approaching the Clackmannanshire Bridge when his mobile rang – a number he didn't recognise. He took the call through his car's speaker system, and said, 'Hello?'

The line hissed through the digital ether for several seconds before a soft voice broke the silence with, 'Andy. It's Kristen.' A pause, then, 'I'm sorry to call at such a late hour. I hope I didn't wake you.'

'No, I'm fine,' he said, his mind flaring with a surge of anxiety. Was this about Jack? Had something happened to Linna? He hadn't heard anything more from Dainty's man in Sweden, and the events of that day had pushed all thoughts of Jack to the back of his mind. Now, he realised how remiss he'd been in not following up. 'Is . . . has—'

'Everything's okay, Andy. I just thought you should know that Jack is flying back to Scotland tomorrow morning. He asked me to call and let you know that he's okay.'

Relief surged through Gilchrist, along with a bombardment of questions – Where is Jack? Why couldn't he call? Is he out on bail? But he couldn't find the words, and was only able to mumble, 'What's the . . .?'

'Jack's not going to be charged, Andy, so please don't worry. And Linna's fine, too. I told Jack that you called yesterday. I'm sorry that I didn't say anything to you on the phone, but I was still upset and not sure what I was going to do. But your call reassured me. And for that, I thank you.'

'But I thought . . . Jack was arrested. At the airport.'

'It was . . . how do I say? . . . an *informal* arrest.'

'I see,' Gilchrist said, as he came to understand that the informal arrest – if there ever was such a thing – had been a ploy intended to give Jack a fright. Being arrested in a foreign country will do that to you. 'What about Linna?' he said.

'Linna's safe. Jack handed her over without any . . . any resistance.'

'So you were there? At the airport?'

A pause, then, 'Yes. I was.'

Now he thought he saw it. The set-up. Jack being met at the airport by Kristen where he'd agreed to return Linna, then the shock of being arrested – in inverted commas – by Kristen's police friend.

'Jack was escorted to the local police station and questioned.'

'Did you go with him?' he said.

'No. I took Linna home.'

Of course you would, he thought. It added to the shock factor.

Kristen pressed on. 'Jack said he'd regretted what he'd done, and my . . . my *contact* in the local police was able to push it all . . . how do you say? . . . under the table.'

Gilchrist knew that her *contact* had to be her boyfriend from years earlier, the police officer with whom she'd resurrected a long-lost love affair, and whom Dainty had said was a nasty piece of work. Making an *informal* arrest at the airport, then pushing a charge under the table would have been a simple matter for an officer with few qualms about bending the law. Not an ideal solution, far from it, but it was a solution to Jack's problems nonetheless, and one for which Gilchrist could be thankful, even though the thought of Jack being played by Kristen and her partner that way riled him.

'And Linna?' he said, more in control of his emotions. 'You know Jack loves her. He'll be devastated if he can't see her.'

One beat, two beats, then, 'Jack can see Linna anytime. But only in Sweden.'

Well, there he had it. The compromise. Jack was being returned to Scotland with his tail between his legs, but with no charges being brought against him. He couldn't see Jack ever leaving

Scotland to live in Sweden to be close to his daughter, because it would pain him too much to see Kristen in a new relationship, and to witness Linna's interaction with her surrogate father. No, Jack would remain in Scotland and throw himself into his work again – like father like son – and fly over to Sweden to see Linna at a time and place to be agreed with Kristen. After all that Jack had done, he supposed it was as good an outcome as any he could expect.

As those thoughts fired through his mind, the road ahead seemed to come at him out of the night darkness in a dizzying rush, and he realised he was approaching a roundabout too fast. He flipped his head lights to full beam as he slammed on his brakes and managed to take the roundabout without mishap.

Kristen broke into his thoughts again. 'I'm sorry for what has happened, Andy. I still care for Jack, and when he's with Linna, I can see he adores her.'

Thoughts of his own missed years of parenthood swamped him, and all he could say was, 'It's all so sad.'

'Yes,' she said. 'It is.'

And with that, the connection died, leaving him to negotiate the country roads in dark and lonely silence.

CHAPTER 57

Ten days later
St Andrews Community Hospital, Largo Road, St Andrews

'Never seen you in a beanie hat before,' Jessie said. 'Not sure if it suits you.'

Gilchrist smiled, then removed it to reveal an almost shorn head. 'Or a number one either,' he said.

Jessie stifled a laugh, then said, 'Now that's *definitely* not you.'

He tilted his head to show her an L-shaped wound that still looked red and sore. 'Six stitches,' he said. 'Not as many as you.' Irene had insisted he have his hair cut short, to match the shorn hair around his head wound. *You can wear a hat*, she'd said, *until it grows back*.

He'd resisted at first, but of course, in the end relented.

Jessie made an effort to raise her hand to touch the side of her own head, but her fine motor control skills had not fully recovered, and he reached out and helped her by leading her hand gently to the scar that ran from behind her right ear almost to her crown. Her fingers tapped the wound. 'It feels lumpy,' she said.

'That's the staples. When your hair grows back, no one'll see a thing.'

'You think?'

He tapped his own wound, and said, 'I know.' He smiled again as he took hold of her wrist and placed her arm flat on the bed. 'You shouldn't touch. Might cause an infection.'

'Quite the bedside manner in your old age,' she said, then livened. 'Robert came to see me yesterday. Who would ever believe he's my son? Have you seen his shoulders? And the height of him? My goodness. And he's grown a beard, too.' Her smile faded, then shifted to a frown. 'Didn't have much of a chat with him though. Too one-sided. I couldn't . . .' She looked at her hand and grimaced as she tried to move her fingers. 'I couldn't sign very well.'

Gilchrist took hold of her hand again, gave her fingers a gentle rub. 'It'll take some time to regain your fine motor control skills. But the doctors are hopeful you'll make a full recovery.' He tilted his head and eyed her over an imaginary pair of specs. 'Provided you do as your told.'

'Dammit,' she said. 'I knew there was a catch.' She laughed at that, and he noticed a slight lop-sidedness in the way her lips parted. Then he felt her hand move, and her fingers try to take hold of his. 'How's Irene?' she said.

'She's good. She really is.' He raised his eyebrows, scratched his head. 'Ever since she said she was refusing all further treatment, she's almost back to her old self. Keen to do some more photography, expand her portfolio. It's good,' he said. 'It's good to . . . to see her . . . to see her like that.'

Jessie offered a sad smile, then said, 'I can read you like a book, Andy.'

He held her eyes for as long as he could, then diverted his gaze. He dabbed a finger at each eye, sniffed, and shook his head. When he looked at her again he saw she would accept only the truth.

His lips flicked a quick smile. 'She wants to . . . to *leave* . . . on her own terms. She says she's tired, and had enough, and no amount of me trying to convince her otherwise will make her change her mind.' He took a deep breath, flicked another quick smile, and said, 'And no pain. No pain.' He shook his head. 'She's got pills for that . . . for when the time comes . . .'

She squeezed his hand. 'I'm sorry, Andy.'

He nodded, sniffed again, dabbed a hand at his eyes.

'Right. That's it. Enough of the morbid stuff,' she announced. 'Cheer me up. What about that bastard whatsisname . . .? John Green Duffy . . . or whoever the hell he is. Please tell me you've nailed him.'

'Oh we've nailed him all right,' he said, relieved by the change of subject. 'And the investigation's stirred up a right hornets' nest. Those Spanish names I mentioned? Ana, Maya and Lucia?'

'What about them?'

'Ana, Ana Moreno, from Almeria in southern Spain, reported missing four years ago. Her body was never recovered. But DNA from the . . .' he almost said nipples, but managed to say, '. . . contents of the suitcase, confirmed her ID. And Lucia Aguilar from Palma, Mallorca. Her body was found two months later on the Spanish mainland less than five kilometres from where Ana was last seen. But without any physical connection to Ana, the Spanish police were unable to link the two, so never realised they had two murders with the same MO.'

'Jeez,' Jessie hissed. 'And what about . . . whatshername . . . the other Spanish one?'

332

'Maya,' he said. 'Maya Hernández. Not Spanish. A Cuban national living in Miami at the time of her murder five years ago. We believe she was Duffy's first victim. Same MO, same missing body parts, but with no traceable DNA her case turned cold.' He shook his head. 'But when Jackie gets the bit between her teeth she's unbelievable. Within twenty-four hours she'd tracked Maya's case down to the States, and printed out Miami-Dade County's report on her murder. Which . . .' he offered Jessie a victory smile, '. . . as it turned out, was the key to convincing Patrick Duffy to confess.'

'Because she was his first victim?'

'No. Because Florida has the death penalty.' He nodded when she opened her mouth in a silent *Ahh*. 'Yep. Dainty told Duffy he was considering beginning proceedings to have him extradited to the States to be tried and convicted for Maya's murder. As her DNA was in his suitcase, Dainty told him the US authorities would consider it a slam-dunk for the death penalty. You should've heard Dainty, telling Duffy he'd spend years on Death Row, waiting for his date with Old Sparky, and when the day finally came his brain would be fried to a crisp by a million volts of electricity zapping through his body from his head to his toes. And see what they say about not feeling a thing? That's all crap, he said. It hurts like . . . and I don't need to tell you the words Dainty used.'

Jessie chuckled. 'So Duffy's happy to spend the rest of his life in a prison in the UK, rather than risk being tried in the States,' she said, more statement than question.

'Precisely.'

She frowned. 'Do you sometimes think we're too soft in this country?'

Gilchrist gave some thought to that, then said, 'I think it

333

depends on the individual. Duffy's more than happy to spend his life in prison, whereas Hutton's been crying his eyes out every day for the last week at the prospect of spending twenty years behind bars, even though there's a strong possibility of him being released before he turns seventy.'

'So he didn't die from a heart attack?'

'There was a bit of kidology going on with him. Faking it, in other words. But he couldn't fool the tests. Nowhere near as ill as he claimed he was. Heart disease did run in his family, but apparently he's made a full recovery, and is fit to stand trial. His lawyer's already convinced him to plead guilty in exchange for a reduced sentence. But still . . .'

'I knew from the get-go he was a slimy bastard.'

'Oh, and you're going to like this,' he said, and watched her lips pull into a lopsided smile. 'Remember that Home Electronics white van?'

'What about it?'

'The SOCOs found a couple of white crumpled-up sticky-backed sheets stuffed into the bins in the yard. They matched traces of glue on the sides of the van where the sheets had been plastered over the company name.' He let several seconds pass, hoping Jessie might be well enough to work it out for herself. But her eyes told him she was still struggling, and he said, 'We suspect it was the same van that was caught on CCTV in the vicinity of Jennifer Nolan's abandoned car.'

'Ah . . .' she said.

'That's right. We think it might have been used to pick up Jennifer after she parked her car. Who was driving it? Feehan or Duffy? We don't know yet. But forensics are going over it with a fine-toothed comb.'

Jessie nodded as if satisfied, then frowned for a moment, and said, 'Another thing I can't work out, is how Nici Johnson ended up being murdered in the rough near the Fairmont. I mean, she knew John Green when he was Timothy Johnson, so she would've run a mile if she ever saw him again. So why would she go there? Unless he took her there by force, of course. But even so, why there? Why the Fairmont? I just don't get it.'

'I've asked Duffy that same question,' Gilchrist said. 'But he's clammed up again, so I suppose we'll never really know for sure.'

'We could try bamboo shoots under his fingernails. That might work.'

'If I didn't know you better, I'd say you were joking.' He smiled with her, then said, 'But here's what I think happened. Remember Carey Connors telling us that Jennifer Nolan invited herself to a get-together over dinner at the Fairmont, then didn't even show?'

'Memory's not completely shot, you know.'

'Well . . . if Duffy targeted Nici, he could've persuaded Jen to befriend her. Then once they get to know each other, Jen and Nici arrange to go out together one night, in this case for dinner at the Fairmont.'

'Where that bastard's lying in wait for her, in the rough.'

'Precisely.'

'Jeez,' Jessie hissed. 'That poor girl,' then whispered another curse under her breath, as her gaze shifted over his shoulder and her lips formed a lopsided grimace. 'Aw, shit. Here comes Laurel and Hardy. Pair of laugh-a-minutes, I must say. Physiotherapists my arse. More like bloody sadists.'

Gilchrist gave her hand another gentle squeeze, then pushed to his feet. 'I'd better love you and leave you then.' A quick peck on the cheek, and he stepped away.

She tried to give him a toodle-do wave, but her fingers didn't work the way they should, and it ended up being more of an air flap.

At the door, he turned, blew her a kiss, then pulled on his beanie hat, which brought a smile to her face, even though it still seemed a tad lopsided.

CHAPTER 58

Gilchrist found a parking space outside Irene's on South Street, and when he entered the living room was surprised to find her buttoning her jacket, scarf already around her neck, as if preparing to go out for a walk.

'There you are,' she said. 'I was just about to call you. We have a date.'

'We do?' he said, struggling to remember what he'd forgotten.

'An impromptu date,' she added, as if that explained everything.

Movement from the hallway had him turning his head, and smiling in surprise when Maureen stepped into the room. She gave him a hug and a quick peck on the cheek, leaving him to say, 'I didn't know you were coming.'

'Wangled a couple of days off. Thought I should drive up to the old town and see how it is.' She scowled at his head. 'And Irene said you'd been assaulted. Why didn't you tell me earlier?'

'Looks worse than it is, and I didn't want to worry you.'

'For crying out loud, Dad, you need to let me know what's going on.'

'I know. I'm sorry. I'll do that next time.'

'There'd better not be a next time,' she said, then added with another scowl, 'Don't you think you're getting too old for this now?'

Well, what could he say? Nothing, other than a shrug, as it turned out.

Irene saved him with, 'Joanne's expecting us. Shall we go? Or do you want to freshen up first?'

'Is that you dropping a hint?' he said, and gave her a chuckle in support.

'Of course not. It's just that it's such a rush for you, being so unexpected.'

'Let me brush my teeth then.'

Five minutes later, teeth cleaned, face washed, and a fresh shirt pulled on in a hurry, he stepped into the cool evening air. Overhead, cloudless skies were darkening for the night, and he was pleasantly surprised when Irene took one arm, Maureen the other, even though it felt a tad awkward walking side by side. But they didn't have far to go, the Criterion across the street as it turned out.

Joanne almost leaped to her feet when they entered, waving wildly at Maureen, then taking her time to hug Gilchrist first, and her mother next. Gilchrist made sure everyone was seated before he took their orders and stepped to the bar. A few weeks had passed since he'd last been in the Criterion, even though it was the closest bar to Irene's. Or perhaps that was reason enough to steer clear of it – too handy, by far. He ordered a pint of Deuchars and three glasses of wine – small white for Irene, and large red for Joanne and Maureen.

When he carried their drinks over, Irene and Joanne were huddled in conversation, while Maureen had left the table to take a call on her mobile outside. He sat down, picked up his pint, then waited until Irene and Joanne lifted their glasses before saying, 'Cheers.'

Glasses were chinked around the table, and he'd just taken that first sip when Maureen returned, seized her glass of red with a, 'Cheers, everyone,' then took a mouthful that almost drained it. Well, he supposed she did have a couple of days off.

He nursed his pint and half-listened to the three of them chatter. He smiled when he caught Irene's eye, and she gave him a smile in return. He thought she looked well despite her illness – some colour in her cheeks, or was it blusher, and a sparkle to her eyes that he hadn't seen for some time. And it was lovely, too, to see Joanne interact with her mum. His mobile rang – ID Dainty – and he excused himself to take the call.

'You're not going to fucking believe this,' Dainty said, without introduction. 'But that bastard Tony Feehan's trying to cut a deal with the procurator fiscal.'

For a moment, Gilchrist struggled to put a face to a name, then it came to him: Home Electronics, and a body somersaulting over the handlebars. 'Well he would, wouldn't he?'

'Yeah, but listen to this,' Dainty said. 'He's dobbed Duffy in for another two murders. Says he only found out about them the day he was arrested. Says he was so shocked he was going to report Duffy to the police. He's lying out his hairy arse, of course, but it's the only chance he's got of not being charged as an accomplice.'

'Do you think he's lying about the two murders?'

'Says he doesn't know their names, but can show us where they're buried.'

Gilchrist paused for a moment, while his mind rattled through the logic. None of Duffy's victims were buried. Which suggested . . .? 'Does he know about the body parts?'

Dainty chuckled. 'You never miss a trick, do you. No, he knows fuck all about them. We're trying to work out how to handle it, and I wanted to run it past you first.'

'I would play along with him,' Gilchrist said. 'If he's lying, it goes nowhere, and he's charged as before. But if he's telling the truth, then you've nothing to lose and everything to gain. Once you recover the bodies – if there are indeed any bodies to recover – and confirm the MO doesn't match Duffy's, then charge Feehan with both murders.'

Dainty laughed. 'Great minds think alike,' he said, then ended the call.

Gilchrist slipped his mobile into his pocket, and was about to return to the bar when a hand slapped onto his shoulder, and a familiar voice said, 'Hey, Andy.'

He turned, stunned to see Jack grinning at him.

'Mo called. Said she was coming up for the weekend. Thought I should join her. So, here I am.' His gaze flickered to Gilchrist's head. 'Nice haircut.'

Gilchrist ran his hand over his scalp, almost as an apology, and said, 'It's a long story. But not as long as yours, I'm guessing.'

A smile touched the corners of Jack's lips, then vanished with a shake of the head.

And in that moment Gilchrist realised he was being too harsh on his son, that every time they met up he only ever had words of disapproval. Jack had acted on impulse for the love of his daughter, a father's misguided action that had not only broken the law, but could haunt and hurt him for years to come. The last thing he needed to hear was criticism from a father who'd barely been around when his own children were growing up. So he tried another smile, and made a conscious effort to lighten his tone.

'It's great to see you, Jack. It really is. But stories like ours are best told over a few beers.'

Jack returned his gaze for several long seconds, then grinned. 'In that case,' he said, 'we'd better get started, then.'

Gilchrist slid an arm around his son's shoulder, and escorted him into the bar.

ACKNOWLEDGEMENTS

Writing is without question a lonely affair, but this book would not have been published without the considerable help, advice, and support from the following: Alan Gall, retired Chief Superintendent, Strathclyde Police, for police procedure; Howard Watson for professional copyediting to the nth degree; Peter Jacobs, Project Editor, Rebecca Sheppard, Editorial Manager, Sean Garrehy, Art Director, Brionee Fenlon, Marketing Executive, and John Fairweather, Senior Production Controller, for working hard behind the scenes in Little Brown to give this novel the best possible start; Krystyna Green, Publishing Director, Constable, for placing her trust in me once again. And finally Anna, for putting up with me, believing in me, and loving me all the way.